The Essex Murders

Vernon Loder

First published by Collins in 1930

This edition published 2022 by

OREON

an imprint of

The Oleander Press
16 Orchard Street
Cambridge
CB1 1JT

www.oleanderpress.com

A CIP catalogue record for the book
is available from the British Library.

ISBN: 9781915475053

Cover design, typesetting & ebook: neorelix

The Essex Murders

For first news of
titles, give-aways and
discounts, sign up to our
infrequent newsletter at:
oleanderpress.com

Chapter I

THE house of Fen Court was aptly named. The marshes stretched away to right and left of it, before and behind. The substantial old building, with its three acres of lawns and gardens, stood like an island in the middle of a vast expanse of rushy fields, lakelets, drains, and water meadows. The sluggish waters of the river Lum formed the northern boundary of the little property, running down to the sea, which beat in on the low coast four miles away to the east.

The house was moderate in size, containing three reception-rooms and six bedrooms, with the usual complement of kitchen offices. It had been a beautiful thing in its day, was indeed still lovely in the half-light of evening. But time and neglect and decay had put in their devastating work. Two of the glorious chimneys had been blown down in a gale, the mellow tiles of a portion of the roof lay shattered and fallen upon the lawn at the rear. Some of the lead-lights in the windows had been starred or broken, and a profusion of lichens and obstreperous climbing-plants covered the dull cream brick of the old walls.

The garden at the back was full of the rotting relics of what had been a prosperous kitchen-garden. The grass on the lawn at the rear called loudly for the scythe, and, beyond it, forlorn gooseberry bushes extended their drab, thorny fingers.

The front showed the informal wreck of what had once been a formal garden. There was a wild, grassy terrace, parallel with the main facade of the house, then a stone balustrade, then another terrace, divided down the middle by mossy, brick steps.

From the end of these steps ran a path which accurately divided the garden to its boundary, a hedge. Flower-beds had been cut symmetrically in the lawns to either side; and a fountain stood in the middle of the path, which was broadened out at that point to pass by it on both sides.

There was also ornamental water.

Fen Court stood where water was cheap. Four portions of this most common fluid formed ponds in the garden. There was a pond to each side of the path below the terrace, there was another pond on each side of the path, below the spot where the fountain stood in its island, a lichened piece of statuary bolt upright in the dry basin.

The east coast is the paradise of the bargain-hunter, and Fen Court had gone as a bargain. It had cost some thousands of pounds to build, when building was cheap; it had sold for the sum of seven hundred and fifty, with its three acres, its diminished glory, and its four circular ponds.

On a day late in March the owner got out of a little two-seater car, helped his companion to get down, and waved a happy hand.

"What about it, old thing?" he asked.

The girl with him was tall and slim and dark. She had let him help her out of the car because she knew he liked doing it, but she was as agile as he and good at most games.

"You've swindled someone, Ned!" she said with conviction.

2

He led her into the garden, "Think so? You may be right. Seven hundred and fifty pounds for an estate! If it had been more, I couldn't have afforded it."

She nodded, and approached the house, to peer in at one of the lower windows, "Wants papering," she suggested.

"It wants a great deal that it isn't going to get just now," he replied, and added, half-whimsically, half-wistfully, "like me, you know."

"Then you must both learn to wait," she smiled, "I say, some of the roof's off."

"I am going to live in the lower storey at first till I can get someone to join me. I can paper the drawing-room myself, also what was a morning-room. I propose to make a bedroom of the dining-room."

"Let me paper. I'm an awful dab hand at it," she said.

He nodded, "Perhaps that would be better. I practised a bit on my garage wall, and the brush would tangle up in the paper – spoilt the effect of the pattern rather."

"It would! I'll come down every day for a week and see you through, Ned. You ought to be able to work here, it's romantic."

He grinned, "That's the idea – work. The moment my amateur paper-hanger is finished, I begin my new novel. It will start here. I always like to paint from a model. 'The Secret of Fen Court!' How would that do, eh?"

"Topping," she said, "but there seems to be a lot of water about. You would think the chap who built it would have been content with the river and the fens. But he stuck in ponds as well."

"Fish ponds, perhaps," said Ned.

"Well, let's see if there are any fish left. There ought to be hoary old carp."

"House first, garden after," he said. "Come on. I have a fine key here; the father of all keys, I should say." They hurried to the front door, and let themselves in.

The new owner of Fen Court was a novelist. He was moderately well-known as a writer of detective fiction, and prospects justified him in buying the dilapidated old place as the nucleus of what would one day be a pretty property. He bought the house on his twenty-sixth birthday as a present to himself.

He was a little taller than his companion, and had a healthy complexion. His eyes were blue but not light. His mouth was somewhat full, his nose straight, his chin strong but not heavy. Always he looked amused at his world, but with a quite unsubtle amusement, devoid of any cynicism.

Nancy Johnson was decidedly pretty, very alert with kind eyes, a roguish mouth, and a nose that had just missed being retroussé. She had an income of two hundred and fifty a year, and nothing to do. That is officially. Actually she sketched a little, and acted as mentor and counsellor to half a dozen young men, of whom Ned was one. If she was romantic, she had cause to be, for most of her half dozen infant Telemachuses fell in and out of love regularly, and brought their cases to be adjudged by her.

Ned was the only one who stared steadily at one star. She did not adjudicate upon his case, because it was, incidentally, her own. Which made the matter a delicate one.

Ned outlined with artistic enthusiasm his various plans for the furnishing of the lower rooms. Nancy's eye for colour, and her woman's instinct for combining the homely with the artistic, enabled her to give him very excellent help.

He smiled and felt happy about that. At the back of his mind lay the idea that this might one day be hers as well as his, and there was no harm in getting it harmonised with their joint tastes.

"It'll be a jolly old place when I'm done," he said, as they left again by the front door. "Now, what about your immemorial carp?"

She stood for a moment on the upper terrace against the balustrade, and admired the open view, with the high sky that seemed to tower up endlessly from the watery flats.

"Gorgeous," she said. "Water, water, everywhere! Beautiful in the sunlight, old thing, but apt to overdo it when the winter comes. You must keep a canoe and a punt, and you will grow web-feet, in time. But it's lovely all the same. I like this brick flight of steps. Do you remember Hood's 'Plea of the Midsummer Fairies,' or 'The Haunted House?'"

"I don't," said Ned, "I always associate poor Tom with the young man who used a wiry terrier to set a snare."

"Then you've heard the worst of Hood," she said and began to murmur: "*With shattered panes the mossy grass was starred, Nettles and thistles struggled for espial, While vagrant plants, of parasitic breed, Had overgrown the dial...*"

He nodded, "That's fine! I must read it – romantic, what?"

"I never see an old house but I think of it," said Nancy. "Now I've put you on the track of Hood's unforgettable faery land, let's go and feed the carp."

"I forgot the crumbs," said Ned.

"And I'm not sure of the carp," said she. "They symbolise – what? I think something old and sinister, ambushed in those dear, dirty ponds. I like to think that they're bottomless pits."

"I don't – if I decide to fill them up," he replied, taking her arm lightly, as they descended the brick steps, and turned aside across the grass. "My romance takes a dry form. I prefer dryads to nereids, and a dry toad to a slimy frog."

Nancy laughed, "Then you have chosen the worst place for a nest."

"I have to compromise," he said, looking at her. "Some people prefer a low horizon. Here it is. Do you like it?"

But Nancy refused to look. She did not wish yet to be subject to classification, but she was wondering if she had ever told Ned that she liked oodles of sky. Or had he merely guessed? The pond they were now approaching was like the others, fifteen yards across, circular in shape, bounded by a rim of closely-set stones. These stones were now mossy, slippery, damp. The pond was full, to within a foot of the flags, of muddy water, on which floated weeds, and scum, melancholy, half-rotted.

"No place for Ophelia," said Nancy, as she looked down, "but, like so many of us – fair at a distance getting wuss as you get nearer. No, I am not fishing, Ned! We're whited sepulchres, and this isn't white. That's all the difference."

"I'm going to christen you Nancy Nietzsche Johnson," he said. "Get away, you little pessimist!"

"I'm a moving on, sir," said Nancy, "I want to see the lower ones. On the whole, I think these will be mosquito crèches in the season. Unless some unexpected prettiness discloses itself further on I am afraid I shall have to advise you to drain and fill."

He nodded, "I am afraid so. There's plenty of casual water without them. But what an unimaginative brute the designer was! He's made one exactly like t'other."

They were now on the edge of the lower pond on that side. Nancy was staring at the further side and her gaze was curiously tense.

"Is that a carp or something?" she demanded, pointing.

He followed the direction of her gesture, "Hello! A blanched carp, if it is a carp, and they do blanch. On its side too – dead as Cæsar! Must be. Our friend the John Dory is the only fish I know that swims upside down, or downside up, with facility. But that's camouflage. He convinces the little fish he's a sunken paper."

But Nancy did not appear interested in his natural history lecture. She was staring hard, and licking her lips, which were dry.

"I suppose it looks white against the muddy water," she murmured, "but, old thing, it's like – it's faintly like a—"

She stopped and shuddered a little. He caught the urgent note in her voice and laughed.

"No guessing needed. We'll just toddle round and make sure." He took the lead now. Nancy was a pace to his rear, and seemed reluctant. He had noticed that fugitive resemblance, but his logic told him to scout the idea. How should such things come into his deserted ponds? Of course it was absurd, he told himself, and then he looked again and saw that it was absurd enough to be true. He tried to keep Nancy back, but now she was more eager, and slipped past him, and stared down into the muddy, weed-haunted water of the pool.

"I think I'm going to be sick!" she said, in a very small voice, and very suddenly.

Ned turned to her, grabbed her about the waist, and carried her rapidly back to the brick steps where he set her down.

"Don't dare to move till I come back!" he commanded. "Head between knees! Keep it down! I firmly believe it's a poisoned pup."

He left her, and ran back to the lower pond. As he approached the place where Nancy had announced her plight, he nearly slipped and went into the slimy depths of the pool. Saving himself by a convulsive movement, he stepped forward two paces, and looked.

It was a face that looked up at him out of the water, a grim, old face, with a short white beard. The rest of the body was entangled in the weeds, and was invisible in that murky medium.

He was not prone to sickness, but he quite understood Nancy's nausea when she caught sight of that floating face. It lay just below the surface, glimmering pallidly, the short, pointed beard tilted slightly upwards, as if its owner and wearer had tried vainly to get his mouth above water.

He made up his mind immediately. This was his place, but what lay in it was the concern of others. No second glance was needed to tell him that the man was dead; had been dead some time. It remained to fetch those who troubled themselves with the unexplained dead. If this wasn't a case of suicide, there was the slippery stone rim of the pond to demonstrate how easily an accident could take place. He was disgusted, as he was shocked. This was a nice sort of thing to do! Was it the Chinese or the Japanese who committed suicide on their enemy's doorstep, to put a curse on the house? And he wasn't even an enemy of the poor old chap who had spoiled at least one piece of ornamental water.

He went back to Nancy, who was sitting up very straight now, and apparently quite composed once more, though her face was as pallid as a sheet of paper, and her eyes showed scared whites.

"Looks like a suicide, my dear," he told her, "no one hops into strange gardens for fun."

"Then it really is – someone?" she breathed.

He nodded, "This is an ugly, nasty business, Nancy. But what we have to do is clear enough. I suppose the nearest policeman is at Costable?"

She bit her lip, "I saw the constabulary notice on a cottage as we passed through."

"Feel fit enough to get up?" he asked.

"Oh, yes;" she got to her feet, and he put an arm round her shoulders, and helped her back to the path above.

"Lean on me. That's the ticket! You may feel groggy for a few minutes. But we'll drive over to Costable, and the air will make you feel better. Come on."

They left the grounds, and he helped her into the car, tucked the rug about her tenderly, and climbed into the driving seat. After a little backing and manœuvering, he was about to drive off when a high and rather shrill voice, made him turn in his seat.

"Welcome to Fen Court, sir!"

A small man, rather stooped, with a weazened face, and washed-out blue eyes, had come across a marsh path, and was standing slightly to the rear of the car. Ned glanced at him with distaste.

"Ah; thank you," he said. "Nancy, we'll be off now."

The little man came closer, his face beaming, "I'm your nearest neighbour, sir. Hench is my name, Cornelius Hench. I saw you had come last night, but I was busy. I hope—"

But Ned had a job of necessary work to do, and he started at once with the roar of a fast revving engine.

Nancy looked curiously back over the dickey. The little man was staring after them, his hand wavering uncertainly near his hat.

Chapter II

NED and Nancy recovered a little as they drove over to Costable. The shock of finding the body in the pond began to wear off. For some unexplainable reason, suicide makes less impression on the human mind than murder, and both of them had come to the conclusion that either suicide or accident accounted for the old man's appearance in the pool.

Ned, drove on, his face rather set. Nancy was the first to break the silence in an attempt to divert her mind from the tragedy.

"What a weird old bird," she said.

Ned half turned his head, "Hench? Rather! Hope he didn't think me rude. I hadn't time to stop and explain why we cut off so fast."

She nodded, "Of course not. You can explain when you see him again. By the way, where the dickolino did he spring from? I never saw a sign of the man, or anyone else, when we were in the garden, and it's flat enough round about to show up anyone who isn't hiding."

"Hiding my hat!" said Ned, "did he look the kind of man to hide? And why should he, old thing? And if he did, why be so anxious to rush up and introduce himself?"

Nancy admitted these mysteries. "What he said was funnier."

Ned had been pondering over that very point, which in part explained his silence at first.

"So I thought. How did he see that I had come last night?"

"Since you didn't, it doesn't matter much, Ned," murmured Nancy.

"But I did," said Ned, deliberately, "I left my cigarette case on the window ledge inside, the last time I was down. I couldn't remember where I had left it. I searched dozens of places before I thought of it. Then I got out the car last night about seven, and barged down here. I showed a light, no doubt, but it was in the sitting-room to the front. There aren't any houses to the front, so how could he see me?"

"In any case, it isn't of any importance, Ned. I expect you forgot to tell me."

"Just because it wasn't, yes. I say, you may be wanted to give evidence at the inquest, Nancy. Rotten for you, but you saw it first."

"I did see the poor old thing," she admitted. "Such a beastly thing to happen when you've just bought the place."

He nodded, "Look here, I know they have a proverb about the dead, and it may sound callous and all that sort of thing. But the old man did not strike me as prepossessing. If I'd seen him alive, I should have said he had a vicious sort of face."

"Well, don't say it now!" Nancy protested, with a little shiver, "perhaps some people look different when they're dead, go by contraries, so to speak."

He did not reply to that. The village of Costable was in sight, and he ran into the little main street, and pulled up at the country constable's cottage before he spoke again.

"You stay here, old girl. I shan't be a minute."

The oldest inhabitant, surrounded by a flock of inquiring lads, stood by the car when Ned came out again.

Police constable Hoggett was behind him, a tall spare man, with a serious air. He dismissed the curious to a distance, and then had a good look at Nancy, to whom Ned was explaining what had been done.

"Hoggett's telephoned his Superintendent, and asked him to come out with a drag. Now, you can either stay here, and have a cup of coffee, or jog back with us. Hoggett's wife will do the honours for you if you stay. If not, we'll open the dickey. At any rate I'm taking Hoggett over at once to Fen Court."

The air had recovered Nancy, and she decided against staying in the village.

"I'll come," she replied, "I don't think I'm morbid, but I do want to know what's happened."

"Right," said Ned, "Hoggett, will you open the dickey, and pile in. I'll run you over at once. By the way, this is Miss Johnson, who saw the poor devil first."

The constable got in, and they drove off. When they reached the gates of Fen Court again there was no sign of Mr. Cornelius Hench. They entered the garden, Ned in advance, and went down to the pond. Nancy stopped at one side, the two men went to the other. Hoggett got out his notebook and made an entry or two. Then he speculated on the chances of getting the body to land without waiting for the drags. A slip or two as he bent forward to reach, convinced him that the attempt would be premature and dangerous.

"I reckon he slipped, sir," he said. "This bank's very slimy, long of the moss on the stones, and the damp too. Here's a bit of moss scratted off on the sides. Likely that's where his foot went wrong."

"But what was he doing in my garden?"

"Couldn't say, sir."

"Have a cigarette. We have to wait," Ned observed, and offered his case. "By the way, constable, do you know of anyone living near here called Cornelius Hench?"

Hoggett lit up, then nodded, "Weazened, scrawny little man, sir? Ah, he lives over in Pear Cottage. That's back of the house here, and part hid in a half-dead orchard."

Ned puffed, "What does he do?"

"Nothing, sir. He's a gentleman."

"Curiously qualified, Hoggett! Wanders about the marches, does he?"

"Oh, that, sir. After birds he is. Kind of hobby. I don't offen come this way, but I hears he is always round after birds."

"An ornithologist?"

"Very likely, sir, but very humane. He doesn't kill them, but just looks at 'em." Ned glanced at his watch. "As we may be here some time before the Superintendent arrives, I vote we adjourn to the house. It's a lovely day for late March, but not what I should call hot."

They walked round the pond, rejoined Nancy, and went towards the house. As they were about to enter the door, Mr. Hench suddenly appeared round the side, and came towards them, beaming.

Ned eyed him with mixed feelings, Nancy with curiosity, the constable nodded to him.

"Where'd you spring up from, Mr. Hench?"

Hench beamed, "I wanted to introduce myself to my new neighbour," he said, raising his hat to Nancy. "He was in an obvious hurry just now. But better late than never. I believe there is a rarish bird that frequents his garden, and—"

"Just a moment, sir," began Ned, rather heavily. "You spring up so extraordinarily from the vague that I am anxious to know how you do it."

The constable repressed a guffaw. Mr. Hench frowned a little, and then his face cleared.

"Ah, I was in my hide."

Ned nodded, "Obviously, but what is it?"

"He means a bird hide, sir," said the constable; "place where you makes a hole, and puts rushes and reeds round it, and sits in it."

"That is so," agreed the little man, "it is situated about two hundred yards to the rear of this house. I am keeping the nest of a marsh harrier under observation, and I have been there every day for ten days."

Ned thanked him half ironically for the information, "Then, perhaps, you saw an elderly man, with a short pointed beard, wandering about here? Or climbing over my hedge, or opening my gate?" he said.

"Certainly not," replied Hench. "No harrier about would sit so steadily if people were walking about here at random. Indeed your arrival spoils my opportunity for the day."

"I am sorry to have disturbed your pet harrier," said Ned, "but I don't quite see how I can avoid it in future, short of selling out again."

Mr. Hench let the irony pass over his head, "I don't blame you. With all my love for birds, human beings must come first. It was only the light you showed last night that gave me the idea you were moving in. I see that I was mistaken. I hope you and your wife will allow me to call later on. I am a gregarious creature; the more so that my daylight pursuits render it necessary for me to be much alone."

Nancy coloured. Ned explained that he was a celibate so far. But Hoggett had his book out again, and turned to Ned.

"You were here last night, sir?"

Ned bit his lip. Confound the prosy and officious old ornithologist! With some faint vexation in his tone, he told Hoggett why and when he had visited the house.

The constable noted it down, "Leaving, as far as you know, about ten, sir?"

"That's about it."

But now the ornithologist was observing the unusual bird in blue.

"May I ask if anything has happened?" he asked.

"We'll see if you can identify him," said Hoggett. "Come with me down the garden, sir." Hench looked at them all wonderingly, then accompanied the policeman. Ned heaved a deep sigh.

"Silly little beast! What the devil did he want to butt in for? I'll see that he doesn't get on to my visiting-list later on."

They watched the two, who had now arrived at the pond's edge. They saw Hench glance down, then start up, and wave his arms about excitedly.

"Is that recognition, or hysteria?" said Nancy, succinctly.

Ned did not reply. He saw that Hoggett was writing rapidly in his inevitable notebook, and gathered that her first guess was the right one.

"And we asked him if he had seen an old man with a pointed beard!" Nancy cried, reproachfully.

"If he'd seen him here," Ned supplemented.

"They're coming back," she gasped.

They came back. Hench was excited still, and very loquacious. The constable had the air of having seen dead old men in ponds every day of his life, and being rather bored with them.

"If patrons were known today," Hench was saying as he came up, "I should call him my patron. My resources are limited. My name is unknown. The work would be exceedingly expensive. This is a tragic moment for me."

Ned did not feel very sorry for him, "May I ask if you knew him?" he ventured.

"I have just been telling the constable so. It is undoubtedly, Mr. Henry Habershon."

Nancy raised her eyebrows, "No relation of yours, I hope?"

"None, my dear young lady," replied Hench, "but once standing *in loco parentis* to my half-written book on the nidification of our larger falcons, and hawks."

Hoggett was more interested in concrete facts, "And lived where, sir?"

"At No.11 Gale Street, Bloomsbury, London."

"Perhaps he was coming over to see you, and lost his way," Ned suggested.

Hench nodded, "Perhaps so. This is difficult country for a stranger. Perilously so. Bogs, holes, ditches, drains, swamps. Treacherous in the extreme. This means the ruin of my life's work."

Nancy uttered an exclamation of pity. Hoggett remained stolid.

"You had no idea that he intended to pay you a visit, sir?"

"None. I usually went up to see him."

"He was well-to-do?"

"I imagine so."

Hoggett closed his book, "We've got to wait for my Superintendent, and the drags. He may be here any time now. I expects the poor gentleman thought this was your house in the dark, got in, and slipped into that there pond. If he'd come by day you'd have seen him, sir."

"Most likely," said Hench, dejectedly.

They entered the house together, and remained in a front room talking over the affair until a car was heard approaching, when they went out, and saw Superintendent Langley, of Upperton, descending from a car on the main road. He had a policeman and a detective inspector with him. The policeman remained behind, getting the drags out from the car, while his superior advanced, with the inspector at his heels.

Hoggett introduced his companions. The Superintendent, a weighty man, and over six feet in height, bowed to each in turn.

"Very good. Now I know where we are. Next thing is to get the poor old gentleman out. Smith!" he looked back at the car, "come along with that stuff. We're waiting."

Nancy stood on the upper terrace while the men, followed by the new constable with the rope and grapnel, went down to the lower pond. There the Superintendent made Hench and Ned stand back, while he and Inspector Brews had a look at the submerged corpse, and made their dispositions.

"More like accident than suicide," said Langley, as he glanced down at the pallid object in the water.

Brews was a man of middle-height, very quick, very alert, with a cheerful face, and a mouth that was always suppressing a smile.

"That's right, sir," he said, "and he might have had a chance to get out if it wasn't for the weeds. You see, he wouldn't come to the top if he went in lately. He doesn't look like a man who has been in long either. He's stuck more or less upright in the weeds."

The constable now came up to the edge, and began to make his preparations for recovering the body. Nancy went quickly back to the house. The dragging up of Mr. Habershon was not going to be a pretty business.

No one spoke while the constable made a cast. The grapnel fell beyond its mark, and the officer drew in, hoping to get a grip on the clothes. But the grapnel came up easily and bare, and the Superintendent took the drag himself.

He threw, but overdid it. The grapnel went even further this time; only, as he drew it in, it caught and held. He gave a tug, and Brews exclaimed.

"Hasn't moved him, sir. You're on to the weeds at the bottom.

"Weeds be hanged!" said the other, and pulled hard. "Wait a bit. Weeds couldn't hold like that."

Ned and Hench edged forward. There was no possibility that Habershon had intercepted the grapnel. He was in exactly the same position as before. Brews now took a hand on the rope, and he and the Superintendent began to haul in very slowly and laboriously, the mud rising from the bottom in clouds, as they pulled.

The constable tailed on too now, and they made better going.

"You'd think it was an elephant," said Ned in a whisper to Hench, "perhaps there is an old lead tank at the bottom, and they've caught it."

"There's something in the bottom hitched up," said the Superintendent suddenly, "move two yards to the left, and we'll clear it."

They all moved on, and pulled again. There was a disturbance on the surface of the slimy water. A band of weeds heaved up, and the three men hauled away with fresh vigour.

"It's another!" said Ned, in a high voice that surprised himself.

"Two!" said the Superintendent, drawing in a deep breath.

"I'm glad Nancy bolted!" Ned confided to the air.

There wasn't a doubt of it now. There were two more bodies visible on the surface of the muddy water, and one looked like a woman.

Chapter III

HENCH made a wry face, and went off hurriedly to rejoin Nancy.

"If you tell her I'll kill you!" Ned called after him, with extraordinary ferocity.

The policemen ceased hauling, and looked at one another gravely. The constable was white and uneasy. Brews and his superior had had a shock, but kept it to themselves.

The superintendent spoke first, "Hoggett, you can drive. I am sure Mr.—"

"Mr. Hope," said Ned, "of course."

"Then you borrow Mr. Hope's car, since he's so kind, and take Miss Johnson back to your wife. She must go, Hoggett. The doctor and the ambulance may be here any moment."

Hoggett saluted and went. The Superintendent hauled at the rope once more.

"Now all together. That's it. Ease a bit," he glanced at the queasy face of the constable, and turned to Brews, "Brews, get down, and get them out when they're at the edge – Mr. Hope, would you give us a hand while he does it?"

Ned nodded, and tailed on to the rope. Brews knelt down on the rim of the pond, and reached forward. In five minutes they had laid the bodies side by side on the ground.

"This is suicide all right," said the Superintendent, biting his lip. "Their hands are tied together with a silk scarf. Both about nineteen or twenty, I should say."

Brews nodded absently. He stared at the young man, then at the pretty young woman.

"Well-dressed, well-fed, better-class," he murmured.

"Get that man Hench," said the Superintendent, through clenched teeth, and turned to Ned. "Recognise them, sir?"

Ned looked white and strained, but was holding up wonderfully. "No, I never saw them before, as far as I am aware."

The other nodded, "This is a pretty recent business, sir. Damned if I know what to make of it." He knelt down and began methodically to search the clothes of the young man. As he worked away, Brews came back with Hench, who had a scared look.

"Have you ever seen either of these people before?" he was asked.

"Never," he affirmed, staring wildly, "who are they?"

"What we've got to find out," said the officer grumpily, and went on with his examination. He accumulated a few insignificant objects, a cigarette case, a wristwatch, matches, nothing else. He found on two of the objects engraved initials, and read them out.

"I.R."

Brews was not watching him, he was bending over the young woman. He bent suddenly and pointed. Flattened against her soaked garments, pinned on to them, was a sodden scrap of paper. He detached it with extraordinary care, and laid it flat on his palm.

"A note on her, sir."

They all gathered round him, the Superintendent springing to his feet to look.

There were some words pencilled on the paper. He read them out in a low voice:

"We are tired waiting, and hoping.
There must be an end to it soon."

"Poor devils!" said the inspector gently.

The Superintendent nodded. He seemed to feel the need for fresh action.

"Put that away carefully, Brews, and get busy. We have to get Habershon out."

Brews put the torn scrap of paper away in a flat box he carried. The Superintendent detached the grapnel, and threw it in again. Ned jumped to help him. Hench stood back a little, staring and afraid.

This last cast was successful. Mr. Habershon's body was soon on the bank. But there was nothing on his person to give a clue to his tragedy. He had some papers, of which the police took charge, watch and chain, matches, a pipe and pouch, and the sum of one pound fifteen shillings in his pockets.

As they were examining him, Ned heard a car drive up the lane a little way, and stop. It was the ambulance, and a doctor had come with it. Sant by name, he was a recent arrival in the district, who had retired from the R.A.M.C., and 'squatted.' The usual police surgeon was in bed with bronchitis.

When he saw the task which awaited him, he whistled loudly, and then sucked in his lips.

"What sort of filthy job have you here, Superintendent?" he demanded.

"Isn't it beastly?" stammered Hench.

The Superintendent shrugged. "Funny coincidence, sir. Two of them are suicides. You can't get away from that. We found a note, and look at their wrists tied together. But the old gentleman is a problem."

"It seems to me a pretty problem altogether," replied Sant, as he kneeled down beside the young woman, "get their wrists untied, will you. I can't make a proper examination this way."

The wrists were loosened, and Sant made an examination. Then he turned to the body of the young fellow and finally to that of Mr. Habershon.

"Coincidence in time, and in place," he said, wiping his hands, and getting up. "None of the three has been dead more than, say, fifteen hours. Is it possible that the old man saw them going to make their dive, rushed up to stop them, and went in?"

"Dimly possible," replied Langley. "Then you mean it was last night?"

"I should certainly say so. Why?"

The Superintendent wheeled on Ned. "You were here last night, Mr. Hope."

"I was. I left at ten. But, if I had seen anyone here, I should have told you."

Langley shrugged, and looked at Hench, "You saw a light here last night."

Hench had pulled himself together, "Yes. I thought it was this gentleman moving in."

"How could you see a light in the front room when you live away behind this house?" Ned asked, angrily.

"That's a point, sir," remarked Langley.

"I walked over to Hitherland, and was coming back," said Hench, "I met Constable Hoggett at the crossroads near Pulley's farm, and spoke to him. You can see the front of this house from there. At least I took it to be this house, because it's the only one near except my own, and I wouldn't leave a light on."

"What time was this, sir?"

"When I met Hoggett? Let me see. I think it was about nine forty-five. But you could ask the constable. He must have some timetable for his beat."

"Did you tell him you saw the light?"

"No. I saw it after he had left me. He was on his bicycle."

Langley nodded, and turned to Ned, "We had better have your address, sir."

Ned gave it, "Guy Mansions, West End Lane, N.W."

Sant was looking impatient, "Let's get the bodies into the ambulance. I suppose, if Smith is ill, you'll want me to do the P.M."

"We may have to ask you, sir," replied Langley. "Here, Jeff, run and get the men from the ambulance, and we'll get it away. Mr. Hench, we know where you live. We'll have a talk with you later."

"I can't be of any help?"

"None at all, thank you," he turned to Ned again, as Hench walked off. "We'll need your evidence, sir, at the inquest, and the young lady's. Are you staying here, or going back to town, may I ask?"

"Back to town," said Ned, uncomfortably, "but I can run down in my car any time you want me."

"Good. As you were kind enough to lend your car, you must wait till Hoggett gets back. After that I don't think we need detain you."

The ambulance attendants came up, and the three bodies were reverently removed. The doctor nodded to Ned, gave him a curious glance, and went off. Brews was glancing at the scrap of paper in the box.

"Looks like a bit torn off a letter," he said.

"You'll have to dry it out carefully, Brews. It may be very important."

Ned had noticed that little bit of paper too. It seemed to him to be a bit of notepaper, cream-laid stuff. But he did not interfere. To him, as to the doctor, it appeared that Mr. Habershon, possibly wandering in search of Hench's cottage, had seen the young couple preparing to leap into the pond, and had lost his own life in an attempt to stop them.

"I'm sorry I told Nancy the old chap had a vicious face," he said to himself, remorsefully. "He did his best, evidently."

The inspector paid no further attention to him. He had gone down on his knees, and was examining the edge of the pond, measuring tape in hand. For once his cheerful face looked grim and grave, and there was not the ghost of a smile on his tight lips.

Langley touched Ned's sleeve, "You are aware that this is necessary, sir. No doubt you give your permission to our remaining in your grounds. You do? Good. Now I think I hear a car. It must be yours coming back. Just give me the address of the young lady too, and I needn't keep you."

Ned gave Nancy's address, said goodbye to the Superintendent, and went to where Hoggett had drawn up the car.

"You left Miss Johnson with your wife?" he said to the man, as he got into the driving-seat.

"Yes, sir," replied Hoggett.

Ned thanked him. He wanted to get back to Nancy. The whole thing must have been a frightful shock for her.

He found her waiting outside the cottage. She had had a cup of tea, but her impatience had been too much for her. She felt that she could not sit in the tiny room, listening to Mrs. Hoggett's well-meant, but loquacious, outpourings, and the flood of questions about the tragedy at Fen Court.

"I want to go back at once, Ned," she told Hope excitedly. "I must lie down and rest. What a hateful day this has been, hasn't it? Simply loathsome!"

He nodded, and set off again the moment she was beside him. She stared straight ahead. He minded his steering, and did not attempt to discuss what had taken place that day. Poor dear, she wanted to get it out of her mind, no doubt. Rotten enough that business of seeing old Habershon floating about in the pond, but the rest was worse. She had been back on the terrace by then, but no doubt she knew what had come after.

She lit a cigarette suddenly, and smoked fast. When she had finished it, she glanced at him sideways. "Is it true there were two?" she murmured.

"Absolutely."

"Young?"

"Yes."

"How utterly foul!"

There was a long silence then. They were near London, when the air, and the comfort and support of having Ned beside her, recovered Nancy a little.

"Does anyone know why it happened?" she said.

He shook his head, "No one can say definitely. There's a likelihood that they were lovers – young enough to have no patience, poor devils. Unless the old man saw them and tried a rescue, I can't understand him."

"In the dark?" said Nancy.

"Yes, that worries me. It must have happened after dark, if the doctor is right. How the dickens could he see them?"

25

The subject languished again. They drove in through the suburbs, and presently Ned stopped his car at the door of Hampstead Mansions, where she had a tiny service flat.

"Let me see you settled, old girl," he said, as he got her out.

"I would rather you didn't, Ned," she said. "Come round later if you like – in the evening."

"You'll be all right? Sure?"

"Oh, quite."

He looked dissatisfied, but saw that she walked in steadily enough, and started his car again. Ten minutes later he had garaged it behind his flat in West End Lane, and went in.

Nancy had a wireless set. He himself was not very keen on the radio, but it was useful when you wanted late news. He determined to run round to see her about nine. That was the time they switched on the latest doings.

Nancy's flat consisted of a sitting-room, bedroom and bath-room, on the fourth floor of the mansions. When Ned called at ten minutes to nine, she led him into the cosy little sitting-room, and brought out a silver cigarette-box. She looked better now, and her voice was clear and steady.

But she did not speak for a few minutes, after he had settled in an easy chair with his cigarette alight. She stared into the fire, while Ned let an absent glance wander round the room.

His gaze came to rest at last on her one picture, a shimmering river scene in watercolours over the mantel. He turned away from it with an odd distaste.

He had seen water enough that day to last him a lifetime! How could he live down by those beastly ponds after that? And who would take the house over from him? It had been ages in the market already, and, with three fresh ghosts to overweight it, it might remain there for another century. Rotten!

He looked at Nancy, "Isn't it about time for the News?" he asked.

"Do you really want to hear it?"

"Of course. Don't you?"

She shivered a little, "I don't – but I must, Ned. I say, I am most awfully sorry about your house. It seems a trifle when you think of this dreadful thing, but I know you can't afford to drop seven-fifty."

He shrugged, "I should say not. Unless I can get some morbid person to buy it, it's a bit of a blue egg for me."

Nancy got up.

"I suppose you could stick it if you had to."

"I could – I suppose. But I'll have a shot at selling first. You going to switch on that gadget?"

"Yes. It may start any time now."

She went over to the cabinet, and tuned in. They waited. They heard the weather report, then came an S.O.S.. They exchanged glances. The sober distinct voice of the announcer begged anyone who could identify a young man, whose description he gave (a young man upon whose cigarette case and matchbox were engraved the initials I. R.), to come forward, or communicate with the Chief Constable for Essex, or Superintendent Langley of Upperton. He followed by giving a description of a young woman, age about nineteen, and of the costume she wore. This young woman was a friend of the young man already mentioned. If any listener could identify her, would he come forward or communicate with the officials already mentioned.

Nancy sighed deeply, "Ned, what a ghastly thing!"

He nodded, and then motioned for silence, "News coming through! – Yes; Fen Court – *Listen!*"

Chapter IV

T HEY listened in silence, their faces tense; staring straight before them, and, for the moment, unconscious of each other. The announcer gave brief particulars of the tragic discovery that day. Ned started slightly when he heard the words: Fen Court – property of Mr. Edward Hope, the novelist. That was annoying publicity. He would have shoals of pressmen after him for the story. He couldn't be such a pig as to capitalise on his experiences that afternoon.

The thought passed through his mind in a flash. He listened again. Ah, here was news... a car had been found on the highway two-and-a-half miles from the scene of the tragedy. It was abandoned, the police had traced the registered number to Mr. Habershon. It was reported that an elderly gentleman, with a white beard, had entered a café in Upperton on the previous evening, in the company of two young people, a man and a girl. Further investigations were afoot. In view of the possibility that the three people seen in the café at Upperton might be those afterwards found drowned, would listeners please remember the S.O.S. already given out.

"By Jove!" said Ned, and drew a long breath.

Nancy got up, and switched off the even voice, now relating the experiences of a Communist seized in possession of a pistol at Geneva.

"What do you make of it?" she asked, as she returned to Ned.

He shrugged. "Sounds perfectly potty! They couldn't all have gone down there to commit suicide. And coffee first too."

"If it was the same crowd, no," she agreed. "Would people take coffee before committing suicide? Don't people about to be executed sometimes have breakfast?"

"Believe they do, sometimes," he murmured. "I can't understand it, but there it is. Then the car was two and a half miles away. Did they all walk over and get in? And why my place. Isn't there enough water elsewhere?"

Nancy nodded. "Unless the old man was her father. It couldn't have been his father, with the initials I. R. Do you think he wanted to marry her, and Mr. Habershon objected, and they bolted, poor things?"

"With the old man in pursuit, but just too late to save them?" he mused, "I don't know. I'm horribly sorry for them, but they've done in my little property, and dragged you and me into this inquest. I'll run you down when it comes off. They'll let us know."

Nancy bit her lip. "Sure to."

He had an inspiration suddenly, "I say, may I use your telephone? I might ring up Bell – he's assistant news editor on the *Record*, and a very decent chap. He may have some news. All the offices will be hopping with excitement."

"The phone is out in the lobby, old boy."

Ned went out to the telephone, and got on to his friend Bell after a time. Bell made a wild attempt to get the promise of the 'story.' He said he had already rung up Ned without success. Ned, who was determined to sidestep any promise of the kind, temporised. Would Bell let him know if anyone had got the identity of the two young people.

"It ought to be easy," he added.

"It *was* easy," said Bell, "a man we sent round to inquire about old Habershon has just come in. He says the fellow was Ivor Rainy, and the girl Maysie Rowe. Both relatives and wards of old Habershon – I say, where are you speaking from? I'll send a man round."

"Piccadilly Circus, and I'm leaving for Folkestone just now," replied Ned, mendaciously, as he rang off.

Nancy was waiting anxiously for the news. He sat down beside her, and raised his eyebrows, "We made a good shot. Those two were wards of the old man. Don't suppose their elderly guardian thought it wise for two such young things to marry."

"But why couldn't they wait? Nancy cried, "they were about nineteen or twenty, weren't they? In a year or two they would have—"

She stopped, as Ned laid a hand on her knee heavily, "I *say*, Maysie Rowe! Could it be the same girl that Jimmy Huston knows? I've never seen her, but there was someone of that name he was rather smitten with."

"It may be," she cried, "I never thought of it. Funny thing how one never imagines our acquaintances can get killed, or commit suicide. It is always someone else."

He looked at her now, hearing a weary note in her voice. She was pale again, and there were dark rings under her eyes.

"You've got to go to bed," he announced, getting up, "we may get a subpœna tomorrow, and be dragged up to that filthy inquest."

"I was just going to hint at it," she said, nodding. "I feel like a rag. Sure you don't mind?"

"I'd be angry if you wanted me to stay," said he. "Now don't think over it, see? I'll come round first thing in the morning."

"There may be something in the papers," she said, as he went to the door.

But there was very little fresh information in the newspapers next day, and for lack of it, they had had to spread themselves on the personalities of Mr. Habershon and his two wards; their style cramped a little by the legal caution of their editors.

Ned just glanced at his paper, for he had been summoned to attend the inquest that morning. He went out for his car the moment he had finished breakfast, and drove round to call on Nancy.

He found her much more cheerful. After all, Mr. Habershon and the unfortunate young people were not even acquaintances of hers. The shock of seeing the dead man in the pond, like all other shocks which have nothing intimate in them, had worn off. She, too, had received an official summons to the inquiry, and got in beside Ned five minutes after his arrival.

"One comfort," said he, as he drove away, "these affairs are rotten while they last, but they don't last long. You and I will come in early, then we can vamoose if it suits us."

She nodded. But they had gone a mile or two before she made a remark of her own, "It must be rather terrible to fall in love like that."

"Yes," said he, soberly, "it must. My paper said it was understood in young Rainy's circle of friends that he was engaged to the girl. Habershon must have been against it, or it would have been announced. People are important nowadays, even if they have no rank, if they have money. The two were cousins, and they would have come in for – I think it was a hundred thousand between them."

"So I read. Perhaps Habershon objected on account of their being related. Some people do, you know."

Ned shrugged. "I wonder if we are right off the mark."

Of course, they had been merely speculating on motives. Nancy dropped that, and turned to another side of the case.

"Didn't they say Mr. Habershon was a F.Z.S.? But he was really a solicitor, wasn't he?"

"No; he had studied for the law, but didn't go on with it. He came in for twenty thousand from the sister – that is Miss Rowe's mother – who left part of this cash. Habershon had two sisters. My paper had the bally genealogical tree in it. Looks as if the police weren't letting out much."

"I thought that, too. But mine said one sister left forty thousand odd, and the other sixty. When their husbands died, they lived together in a big house at Hampstead. Maysie Rowe went to school here, and then to finish in Paris, Rainy was at Harrow, and then for a year in Rome. His mother died while he was away, and the other sister died soon after. It seems they were very devoted."

Ned assented. "You do hear of such cases. But we'll have an end to all this newspaper talk very soon. I had half a dozen telephone calls after I got home last night, and two early pressmen looking for a worm this morning. I told them there was nothing doing."

"What'll happen at this inquest?" asked Nancy.

"I've never been to one, but I expect just identification; then we tell about the finding, and the doctor says what he found. Seems to me they'll have two verdicts. The two will be suicide; if it comes out that old Habershon objected to the match. He'll be accident, I expect. Anyway, that will settle it, and no one except the poor devils themselves will be a ha'penny the worse. – Oh, I forgot my miserable self!"

They drove on in silence. The inquest was to be held at Upperton, on account of the lack of proper facilities at Fen Court. They had fortunately not asked Ned to let his ill-starred house be further damned from a selling point of view by holding the inquest there.

32

The little country town was seething with people when they drove in, and made their way to the court. Londoners, and people from three adjacent counties, thronged the streets, with curious natives, pressmen, photographers, the riff-raff that a sensation breeds, and a sprinkling of police officers.

Ned could not drive and bend his head, but Nancy buried hers on her bosom as cameras clicked. An adventurous pressman jumped on the running-board, but Ned pushed him off, and a constable grabbed him, and pushed him further off.

The little court was crowded when they came in, but Superintendent Langley was on the watch, the proceedings opened with the swearing of the jury, and their short absence to view the bodies. When they came back, the court began its proceedings in a wonderful silence, so deep that the Coroner's first words seemed to crash on the air.

After a few remarks, he called on Mrs. Agnes Hoing to identify the bodies. He was taking the case of the two young people first.

Mrs. Hoing, a tall gaunt woman, with an austere face, took the oath impressively. She deposed that she was Mr. Habershon's housekeeper. She agreed that the bodies of the man and girl were those of Mr. Habershon's wards, Miss Rowe, and Mr. Rainy respectively. They lived with their guardian. She agreed that Mr. Habershon had taken both out with him in his car on the Tuesday. He had left home at six o'clock. She thought he drove the car himself. He had not been seen by her again until she had identified his body that morning.

Questioned by the Coroner, she said that she thought Mr. Rainy had been in love with his cousin. She drew in her lips as she said that. She had certainly understood that there was trouble over it. It was not the first time there had been trouble. Mr. Habershon was not a very effusive sort of man, but she was sure he was fond of his wards. She understood that he thought it was unwise of cousins to marry.

"Did Mr. Habershon quarrel with Mr. Rainy over this?" she was asked.

Again that curious drawing in of the lips, "No, sir," she said. "Mr. Habershon was very dignified. He was a good employer and a kind man."

"Let me put it another way, Mrs. Hoing. Did Mr. Rainy quarrel with his uncle. Did he exhibit resentment at this objection?"

"He did, sir. Not that I would say he was a fierce young man, or not what he should be, but he did talk nasty to me about his uncle once, and I checked him."

"But you are not aware that they had any row?"

"I have my own room, sir, and I don't listen at doors, and I don't hear what I'm not intended to hear."

"Quite. I understand. Then there was no open breach, as far as you are aware?"

"No."

"Do you know why Mr. Habershon took his wards for this drive? Or where he professed to be going?"

"No, sir. I never asked and he didn't tell me."

"You never heard either of these unfortunate young people talk of suicide."

"No, sir. I wouldn't have thought it of them. They hadn't anything to grumble at; being so young. If they'd waited a year or two, they could have done what they liked."

The Coroner suddenly wore an air of haste to be done with this witness.

"Thank you. You may stand down," he said, hurriedly, "I shall now call upon Miss Nancy Johnson to give evidence."

Ned had been watching the coroner's face. He thought there was something significant in his expression. Something in Mrs. Hoing's

34

last phrase had made a difference. There was something new in the wind. What was it?

Nancy went up composedly enough, and took the oath in low but distinct tones. Her appearance excited a great deal of interest, but her evidence, while sensational enough, fell flatly on the ears of an audience who had expected to find this pretty girl more intimately mixed up with the case – Mr. Habershon's choice for his nephew, it might be! When she stood down, Ned was called, and told briefly what he had seen, and done. Then came Hoggett, dry and brief, and the Superintendent, who explained what had been done to recover the bodies.

Mr. Hench was not in court, nor, to Ned's surprise, was Inspector Brews. The doctor followed the Superintendent, and proved more timid and hesitating in the box than he had been when he had first examined the bodies.

Questioned, he agreed that death was due to drowning. There were no signs of violence on the young couple, except sundry marks made by the instruments used to drag the pond.

Here Ned noticed another shade of expression cross the face of the Coroner, as he leaned forward.

"Did you examine the organs, Dr. Sant?"

Dr. Sant drew in his lips, "Cursorily, sir."

"As a result of what you found there, you have had to call in the services of the Home Office Expert?"

The court buzzed for a moment, and every eye was fixed on the doctor. He replied very slowly and softly, "That is so, sir."

"But you are still of opinion that death was due to drowning?"

"I am, sir."

Superintendent Langley was whispering to the Coroner now, who nodded. Ned felt Nancy's hand clutch his under the table at which they sat. He returned the pressure, but kept his eyes fixed on the Coroner's grave face.

The Coroner spoke briefly. The police had requested an adjournment, to make further inquiries. The case was adjourned for a week. They would now consider the question how the late Mr. Habershon met his death. A fresh jury would be sworn.

"What's it all mean?" whispered Nancy to her companion, as the business of empanelling another jury was gone through.

"Don't know! Looks ugly," he whispered back.

The Coroner took up the tale once more. He remarked that it would be necessary for three of the witnesses in the first case to be recalled. Superintendent Langley repeated his evidence word for word. Then Dr. Sant was up again, and giving the result of his examination.

He said that death was due in this case to drowning. He had found marks on the body due to the grapnel being used. Also he had found an abrasion and a bruise on the back of the neck. That might be due to a fall. He believed it was so. Asked to explain more clearly he observed that Mr. Habershon must have slipped in. His feet going from under him, as he stood on the slimy moss-covered bank, he might have shot forward into the water, his neck striking the stones which made a rim round the pond, and so causing the bruise.

Pressed for details, he deposed that he had made some experiments. If a man ran up to the edge of the pond, and there checked himself and slipped, the lower limbs would shoot forward as it fell, the head falling back a little as the body dropped.

"But there was nothing in the organs of the deceased to suggest that his death might have been due to any cause other than drowning – violence, for example, or drugs?" asked the Coroner.

"No, sir. I am of opinion that death was due to drowning. It is possible, of course, that the blow on the back of the neck and the lower part of the head deprived the deceased of the strength to get out of the pond. I think he would have found it almost impossible in any case."

Again Langley was at the Coroner's elbow, and again there was a pause, and then the dry announcement that this inquest was also adjourned for a week, for further inquiries. There was a general gasp, a buzz of conversation, then a stern rebuke from the Coroner, who motioned the police to clear the court as he retired.

Ned hustled Nancy out hurriedly. He wanted to get away before the pressmen cornered him. He managed to get clear of the court, and reaching the car, discovered that the only open road was that leading towards Fen Court.

"Hop in!" he said, "we'll run over to the house. I want to see what damage the sensation-hunters have done. It'll be plenty unless someone checks 'em."

As they spun away up the road, Nancy recovered her spirits a little, after the depression that had weighed on them during the court proceedings.

"What did the adjournment mean, Ned?" she asked presently.

He smiled grimly, "Something wrong, old thing. The Home Office fellow signifies some dope or drug, and that hints at murder. The morbid brutes will be pulling my place to pieces for souvenirs later on. Like hounds round the court house, weren't they?"

Nancy nodded, "And it's got nothing to do with them."

"Nothing at all! If I'm interested, it's because I have to be."

Chapter V

N ANCY reflected for a few moments before she spoke again. Then, "But the old man wasn't doped, or poisoned," she said.

"No. And the car was two and a half miles away." She frowned.

"So all three must have been carried there – to the pond."

"Doesn't follow," said he. "The old chap may have driven there, after they had left the car, and fallen in."

They drove on. Presently they came to the point where the short lane to Fen Court met the main road. Here they found a few straggling sensation-seekers, and a stout constable. He pulled up the car and Ned had a short talk with him before he was allowed to go on.

"Intelligent of the Superintendent," he said to Nancy as they resumed their progress. "He discovered that this lane is private property, over which I have a right of way. He won't let any of the crowd get near the house."

When they had pulled the car up at the gate and entered the grounds, they saw a detective at a window, and, in the garden, Inspector Brews. Brews hurried up to meet them, smiling.

"Well, here you are, Mr. Hope," he greeted Ned, raising his hat to Nancy. "I have been very busy here; hadn't time to go over to the inquest. What came of it?"

"Adjournment," said Ned briefly. "Home Office intervention."

Brews nodded, "Well, well. It's a funny case altogether. You didn't know Mr. Habershon, of course. No? Useful if we could make out what he was interested in, don't you think?"

"Mr. Hench said he was interested in birds," said Nancy.

Brews beamed at her, "Birds. Oh, of course. He was paying for the publication of Hench's work on birds."

"It would be a lot more interesting to me if I could discover what you fellows suspect," said Ned.

"We suspect? Well, I suppose it's too early for suspicions yet. Must have grounds for that, you know."

"Of course. But what did the doctor find? Some grounds there, perhaps."

Neither Ned nor Nancy expected the detective to enlighten them, but he replied at once, "Perhaps. It all depends. No need to make a mystery of that. The doctor found dope; not much, but enough. I don't know what kind of dope, but he suspects it was administered in coffee."

"Then it was murder?" said Nancy, in an awed voice.

Brews shrugged. "Doesn't follow, Miss Johnson. You can administer to yourself. Like anæsthetics for dentistry, you know. It's just possible that a suicide might like to lighten the last pangs."

Ned nodded, "I see. Why didn't Hench turn up at the inquest?"

"Wasn't needed. He saw nothing until you had made the discovery. I am going over there now. Would you care to come with me? He was over here first thing this morning, and said he would like a word with you."

Ned glanced at Nancy, "Care to come?"

She agreed, "I wonder what he wants."

As they left the garden together, and set out towards Mr. Hench's cottage, Brews surprised them by talking quite freely about the case.

"People have odd ideas about us," he confided to them. "Mysterious, sinister fellows, detectives – that sort of thing! Absolute nonsense, if you ask me. We're plain men, doing a plain job. Take me, for instance. I can't see through a brick wall. If anyone can, let him come forward, and give me his views! Every one has a view. It may be wrong or right, but it's a view. Now what would be your ideas about this case, if it was your duty to go into it?"

Nancy stared at her companion, then at Brews. Ned laughed.

"My views? At a venture, I should say it was suicide; with your anæsthetic twist to it, and Mr. Habershon coming along afterwards to see what had happened to them."

Brews nodded, "And you would think they tied their wrists together – when? After taking the dope, or before?"

"After, I should say."

"Then they brought their coffee down to the pond, eh? In a thermos evidently."

Ned bit his lip. Nancy replied quickly, "But didn't they have coffee in some place at Upperton?"

"They did," said Brews, "but there was a thermos in the car. More coffee, you see. Odd that!"

"Very odd. But can it be proved that there was coffee in the thermos?"

"There was, Mr. Hope. And the doctor suspects that it was tinctured with some dope. Now, how did they tie their wrists together if they were under the influence of that?"

Nancy ventured an objection, "But if they were doped in the café, or in the car, and Mr. Habershon was driving it, they must have been carried to the pond."

Brews agreed, "Exactly – *if!* Habershon was sixty-six, but the doctor reports him a strong, well-muscled, healthy man, quite capable of carrying two light young people – one at a time, of course – to the pond at your place, Mr. Hope. From the gate, that is."

"But the car was two and a half miles away?"

"When found. Quite. But what was to prevent anyone from driving it there, leaving it, and going back to the pond."

"Then it was murder?"

Brews smiled. "Now you see what a tangle it looks, even to us. We see the opportunity, but not the motive. We don't know why Habershon drove down here, or why the two accompanied him; or why, having had coffee at Upperton, they had more in the car. We don't know why Mr. Habershon, if it was he, went back, and risked discovery."

Nancy nodded, "He might say they had run away, and he had followed them, suspecting that they contemplated suicide."

"He might have done. It might be true. But who is to tell us? They are all dead, you know. Still, I like to hear everyone's point of view. Here we are at Mr. Hench's. No doubt he will have his ideas too. It may be interesting to hear them."

Ned concluded that the local inspector was a master of wild and whirling words, but of little else. He looked a thoroughly decent, cheery fellow, but there was nothing in his countenance to suggest an overplus of grey matter behind and above it.

"Funny old cottage," he said, dryly.

They had been walking down a field path, and were now at the gate of a straggling and neglected little orchard, in the middle of which a tiny black-and-white cottage stood. Hench hurried out of the low doorway to greet them, but Ned had an idea that the little man was not too pleased to find Inspector Brews with the party. When they had exchanged some commonplaces, Ned went to the point.

"Mr. Brews said you wished to see me, Mr. Hench."

"That is why I came over." Brews beamed.

Hench scratched his head perplexedly, "I do hope the Inspector didn't suggest it had anything to do with that dreadful affair, Mr. Hope?" he twittered, and, seeing the wonder in his visitor's eyes, added hastily, "I thought, as you were a literary man, you might know of a publisher to take up my book, now that poor Mr. Habershon is gone."

Ned suppressed a gasp. Apparently the selfish little blighter thought of no one but himself.

"I'm afraid I have no influence with publishers," he said, dryly, "not in that line, at least."

Brews intervened genially, "Evidently a misunderstanding, gentlemen. I thought I would show Mr. Hope the way over, Mr Hench, but, now I am here, perhaps you can help me. No mystery, you know. Just got to look at me to know I'm no Sherlock Holmes, Mr. Hench! But you're a man of the world, and trained in observation too. What do you think of this little case of ours?"

Mr. Hench scratched his head again, "Doesn't look like suicide to me."

Brews cast a gratified glance at Ned, "Well now, I am glad I asked you. This gentleman here says suicide; you think—"

"Not that I'm quite sure," interrupted Hench hastily, "If it had been anyone else, I would have said murder. That's what it looks like."

Brews drew forward a chair for Nancy, and she sat down. Ned followed her example, his expression perplexed. The inspector bent an earnest gaze on the little ornithologist.

"I'm at sea again. I expect you know what you mean, sir, but you must put it plainer for me."

"I mean I cannot imagine Mr. Habershon committing murder."

"Mr. Habershon, sir? Well, that's an odd idea. How would you make that out?"

Hench made a diffident gesture, "Probably it's nonsense. But I could imagine a guardian, who had charge of his wards' money, getting rid of them – only *not* Mr. Habershon."

"Why, of course not," said Brews, "you town gentlemen are too ingenious for me. Mr. Hope here is a story-writer, I believe, but you have got on to a more difficult theory, Mr. Hench. I don't know how such a plan could be worked out, even if it was a callous ruffian, and not Mr. Habershon."

Mr. Hench looked doubtful, "I don't know. What I meant was that a man who wanted to get rid of his wards – say had made use of some of their money – might bring them down in a car to a lonely place like this, dope their coffee, and then push them in, after tying their wrists together to make it look like suicide.

"But he went in himself, sir?"

"Mr. Habershon, yes. But it's slippery there, and it was dark."

Brews whistled softly, "Why, yes. That is true."

"I nearly went in myself yesterday, when I was hurrying along the flags at the edge," said Ned.

Brews scratched his chin, "Of course it could be so. I don't deny that you have given me something to think about. But there was the scrap of paper. That does your theory in, sir. Unless the guardian was a forger, eh?"

Nancy broke in, "We'd forgotten that. It was in – but do we know if it was in the writing of either of the people, inspector?"

"Mrs. Hoing identified it as that of the young lady, miss," said Brews. "You can't get over that, Mr. Hench. It would mean two coincidences. The guardian would have to have made free with the funds, and want to get rid of his wards, and simultaneously the wards would have wanted to get rid of themselves."

Hench shook his head, "I don't see that. What did the note say?"

Brews repeated it, "That's all. No end to it."

Hench stared. "But that might be a bit torn out of its context in a letter, inspector. It sounds like it."

Brews started, and an anxious expression came into his face, "Why, yes, that's another way of looking at it. A scrap torn out of a letter. It had that appearance. You see, Mr. Hope, how wise it is not to turn down amateurs' theories. It isn't that they know our work, or are any smarter really. But they come to it with a fresh eye."

Hench looked gratified. "You see what I mean then. To make it look still more like suicide there was that scrap pinned on. Not addressed to you police, or to the Coroner, as it would be. Just made out to give an impression that they were both tired of life, and about to end it. Only, as I say, I couldn't believe it of Mr. Habershon, and I was only speculating about the money."

"We'll soon see about that," said Brews, cheerfully. "One of our people has gone to the house in London to make a search of it, and go through the papers. If there was any money out of order, he'll find all about it. But I must say, you have a flair for detective work, sir. With all respect to Mr. Hope here, you've hit on a more workable theory."

Hench swelled himself out, "I may be quite wrong. Quite out in my reckoning. But it just struck me. Then, inspector, there was the wristwatch found on the young man, wouldn't that give you the time he went in?"

Ned and Nancy looked at the detective. He nodded, not unhappily.

"Well, of course, we looked to that. We know the ropes as far as routine is concerned. We have the technique all right, though our ideas may run in the same groove too much. It had stopped at a quarter past nine."

Ned started, "But I was here shortly before ten, inspector."

Hench intervened, "It was your light I must have seen. It must have happened before you came, Mr. Hope."

Brews nodded. "That's it. Mr. Hope came along after. It was all over then. Well, I am much obliged to you, Mr. Hench, and I must be going."

Hench nodded and smiled, then he turned to Ned.

"I wish you would stay for a little, and look at my illustrations for my book, Mr. Hope. I must say they're unique. If you came across a publisher any time, and he wanted something of the kind."

Ned got up, "I am sorry, but I must take Miss Johnson back to town. I may come in tomorrow, though I can't promise."

Hench had to be content with that. He sat down to resume some notes which their arrival had interrupted, and Brews walked with his companions back to the main road, where he left them.

"That's an observer – trained too, Mr. Hope," he said, as he raised his hat. "Mr. Habershon, or no Mr. Habershon, there may be something in his theory; part of it anyway."

"What do you think of him?" Nancy asked, as she and Ned went back to the car, "if a man tells you he's clever, he is very probably a fool; and if he says nothing he may be a fool; but, if he gives himself away openly, the odds are that he isn't."

Ned agreed. "No man could be such an ass as he seems to be. What struck me about his method was this. He asked my opinion. Why? I have nothing to do with it. I didn't even know Habershon. Does he suspect me simply because I came here that night to get my cigarette case?"

"I suppose he does," said Nancy, as she got into the car, "You see, we are still only names to him. He has no proof that you never met Habershon. He's bound to keep you on the list till he knows more."

He started the car, looking thoughtful. "Yes – I suppose so. I say, Nance, what do you think of having a spot of lunch at Upperton. It's getting late, and I want to have a chat with the fellow, the agent who sold me the house. I didn't get that seven hundred and fifty without a bit of a screw, and I want to know if it's all thrown away."

She nodded, "I think you are wise to see him. I am sorry, old boy. It's a nasty jar for you, with your other lease still running."

"I'll sell right away, if I can get any kind of an offer," he returned, as he got into top gear, and accelerated. "I can't afford to lay out the money, unless I go to live there."

Nancy shivered at the idea. "Ned, you saw that scrap of paper. Did it look like a bit of a letter?"

He nodded, "I must say it did. Jolly well like it."

"But is Mr. Habershon the type to murder?"

He shrugged, "There's a lot of clotted nonsense talked about types. One chap makes out that a public schoolboy, or a gentleman, would never commit premeditated murder; isn't the type. People aren't types in that sense. Every person you know is a mass of contradictions. A man is made up of cross sections of dozens of so-called types. And how are we to classify anyway? What do we know of each other? To bring it closer home, what do you know about me, old thing?"

"I suppose I don't really know much," she murmured.

"As little as I know about you. You know what you think I am. But you won't really know till the Day of Judgment."

Nancy nodded. "I don't think I want to know too much about anything."

"You're wise," he said. "If we all were omniscient we'd go mad."

Chapter VI

T HEY lunched at the best hotel in Upperton, and though the food was good and the cooking excellent, they had a rather worried expression on their faces when the waiter came in with coffee.

Frankly, the interview with the estate agent had been as unpalatable as it was brief. He was sorry for Ned, but that was all there was to it. Neither he nor anyone else, he averred, could sell that house again for a year – it might be more. People were superstitious. There was no gainsaying it. They didn't believe in ghosts, but they wouldn't go where ghosts were.

"Now, what I am going to do is nebulous, to say the least of it," Ned remarked, as he put sugar into his cup, "it's either live in it, or sell it. I can't sell, and no one—" he glanced at Nancy, "no one would like to live in it. Damn those ponds!"

Nancy knew what he meant. He could live there at a pinch, but he had not bought the place as a celibates' paradise.

"I could lend you a bit if you're likely to be hard up."

He shook his head, "Awfully decent of you, but – Oh, help! Here's Bell of the *Record*."

Nancy knew Mr. Bell slightly. He was heading for their table, with a significant grin on his face.

"May I sit in at your table, old chap," he asked, when he had shaken hands with them both. "You know, Miss Johnson, I have been trying to run down our friend here for two days, more or less. I even went to Folkestone."

Nancy smiled.

Ned shook his head. "And you can go to Folkestone!" he growled. "Thou art not wanted here, friend!"

Bell pulled out a chair, and asked the approaching waiter for a coffee. "You promised me a story. I saw the old man and he told me to get it."

"Not from me," said Ned.

Bell glanced at Nancy, "Excuse the shop talk, please. Now, old boy, there is kudos for you in this, and better, there is money. The old man says you're a smart fellow. He wants you to go into this. He says a chap who can write detective fiction ought to be able to unravel real life stuff."

"He's mad," said Ned, "the man who writes detective fiction has less chance of unravelling a real case than anyone else. He is so used to making the circumstance fit the crime."

Bell grunted, "Be hanged to that! All the old man asks is that you should take it up. He mentioned the sum of five hundred pounds. Minted coin, darling! All you have to do is to talk learned, bring in bits about that ineffable institution the French *Surete*, crib everything done by everyone else, and steal any police thunder you hear grumbling in the distance."

"H'm," said Ned, and glanced sidewise at Nancy, who was smiling again.

Bell looked at him earnestly, "That's all. Are you on? Make it as high-toned as you like. Our public is one that can't appreciate a tec' novel, unless its fully documented with quotations from Lombroso, classical trials, pseudo-scientific jargon about psychology, and the other tosh with which the uninspired novelist saves his sleuths from doing any real work."

"What do you think?" Ned asked Nancy.

"I don't see why not," she said, "if the editor really doesn't require you to provide the true solution."

"No editor does," said Bell. "Look at the correspondence in all the rags during a *cause célèbre*. Johnnies signing themselves *Criminologist* butt in with the weirdest theories, not one half a mile from the truth. It all goes."

Ned reflected. He was certainly hard hit by the sudden depreciation of his newly acquired property.

"I'll think it over," he said.

Bell smiled. "Don't! Come in and see the old man. By the way, I came down by train. Could you give a poor man a lift back in your jigger?"

Ned agreed, "I may tell you this, my son. If I hadn't fallen down over a deal in real estate, you wouldn't have got my finger engaged in this pie. Not on your life. When you've finished your coffee, I offer you a place in a not very comfortable dickey."

"And I accept it," said Bell, "Miss Johnson, I offer you my heartfelt thanks for turning the trick. I could see that, without your encouragement, he would have retired into his shell."

He gulped down his coffee, offered a cigarette to Ned, took one himself, and beckoned to the waiter.

"The lunch is on me," he added. "I haven't cut into my official entertainment fund this year."

"I think you were wise to take the offer, Ned," said Nancy, as they drove back to town. "But where will you start?"

"Don't know," he said. "Better make a *précis* of events up to date, I suppose. But wait a moment!"

He pulled up the car, reversed, turned, and drove back towards Upperton. Bell leaned forward and touched his shoulder.

"Is this a circular tour, old chap?"

"Forgot something," Ned told him. "I must ask the people in the café where those three stayed for a little," he added to Nancy.

The Royal Café at Upperton was a rather pretentious place for a small town. But the manager was very alert, and very understanding, and when Ned got down from the car and interviewed him, he put things in a nutshell.

"Ah, you're Mr. Hope, who gave evidence today," he said. "I was in Court, at the inquest. Well, I can tell you that Mr. Habershon and a young man and woman came in that night. That was true enough. They reached here at half past seven. But they didn't all have coffee. Mr. Habershon ordered coffee. But the waiter was called back, and told that the young people would have ices instead. Every time of the year is the right time for ices with younger folk, you know."

"Did they all look cheerful, friendly together?" Ned asked, "or would you think there was a cloudy atmosphere?"

The manager shook his head, "I looked in while they were having their refreshments. Mr. Habershon looked calm and serene. The young people seemed interested in their ices."

"Unlike prospective suicides?"

"So I should say. I put it to the waiter, who saw more of them. He says they were not very cheerful, or very gloomy. More or less a normal, quiet party."

Ned thanked him, went back to the car, and set out for town once more.

"Should you say that people about to drown themselves would choose hot coffee or cold ices in advance?" he asked Nancy.

"I don't think they would do either, but people who could eat anything before they committed suicide might choose what they liked best. Personally I don't think suicide and refreshments go together."

"Makes it like murder," he said.

Little more was said about the subject until Ned had dropped Bell at his office, and driven on to the Hampstead flat.

"I'll come in for a little, if I may," he said to his companion, when they reached the flats. "You might help me to get the thing down on paper. A skeleton'll help me to fit on the flesh and bones."

"Don't talk of skeletons," she protested, getting down, "but do come in. I'll give you tea presently."

When they were sitting in her little room, she borrowed his pen, and laid out a writing-pad on her knee.

"I hate this grisly business," she murmured, "but I hate murderers too. If it helps to catch one, I'm on! It beats me why some people are so sensitive about trapping them. They're not half so sensitive about the poor things who are the victims. Carry on!"

Ned lit a cigarette and nodded, "I'm with you all the time. But this job gives me a new respect for detectives. Where do I start? At the beginning, I suppose, which is probably the middle of events. Murders don't begin with the murder. They have roots somewhere deeper down."

"Never mind the roots," said Nancy. "Let's start in the middle, and then we can work up as well as down; root one end, fruit the other."

"Good. Then we'll begin where Mr. Habershon left the house in Bloomsbury with his nephew and niece. Put this down as I go on."

Nancy nodded.

"Mr. Habershon, driving his own car, leaves his house at six o'clock. Got that? Now a query. Did he leave his house in the car, or did he leave the house to get the car? Did he leave with Rainy and Miss Rowe, or did he go before, or after them, to the garage? Find this out."

"They didn't go into that at the inquest," said Nancy, when she had written this down.

"They didn't go into any details. We know why. They were going to ask for the adjournment and the police wanted the details kept dark. Now again. The car, with the three people in it, next drew up at the Royal Café in Upperton. That was at a half past seven. Some pace, for Upperton is twenty-five miles from town. Habershon ordered coffee for all, but Rainy and Miss Rowe countermanded their part of the order, and had ices. Now, a query. Did the thermos found in the car belong to Mr. Habershon? Was it filled at his house prior to his leaving? If it was, and contained coffee, then why did he take the two into the café?"

"Where was he going in any case?" asked Nancy, looking up from her scribbling. "He must have cut dinner. The other two would be hungry, if he wasn't, why didn't they have food in the café?"

"You are running away from me, my dear secretary," said Ned, "I am like Brews, a plain blunt man, with slow brains. You finished with the last bit of script, eh? Good. Then go on: Mr. Habershon and his nephew and niece are then found in the pond. The wristwatch worn by Rainy has stopped at twenty past nine. Query: at what time did Habershon's watch stop?"

"The police haven't thought of that," cried Nancy.

He looked sceptical, "Probably they know all about it by now. Brews told me a great deal that is unimportant. It's what he failed to tell me that counts. Fountain pen forward!"

"All present and correct," she murmured.

"Upperton is nine miles from Fen Court – roughly half an hour in a car at a slow pace. Where were Habershon, Rainy and Miss Rowe in the interim?"

"At the café."

"Well, they enter the café about half past seven, and leave about eight. If they drive straight to Fen Court, they would arrive about eight-thirty. Rainy's watch stopped when he was in the water—"

"Won't a watch go under water?"

He shook his head, "I don't know. Perhaps not for long. Roughly that leaves nearly an hour unaccounted for. We don't know where the coffee in the thermos was drunk. They may have taken it sitting in the car at Pudstey. At all events they finished the flask."

Nancy nodded agreement, "I think not at Pudstey, Ned. That is so far from the ponds. Taking murder as the hypothesis, I want to know why Habershon left drugs in the flask for the police to analyse?"

Ned lit another cigarette. "He didn't. If it was murder, he intended to dope them so that he could stage the suicide fake without a struggle. If it was to be a fake suicide, he expected to dispose of the bodies, return to the car, wash out the thermos, and get away. Perhaps he meant to drive furiously to Costable, get the policeman there, tell him his wards had committed suicide, after giving him the slip, and beg him to help in the search. But one thing he did not intend to do, to fall into the pond himself. No use committing murder unprofitably, is there?"

"No," she conceded, "I forgot that. Go on."

He began again, "What induced Rainy and Miss Rowe to go out for a drive with their guardian, at six on a March evening? Did they usually dress for dinner? Were they going to dinner out of town, and if so, did their hosts usually dress. If they did, why were the three in day clothes? Is it possible that Habershon was going to see Hench? Granted that he was, what attraction would that be to the young people? Memo: see Jimmy Huston, and get any information you can about Miss Rowe, also Rainy, whom Jimmy must have known too. Were either of them interested in birds?"

Nancy scribbled fast, then she looked up, "An awful lot of questions without answers, Ned."

He smiled, "I think I have one answer out of the bran-dip."

"Oh, have you. Good, What is it?"

"Question: Why did Habershon take the pessimists' line of wearing braces and a belt? In other words, why take a thermos of doped coffee, when he treated them in a café as well? My theory is this: he may have hoped to get an opportunity to dope their coffee in Upperton. But they had ices, and even if they hadn't, he may have found the surroundings unsuited for the job. The thermos would be a second line of offence. After ices, they would feel cold; hot coffee from the flask would be suggested, and taken. A smart man would have two strings to his bow."

Nancy frowned, "Suicide of this kind isn't often a premeditated thing, Ned. The scrap of paper was pinned on. Women don't carry pins about, though I expect men think they do. It doesn't seem to me to fit in. Think of it: Miss Rowe, young and lively, if she is Jimmy's Miss Rowe, decides to commit suicide with her lover. She starts out for a drive, has ices in a café, coffee afterwards. All the time she is carrying a scrap of paper hinting that the end has come, and a pin to fix it on with. I don't see her in this Ophelia stunt."

He assented, "That is my idea too. It is just possible Rainy had a pin in the lower flap of his jacket. Some fellows do put one in there, though not many. I'll be able to get some ideas from Jimmy Huston. Meantime, my throat is nearly as dry as my brain. Let me have your notes and then we'll have a spot of tea. After that I have an errand you might do. To try to interview Mrs. Hoing the housekeeper."

"While you see Jimmy? Right! I'll have a shot at it." She handed her notes over to Ned, and went out to make tea. He studied carefully what she had written, and added a footnote.

"How long would that dope take to act?"

The moment they had finished tea, he got up, gave Nancy a short idea of what he wanted her to ask Mrs. Hoing, and left the flat. Jimmy Huston might be in the billiard-room of his club at this time. It was worth trying.

Nancy set out a little later. As she had said she did not care very much for the job. She was not a morbid young woman. But two things figured very definitely in her mind. One was her abhorrence of murder. The other was a, perhaps, mistaken idea that Brews suspected Ned, and might entangle him in some way. Like most outsiders, she did not realise that the police think more of convincing themselves, than of convicting the innocent to make a cheap score. And the disciplined mind of a policeman very definitely disassociates theories from proof, and hearsay from evidence.

In half an hour from her setting out, Nancy was interviewing Mrs. Hoing in the latter's little sitting-room in Bloomsbury. Mrs. Hoing was not so formidable looking at home as she had appeared at the inquest. She appeared glad to have someone to confide in, and that someone a woman.

"I've had such trouble with reporters, you wouldn't believe, my dear," she told Nancy. "Nasty minded people they must be. What has it to do with them? Now, you're different, I can see. And that young gentleman of yours had just taken the house too!"

Chapter VII

"T HAT'S just the trouble," said Nancy, who felt that she was going to like Mrs. Hoing. "No one will want to buy it, or live in it, now."

The elderly woman shook her head, "I said that to myself when I heard the gentleman speak at the inquest. But what is it you want of me, madam? I don't know any more about it than I said to the Coroner."

Nancy frowned a little, "I heard you, Mrs. Hoing. But somehow we could not make out if Mr. Habershon took the car from the house door here, and the young people went with him."

"But why should you want to know that?" Mrs. Hoing demanded now.

Nancy decided to tell her of Bell's offer to Ned, and the latter's acceptance, "It will help him to stand the loss over the house," she added when she had explained matters.

Mrs. Hoing's face cleared, "Oh, now I do see, and I'll help if I can. But wait a bit. Would you like a cup of tea?"

Nancy had an inspiration, "That's awfully good of you," she said, "but might I have coffee, if it is not too much trouble?"

The appearance of "coffee" might enable her to pump Mrs. Hoing about the filling of the thermos found in the car, she thought. The housekeeper nodded. Apparently she felt very lonely and upset, and was glad of one of her own sex to keep her company.

"Of course, dearie," she said in her homely way, "I'll go and tell cook to make you a cup, and I'll have one myself. Mr. Habershon was always very particular about his coffee."

She cut off Nancy's thanks by bustling downstairs. In a minute she came back again, and nodded.

"It won't be long now. What was it you were asking? Oh, yes, about Mr. Habershon and the car. Well, you see, the chauffeur had an evening off, and the car is kept in a garage about half a mile from here. So Mr. Habershon went to get it. He didn't bring it here."

"But I thought you said he left here at six," said Nancy.

Mrs. Hoing nodded, "So I did. But I wasn't asked to speak precise, and it didn't matter, since he wasn't found dead in town. I meant that he left here at six to go for a drive."

"But how did you know he was going for a drive? Did he tell you?"

"No, he didn't. He never went into details. There was no need for them, you see. But he asked to have the big thermos filled for three, and he wouldn't carry that about the streets. He kept it for use in the car."

"Oh, I see. You knew the other two were going since he asked for coffee for three?"

"That's it. I've been here long enough to know what he meant without bothering him."

Nancy smiled, "I expect so. But did Mr. Rainy and Miss Rowe leave with him, or did they meet him at the garage?"

"That I can't say," replied Mrs. Hoing. "You could ask there. Mr. Gray, who keeps the garage, is very polite. He'd tell you. Though, I don't see how that is going to help you. It's down in Essex you ought to look."

Nancy thanked her, "You know Mr. Hench, Mrs. Hoing?"

"I've seen him very often – well, fairly often here. He hadn't much to say to me, but I believe he was mad about birds."

"And was Mr. Habershon interested?"

"I don't know that he was, much, Miss."

Nancy stared, "Mr. Hench told us privately that Mr. Habershon was paying for the publication of a book about birds and their nests."

Mrs. Hoing nodded, "Oh that would be on Mr. Ivor's account. Mr. Ivor was great on eggs. He has a wonderful collection here. I have an idea it was to be mentioned in the book, and Mr. Ivor was only to be told about it afterwards. Mr. Habershon was not one to fuss over people, but he liked to humour Mr. Ivor's fancies, and it was to be a surprise."

Nancy bit her lip, "That was kind of him."

"Well, he may have had other ideas behind it too," mused Mrs. Hoing. "You see, he was dead against the two marrying, and it may have been to be a sort of consolation to Mr. Ivor, for standing in the way over that."

A maid appeared at this moment with a tray. She put out a little table, set upon it a silver coffee jug, a silver jug of hot milk, and a sugar bowl. Then she went out again, and closed the door.

"Black or white, Miss?" asked the housekeeper.

"Black please, and not too much," said Nancy.

Mrs. Hoing poured for her, and then for herself. "I like plenty of milk in mine."

Nancy sipped her coffee, "It's very good," she said, "but I don't think I ever tasted this kind before."

Mrs. Hoing agreed, "Very likely not. Most people like the Mocha blends, or ones that come from the East, but Mr. Habershon always had Brazilian. This comes from a plantation near São Paulo; a friend of his sends it from a special bit he grows for himself. 'Tisn't everyone's taste I know."

"Do you think Mr. Habershon was on his way to see Mr. Hench that night?" Nancy asked, taking another sip.

"It may be, Miss. He didn't tell me."

"Perhaps going to show Mr. Ivor Rainy the illustrations for the book on birds' nests."

"I've been wondering," said the housekeeper slowly. "You see, it would have to be something very interesting to Mr. Ivor that would take him out to Essex at night this time of year."

"I thought of that too. So you don't know where Mr. Habershon picked up Mr. Rainy and Miss Rowe?"

"No, I don't."

"I suppose the police haven't bothered you much?" asked Nancy, who thought she had better go on to the garage.

"In a way they have, and in a way not. There's one in the house now; in Mr. Habershon's study."

Nancy started. "Really? But why?"

"Going through the papers, Miss. He came this morning, and he's been busy since. A quiet man and no trouble."

Nancy rose.

"Well, Mrs. Hoing, you have been awfully kind, answering all my questions. I shouldn't have bothered you, only I do want to help Mr. Hope. I think I will act on your hint, and go round to the garage now. Thanks for the coffee."

Mrs. Hoing smiled, and got up to show her out. "That's right. You ask Mr. Gray, and he'll tell you all he knows. And if there is anything more I can tell you, come round. I'm glad to see a bit of company."

When Nancy had ascertained the address of the garage, she thanked Mrs. Hoing again, and went in search of it. Reaching it about half an hour later, she was fortunate in finding the proprietor in his office. He received her very politely, though he hesitated for a moment when she told him that she was making inquiries on behalf of a paper.

"It depends on what you want to know, Miss," he said, when she asked him to tell her if Mr. Habershon had any passengers on board the car when he set out for Essex. "But I don't see that it can do any harm to tell you that he hadn't. He came in here for the car about a quarter past six. It was always kept ready for him, and he was in a bit of a hurry that night. He got in, and drove away in five minutes."

"Then his niece and nephew were not with him that night?"

"Not with him here, but I understood he had to pick up two people. A dreadful business that, Miss."

"Ghastly," she agreed. "Did he say where he was going to pick up his passengers?"

"No, he didn't. But he was not the kind of man to give anyone information, and of course it wasn't my place to ask."

"I see that. Had he a flask with him – a thermos?"

"Yes. He had one under his arm. He often took it with him if he went into the country."

As there was no more information to be got out of him, Nancy thanked him, and went home. She rang up Ned on arrival, but he was out still, and there was no answer.

On the whole, she decided that the information she had received from Habershon's housekeeper was interesting enough to communicate to Ned without delay. After his fatiguing day he would probably return early to his flat that night. She would ring up once more between nine and ten.

She dressed, and went down to the service restaurant for her dinner. She met a friend from one of the other flats there, and talked with her until half past eight. Then she went to her own flat, and sat down to think things over.

But not much relevant matter accrued from her long reflections. Only one fact, or theory, that was at all significant occurred to her. If Habershon had picked up the young people somewhere, it might be at some house where they had been paying a visit. Could she discover the address? Rainy and Miss Rowe could hardly have been out to dine, since they had been picked up, presumably, some time after six, but they might have had a late tea. If Rainy was so keen on ornithology, and there was a chance of seeing the illustrations for Hench's book, he might in his eagerness have voted for a run out to Pear Cottage at once. That left some time unaccounted for, it was true, but she could not expect to discover everything at once.

At half past nine she rang up Ned's flat. After a few moments, she heard his voice.

"Is that you, Nance?"

"Speaking," she replied, "Ned, I have some news for you. I went round to see Mrs. Hoing just now. She was very helpful – quite a good sort. After that I went to the garage where Mr. Habershon used to put up his car."

"Oh, good!" said Ned approvingly, "and what did you hear from the housekeeper?" She told him briefly, "So you see, if it is of any importance, he did not go direct from his house in the car," she added.

"I know that," said Ned, surprisingly.

"How?" she demanded. "Been at the garage, too?"

"No, but I have had a talk with Jimmy Huston. I'll tell you more about that tomorrow. Is that all you got from Mrs. Hoing?"

"You're jealous," she cried. "How was I to know that Jimmy knew something that we didn't? I would like to know—"

"I'll tell you tomorrow," he said hastily. "I know all about the sanctity of private phone calls, and all that, but must be careful."

"Wait a moment," she said. "There was another thing. That thermos flask was filled at his house. He took it under his arm to the garage. Did you know that?"

"No. That's good, and its news to me. And though Jimmy said Ivor was fond of birds and their eggs, he didn't tell me what a passion it was, or the old chap's reason for acting as patron to Hench."

Nancy felt pleased that she had succeeded in gathering some information which was fresh to Ned.

"Well, Mrs. Hoing said he had the flask filled, and it was Brazilian coffee. She gave me a cup. It was nice in a way, but I don't think as nice as Costa Rica or the Eastern coffees. Matter of taste I suppose."

Ned's voice sounded excited as he replied, "Oh, good egg! We'll try that on the dog – old Brews. Sure it was Brazilian?"

"Quite. She said Mr. Habershon was fond of that kind, and got it sent to him by a friend in São Paulo."

"Splendid. I say, old thing, are you game to go down with me again tomorrow? I want to put it to Brews. I have a kind of vague theory. No, I won't mention it now. I'll tell you privately. Think out a theory yourself now, and we'll compare notes in the morning. You got part of it yourself. Mr. H. took the thermos with him *filled*. Now I must get to bed. I have a job to do early, and I'll call for you at ten."

It was very exasperating. He rang off at that minute. Nancy felt sure he had something up his sleeve. But perhaps it was wiser not to talk too much over the wire. She was not sure if people at the office overheard conversations, nor was Ned.

As she undressed and got into bed, she was thinking of what Ned had asked her to do. Of course she knew that the thermos had been taken off in the car already filled.

Enlightenment suddenly came to her. Mr. Habershon had a chance to drug that coffee. How silly of her not to think of it before! He was against the young people marrying. Perhaps the money came to him if they died? If it didn't, of course, the theory fell flat.

Wait a moment, she said to herself, what about seeing Mrs. Hoing next day, before Ned called for her?

That was certainly an idea. Nancy knew little of the ways of poisoners, and detested that crime beyond most others, but even to her inexperience it seemed foolish to imagine that Mr. Habershon would go to a shop and buy dope. Hadn't you to sign the poison book or something?

On the other hand, Mrs. Hoing would know if there were any drugs kept in the house. The only question was, would she speak!

Chapter VIII

N ANCY rose very early next morning, and hurried to Mrs.
Hoing at a quarter past nine. If she was not back at ten, Ned
could wait. But if Mrs. Hoing was willing to give her the information,
she could hear all she wanted to know in five minutes, and rush back.

As she went she was thinking deeply. The part of Bloomsbury where
Mr. Habershon lived had grown fashionable in the last few years. His
house was rather a fine one, and expensively furnished. He had a staff
of servants, and it must cost him something to live there.

He had been training for the law, but had given it up when he
came into twenty thousand pounds from his sisters. Her arithmetical
faculty was not great, but she knew that that sum, at five per cent,
would provide a thousand a year. She would have to ask Ned if a
thousand a year went very far, living in that style.

She reached the house just in time to catch Mrs. Hoing. The housekeeper, in black, was setting out shopping. Nancy felt that it was rather
daring, and perhaps indiscreet, to hold the woman up in this way just
to get some information about Mr. Habershon. But it was now or
never.

She was relieved to find that Mrs. Hoing did not resent her questions.

"I said, you know, miss, that I was willing to tell you what I could," she remarked, as Nancy volunteered to walk towards the shops with her.

"I wondered if Mr. Rainy could have got the drug in Mr. Habershon's house," Nancy said to the amiable elderly woman, as they set out, "I mean Mr. Habershon may have kept some, and forgot to lock them up."

Mrs. Hoing started, "Well now, of course there was some – sleeping stuff, anyway. Mordinal it was. Mr. Habershon's doctor recommended it to him a year or two ago, when he couldn't sleep."

Nancy felt excited now, "But I thought Mr. Habershon was a very healthy man for his age. Didn't the doctor say so at the inquest?"

"He did, Miss. But insomnia isn't always a sign of disease. Mr. Habershon was as strong as a horse, only he was a bit of the worrying kind. If he couldn't sleep for three or four hours, he would think there was something wrong. His doctor could tell you that. Insomnia's like flu, dearie. Some people call it flu when they have a cold, and some talk of suffering from insomnia when they miss an hour or two's sleep."

"Did he keep the stuff locked up?" asked Nancy.

"No, Miss. He had it in a cupboard in his bedroom. You see, as his doctor tells me when I asked him about it, Mordinal isn't a very strong drug, and not dangerous if you keep to the dose. He said he recommended it more to make Mr. Habershon's mind easy."

They had now reached Oxford Street, and Nancy held out her hand, "Thank you so much for telling me. You have been a great help to us, Mrs. Hoing. I hope the police haven't worried you any more."

"No, Miss. The one I had here worked late last night and hasn't come back since. He took a lot of papers away."

When she left the housekeeper, Nancy flagged a taxi and drove back quickly to Guy Mansions. Ned was already there in his two-seater, and had a fine hamper in the dickey.

"We'll picnic somewhere," he told her. "I have expenses for this stunt, and I thought we ought to do ourselves well for once. Hop in, and I'll tell you about my visit to Jimmy Huston as we drive."

The day was fine. The sun shining. It was difficult for either of them while in the other's company to see the tragedy in quite as grisly an aspect as it had first presented itself to them.

"I don't think I care much for Jimmy," began Ned, as they drove out of the street and turned a corner, "he's a bit of a weed, and conceited enough to think himself a fine flower. He swears Miss Rowe was in love with him, and not Ivor. He says Ivor was a swot, and a highbrow."

"Nasty little man," murmured Nancy.

"So I thought, but this is his yarn. He says Habershon liked him and encouraged him, but somehow Ivor had managed to dominate the girl. The day this happened, he rang up Miss Rowe, and asked her would she come to tea at his flat. He paints a bit, and he wanted to show her some of his stuff. I saw it. Great Snakes, Nancy! Cubism is dying out, but he doesn't know it. He's a perfect ass. But that hasn't anything to do with what I am telling you. It was this: the girl said she wouldn't come without Ivor. He said to bring Ivor. Better to see her even with the other fellow than not at all."

Nancy nodded. "Yes. Did Rainy go?"

"Absolutely, only it turned out that Ivor was busy blowing some eggs, or mounting them, or something, and that kept them late. Jimmy said he was in a bate about it, but he showed them his stuff, and they had a hefty tea at half past five – they hadn't arrived till half past four, and Jimmy was keen for them to see his stuff first."

"That's why they weren't hungry later."

"Seems so. Well, to Jimmy's further disgust, Mr. Habershon rang up about a quarter past six. He was going to call for his nephew and niece in half to three-quarters of an hour. Rainy didn't say why. I expect between ourselves that he had had enough of Jimmy's bragging, and Jimmy's art, and wanted to get away. Habershon turned up with the car. I gather that something Jimmy said to Ivor about taking Miss Rowe away so soon (he practically suggested that Ivor had got old Habershon to come) made a row between them. Anyway Jimmy was huffy and didn't go down with them to the car. He saw them drive off out of the window – looking out I mean."

Nancy smiled. "I can imagine him doing that."

Ned turned his head towards her, "Now what is your theory?"

Nancy told him of her talk with Mrs. Hoing that morning, "You see, that shows us Mr. Habershon could have doped the coffee in the flask. The only question is, was it the same dope – mordinal?"

"There's another question, too," replied Ned, quickly. "Was it the same coffee? I've seen the Brazilian beans, and they don't look the same as the others. I expect an expert could tell us that – I mean the difference."

"You mean the analyst who examined the dregs left in the flask?"

"That's right. Now, unless old Brews has this information, it is something we can swop. I can't see him confiding much more in us. But, if he'll tell us at what time Mr. Habershon's watch stopped, we'll put him on to this coffee business."

There was a short silence, then Nancy spoke again, "Ned, if Mr. Habershon had an income of about a thousand a year, do you think he could keep up the establishment he did?"

He knitted his brows, "Jimmy Huston said it was pretty luxurious. I should hardly say he could, unless he had other resources. But we mustn't forget that the two were living with him, old thing. It is quite on the cards that he was allowed to use the income, less allowances to the nephew and niece until they came of age. But I can't see it likely that the two women who died would mention him as succeeding to the fortunes if Rainy and Miss Rowe died."

"He would be too old, wouldn't he?"

"Well, they would naturally assume that their children would out-live Habershon, and they had already left him twenty thousand. But we'll know all about that when we hear what the will said."

The sun was well up, and the weather extraordinarily mild, when they reached a spot about two miles from Upperton. Ned stopped the car, backed it into a lane, and suggested an early lunch.

"Then when we get to Fen Court we can carry on without any further breaks until it's time to go back," he said.

"What can you do there after you have seen Brews?" she asked, as she began to unpack the hamper.

"Have a look round the garden," he said. "It's my place after all, and the police only object to tramping about before they have examined the ground. They must have got it all measured and taped out by now."

Lunch over, they started again, and reached Fen Court in half an hour.

A policeman was still on duty at the end of the laneway leading to the house, but when they reached the gate, and entered the grounds, the garden was empty, the sinister ponds gleamed in the sunlight.

"Perhaps we ought to have looked for Brews in Upperton," mur-mured Ned, as he went along the terrace.

There was a tap on a window behind them as he spoke, and they both wheeled about, to see Inspector Brews beckoning from the drawing-room window.

"B'Jove! He's got Hench with him," said Ned, in a whisper, as they turned towards the door, "I wonder what's that for?"

Brews welcomed them heartily, "I hear you've turned journalist, Mr. Hope," he said, smiling. "Don't know if I ought to talk to you at all now, but I'll give you the benefit of the doubt."

Ned glanced at him in surprise. He had spent the early hours of that morning writing his first press article on the case, but how did Brews know of his new job? Hench had been bobbing at him, and then at Nancy. He burst out suddenly.

"Then you've heard about Mr. Habershon and the money, Mr. Hope!"

"Hush!" said Brews. "I didn't tell you, sir, to shout it all over the place."

Ned stared at the little man, "Money? What money?"

Brews studied Ned's face thoughtfully, while he made a gesture enjoining silence on the little man, "I may take it, sir, that this will not go into your paper?"

Ned nodded, "You may always take it, Inspector, that I shan't publish anything prematurely that will obstruct you in your work. Now may I hear what exactly is up."

Brews stroked his chin, while Nancy bit her lip, and waited excitedly for his revelation.

"Well, sir, our inquiries in London disclose a rather serious state of affairs. As far as we can learn, Mr. Habershon was not hampered by any restriction to trust funds. He was not a trustee in the technical sense of the word. The fortunes he was managing for Mr. Rainy and Miss Rowe were invested in house and flat property. A great deal of this property was sold two or three years ago. The proceeds were invested in various shares. There were subsequent sales and reinvestments. But within the last three months a sum of sixty thousand went into Bearer Bonds."

Ned had a faint idea of what was coming, "Not dud stuff?"

"No, sir, quite excellent in their way, but, being what they were, as negotiable as bank notes, and no questions asked."

"The kind of thing a man can get away with, and sell at any time," cried Hench excitedly. "I can hardly believe it, Mr. Hope."

Brews silenced him again, "Allow me, sir. But that in itself would be all right if the bonds were to hand. But they aren't."

Hench was irrepressible, "But, I told you, inspector, that that is nonsense. If Mr. Habershon meant to kill them and bolt, he would have had the bonds with him."

Brews shrugged impatiently, "Not if it was to appear like suicide, sir. Suppose that to have been the lay, and Mr. Habershon got away with it. He must have hoped a verdict of suicide would be brought in. Then he would only have to settle down until such time as he judged it safe to get away with the booty. But this is all speculation, Mr. Hench, and you may get into trouble if you let it go any further. That also applies to Mr. Hope here. The affair is still, in a sense, *sub judice*. All we know is that the Bearer Bonds are missing."

"I can't believe it of Mr. Habershon," said Hench stubbornly.

Nancy suddenly found her voice, "I say, Mr. Hench, did you invite him to bring his nephew down to see your book illustrations that evening?"

Hench shook his head, "No. I wouldn't have gone out if I had invited guests. But I certainly did tell him I should be glad to see his nephew at any time."

Why?" asked Brews.

"Because he was a great collector of birds' eggs," replied Hench. "He had great luck and skill in finding, and then he had a good allowance from his uncle, and bought specimens. If you look at my illustrations you will see that some of them represent the gems of Mr. Ivor's collection. But Mr. Ivor didn't know that I was going to mention them. We kept that dark. His uncle wanted to give him a surprise."

Nancy smiled. This bore out what Mrs. Hoing had said to her, "But they might have come down by chance that night. Mr. Habershon may have told Mr. Rainy."

"Oh, that is quite possible. It explains the fact that the car came this way. But it seems a pity Mr Habershon didn't let me know."

"It may have been a sudden impulse," said Nancy.

Brews broke in, impatiently, "Or an excuse to get his nephew down here. Well, Mr. Hench, I am obliged to you for your information. It helps us quite a lot. But I won't keep you any longer."

Hench raised his hat to Nancy, and was about to go, when he turned back to speak to Ned.

"I wish you would come over to see the illustrations, Mr. Hope. When you have had a talk with Mr. Brews, perhaps."

"I may if I can manage it," said Ned.

"Now, sir," began Brews, when Hench had disappeared, "I can see you've got some fresh ideas, probably better ones than that little gas-bag. Something that Mr. Huston told you perhaps."

Ned would have felt inclined to dub the inspector a gas-bag, superior even to Hench, if it had not been for the sting in the last sentence. It certainly looked as if his visit by night to Fen Court might have unpleasant repercussions. Unless Brews had had him shadowed, how did he know that he had seen Jimmy Huston?"

"I only heard from Huston what Hench has been telling us," he said, after a moment's reflection, "that Rainy was fond of ornithology."

"Then perhaps it was something that Miss Johnson here heard from Mrs. Hoing?" said Brews beaming at Nancy, "Was that it?"

Nancy bit her lip, but smiled a moment later, "Fair do's, inspector! You want to know something and we want to know something."

Brews laughed, "What's yours, Miss?"

Ned glanced at Nancy. It was unlikely that she had been shadowed too, but quite possible that the detective who had examined Mr. Habershon's papers had asked who was the housekeeper's visitor.

"We want to know at what time Mr. Habershon's watch stopped," he said, frankly. "That can't do any harm."

Brews nodded, thoughtfully, "And what do I get for this pretty thing?"

"A little information about the dope used," said Ned.

"Mordinal, wasn't it?" said Brews, quietly. "Mr. Habershon's doctor prescribed it for him a while back."

"Then it was in the dregs of the flask too," said Ned, quickly.

"Yes, sir," replied Brews.

"And—" went on Ned. He suddenly recollected that Brews was leading him on without giving anything in exchange, " – well, is it a swop?"

Brews smiled gently, "I haven't heard anything new yet, sir. You needn't tell me that Mr. Habershon had the thermos filled at his house, and took it with him in the car, or that there are ten tablets missing from the mordinal bottle in his bedroom."

"You haven't heard anything new, but I have," said Ned. "You've just told me that mordinal was not only used by Mr. Habershon, but also found in the flask. Now what about the watch?"

Brews grinned, "You're up on balance so far, sir, not me! A swop's an exchange, not a gift."

Ned looked at Nancy. She nodded. Both felt that Brews would play the game with them, and at the back of both their minds was the idea that the inspector, if he turned rusty, might be able to demand as a right any information they had which bore on the case.

"Well, Inspector, I give it to you for what it is worth," said Ned. "Mr. Habershon used nothing but Brazilian coffee. If Brazilian coffee was in that flask you may take it that the thermos was doped between Gale Street and here."

Brews stared steadily at Ned, and then broke out, "What did I say, sir, about a fresh eye. You thought you had a lot of information that we had overlooked. But that was all routine work. We do that sort of thing on our heads, so to speak. You collected a lot of chaff, but you saw a grain of corn, too, that we missed."

"Or a bean of coffee," said Ned.

"Or a bean of coffee, sir," replied Brews. "Now that tip goes to the analyst at once. He'll tell us what kind of coffee was in the flask. Good! I'm much obliged to you."

Nancy beamed at Ned, and he at her, "But now you might tell us about the watches, Inspector," she said.

Brews went over to a chair where he had left his hat, "Oh, I don't mind telling you that, Miss. Mr. Rainy's wristwatch stopped at four minutes after – no, Mr. Habershon's you were asking about, wasn't it? Well, his stopped four minutes after Mr. Rainy's. And now, sir, I must hurry away to see our analyst."

When he had gone, Ned stared at Nancy. She shrugged.

"I wonder why Brews tells us so much," he murmured, doubtfully.

Nancy bit her lip, "I wonder if he tells us the truth. That's more to the point!" she said.

Chapter IX

N ED sat down and began to smoke. Nancy took her place beside him on the wide window ledge, and speculated in silence for a little, her brows drawn down. It was beginning to dawn on her that Ned had been right when he told Bell detective-story writers were not necessarily good at actual detection. Why, any of them could have made a worldwide reputation long ago if they had come forward to solve a single real mystery. But they always waited until the police had made a capture before they rushed in with theories that were anywhere near the mark.

"I say, old thing," said Ned, "I'm quite conscious that I'm not up to Brews' form, but I think I see a little light. All the time I have been asking myself how the bodies were brought here. The theory is by car. Then Brews quite justifiably says his people cover all the routine jobs perfectly. Among them would be tracing tyre tracks down the lane to my gate here."

She nodded, "That would be elementary."

"But Brews never mentioned it to us."

"No, but we can have a look at the lane now. You mustn't forget that you drove down here several times, you drove here again that night, and twice since. In other words you must have muddled the tracks a bit."

He smiled, "Yes, that's my point. Why wasn't I warned off the grass, as I would have been if I had persisted in trampling all round the pond after the police came?"

"Let's have a look before we go any further," said Nancy, getting off the window ledge.

They left the house, and went through the gate into the lane where the two-seater stood. Then they crept between it and the hedge, and made a careful examination of the roadway.

"The tracks here are distinct enough, and there has been no rain for a week," Ned observed, "that's odd."

"You may both have newish Dunlops," said Nancy, "we can check that."

"You're right," said Ned, and they turned back into the house, to take up their former positions on the window ledge.

"On the whole," said Nancy, after a pause, "it seems that Mr. Habershon did not need to worry about a will. He was melting down solid property into fluid cash."

"Bearer Bonds – fluid enough for anyone."

"He then decided to dispose of his nephew and niece, making it look like suicide," she went on. "He had a chance that few guardians have; since his wards wished to marry, he was able to oppose it on the ground that they were cousins."

"Perhaps – if you admit that theory – he made the objection so that Rainy and Miss Rowe would have something to get worried about," said Ned.

"Go on."

She frowned, "But, even if he was able to dope them both, and carry them separately to the side of the pond here, he was obviously incapable of carrying them from the spot where the car was found abandoned."

"A man of sixty-six; no. Out of the question." Grisly as the affair was, and terribly shocked as she had been when the bodies were found in the pond, Nancy was discovering a curious odd pleasure in her ratiocination now.

"But the car needed a driver, or it could not have been found some distance away. Then we must assume that Habershon drove the car to the gate here, did his foul job, got in again, and drove away."

"Afterwards rushing back, intending to make out that he was in pursuit of his wards, who had given him the slip, and manifested suicidal tendencies."

"Quite. He rushed back here on foot, meant to rush off again seeking help, when it was too late, but slipped, and went in. Once in the pond, he was caught by the weeds, and drowned."

"That seems to be the police theory so far, and it had some good points," remarked Ned, "but if the old chap's car has tyres which are neither Dunlops, nor of the same size as mine, then there is a hole in the jolly old ballad. My tyres made a good many marks, and there are no others."

"But the ambulance came and the police came in a car."

"Can't help that, old thing. They must have stopped them at the point where the lane joins the main road. You saw for yourself." As he spoke, he slipped off the sill, and tucked her arm in his.

"Come back to the car again. I must have a map to look at. Unless, as you hinted, Brews is wantonly stringing us along, it was quite impossible for old Habershon to have driven the car here with the bodies – with Rainy and the girl, driven back to where the car was found, and then walked here once more, and slipped in."

"I don't see that," she objected, as they left the house once more.

"I do, Nance. It's as plain as a pikestaff. Say it only took old Habershon ten minutes to drive the car to where it was found, but add to that the time it took him to walk back, and go in. It is presumed that Rainy's watch stopped because he was in the water, and Habershon's for the same reason. But Habershon's watch was stopped only four minutes after Rainy's. Got that?"

Nancy stared at him admiringly, "That is clever of you. Let's run over and surprise Brews."

He shook his head, "You never know if Brews will be surprised. That man is no fool. Besides I want to work out another bit of my theory."

Inwardly Nancy took back what she had said to herself about the uselessness of the amateur sleuth in real life. She followed him to the car, where he searched for a large scale map, found it, and spread it out on the bonnet.

"This is an ordinance map I bought specially," he told her. "Now let me see, here is my watery demesne. Keep your eye on it. Now I want to find the exact spot where Habershon's car was left."

"In a short lane leading to a field near Pudstey crossroads, wasn't it?" she said.

He nodded, scanning the map. "Here we are, this must be it. A blessing on the white head of the man who first ordinanced, also a cheer for me, for my first-time shot! Nancy, do you see this wandering ribbon going serenely from west to east."

"Of course I do. It's the Lum."

"Exactly. It is the far-from-noble river Lum. And it was the proximity of the river Lum that led the estate agents to say that fishing was among the amenities on my estate."

Nancy excitedly studied the map, "Oh, here it runs by that field the lane runs into."

"It does, and it is not five yards from the gate. Now if the old savage wanted cheap and easy transportation, foul ruffian that he was, here it is. Can't you picture it? Draw the car up into the lane, bring out the flask for a little refreshment, serve out cigarettes all round, and wait for the mordinal to do its work. I needn't harrow your feelings with a description of the other events."

Nancy gave a little shiver, "Don't! But how does that account for the bodies being in the pond afterwards? And would they all float down the river so far. It's very slow running, and weedy in places."

He agreed, "That is so, but there are boats. There is a leaky old punt moored near Fen Court. There are no doubt other boats on the way."

"But Mr. Habershon would know that the car was here, and would be found."

"Only for the fact that he did not expect to die there and then, my dear. He fully expected to get back to the car."

"Yes."

"And that is why he left the bodies in the pond. If he had tossed them into the river near here—" Ned paused, folded up the map, and added hastily, "We'll drive over, and have a look. This is where an ounce of practice is worth a pound of speculation. Get in and I'll crank her up. I expect she's cold."

Nancy climbed into the car, the engine was started, and they backed out of the lane and started for Pudstey crossroads.

As they discovered when they reached their destination, the spot where Habershon's car had been found was not so much a short lane as an embayed entry to a field. The gate itself was one of those that are fastened by a spring contrivance. On the ground there still remained the tyre tracks made by the standing car.

"Just the same as mine," said Ned, when they had descended to look, "and there's the river. "And more than that, if my eyes do not deceive me, there is a punt."

They opened the gate and went into the field. The punt was moored to an alder standing on the bank. A strong old rope was fastened to a ring in the stern, and the other end tied to the trunk of the sturdy tree.

"No chain or padlock, nothing to do but slip the knot," said Ned, "Eureka!"

"Not so much Eureka either!" murmured Nancy, who was sorry to break in upon his innocent triumph, but felt that truth came first, "If Mr. Habershon took them down in this boat, how did it come back? The whole thing is very mysterious, but not miraculous."

He grinned, "You are crushing, but not without warrant. A boat is certainly not a boomerang. H'm. I wonder who owns it."

Nancy had caught a glimpse of an old farm house two fields higher up, "Perhaps the farmer."

"Good. Then the farmer for us. He may have heard something."

Ten minutes found them in the farmhouse interviewing the farmer's wife. She was full of the Fen Court affair, and not averse to supplying comment and gossip about it. But Ned mendaciously cut her short.

"We didn't come about that," he said. "We wanted to know if we could buy your punt. We want a cheap one. But perhaps that isn't yours."

The farmer's wife said that it was. Her husband had bought it to fish from years ago, but he was a bit rheumatic now (worried with the screws, was how she put it), and did not use it. She added that other people did, without hiring or paying for it either.

Ned professed indignation. Who had the impudence to do that sort of thing? She shook her head. She did not know. But a couple of days ago, in fact, just about the time of the poor young folks suiciding themselves, it was taken away, and found floating some miles down.

"My husband sent one of our men to bring it back this morning," she added. "Farmer Datchett, down at Poljohn sent word up it was down opposite his place."

Ned and Nancy were now greatly excited, but contrived to hide their feelings. They agreed to have another look at the punt and let the farmer know if they could make an offer. Then they rushed back to the car, to canvas this new discovery.

"Boomerang or no boomerang, I think this was Charon's boat," said Ned. "The old chap no doubt intended to bring it back, or perhaps he thought it would drift on to the sea, and be lost. Now we will race back and examine the bank of the beautiful Lum, to see if we can find any signs that a landing was made there."

"I give you back your Eureka, with my compliments," said Nancy, contritely.

"Thank you," he replied, as he started the car. "But if you hadn't been doubtful we should not have interviewed the farmer's wife and got the actual facts."

Ned drove back rather faster than he had come. He felt that he had made a considerable discovery. Signs of a boat or punt having been moored alongside his garden at Fen Court would pretty well prove that the bodies in the pond had not been brought there by car but by water.

Nancy was as eager as he. She believed that Ned was going to become a very considerable rival to Inspector Brews. What a *reclame* this would bring him, if he pulled it off! Why, his novels would sell like hot cakes; not only, as they did now, like competently made bread.

They pulled up the car at the gate, and jumped out. There was a little gate in the hedge at the side, along which the river ran; it gave on a stretch of grassy bank twenty feet wide. The river itself was fringed with reeds, and they studied this vegetable barrier with interest as they emerged from the gate, and stood on the bank.

"Jove!" cried Ned, "someone has been here. Look! There are broken reeds and that patch of water-weed is torn up. Let's get on and see."

They went down to the water's edge. There they had further evidence of the soundness of their theory. The grass was beaten down, as if something heavy had been dragged along it, and there was a mark on the clay bank that suggested the impact of a broad-nosed punt.

"That's done it," said Ned. "Habershon, of course, expected to tell his story of the young people's bolt to commit suicide, and his futile pursuit. He would make it appear that he had followed them along the road, and down the lane here. Had he lived to do that, no one would have thought of looking for a punt here."

"No," said Nancy, "Let's get back to the car now, and see what Brews thinks of it."

He shook his head as they went into the garden and closed the gate, "Not yet. I want to see Hench now. I promised to look at his illustrations, and we may get some information about Rainy from him. You remember Rainy was so busy blowing eggs, and that sort of thing, when Huston invited them to tea that he came late. Can you imagine the fellow worrying about birds' eggs, when he and the girl had determined to commit suicide."

"It might have been a brainstorm," she murmured, as they got into the car.

"'Ware false psychology!" said he, "brainstorm is a grand excuse for crime; just as Freud and Fraud often figure in the police courts when the swindler had a brainy barrister to defend him. Rainy and Miss Rowe weren't mad. But Hench can tell us about Rainy anyway. When we've seen him we'll give Brews a turn."

Chapter X

HENCH was in deep dejection, and his room dark, when they rang the bell of Pear Cottage. According to him the tragedy at Fen Court had not confined itself to the three persons most intimately concerned, but had wrecked and ruined his own prospects.

His patron had gone, and the money for the ornithological work with him, while his treasured hen harrier had taken flight and deserted her nest, so that he'd had to, reluctantly, fill up the "hide," and abandon his investigations before they had borne proper fruit.

"It's very hard, Mr. Hope," he complained to Ned, rubbing his head slowly with his hand, and staring mournfully at Nancy, who sat by. "Publishers won't spend all the money this thing needs unless you are a big bug with a famous name. But do let me show you the illustrations. They are mostly photographs, with a few sketches."

"We came over specially to see them," said Ned, not quite veraciously, "I know my publisher does a little general work, as well as fiction, and I might put it up to him."

Rather to his embarrassment, Hench seized and wrung his hand. "If you would, my dear sir, I shall be everlastingly grateful." He offered a cigarette case to both, and lit up himself excitedly. "Wait a moment. I will clear the table," here he swept some papers on to the floor, "and lay them out."

"Another batty bird-man," Ned said to himself as he glanced amusedly at the little man, who had now mounted on a chair to reach a high cupboard, and descended again with an immense pile of mounted photographs.

He was less inclined to scoff when he saw the photographs. They were works of art in their way, and marvellously well taken. He and Nancy were loud in their admiration of the little man's skill and patience. The last photograph, of a skua, taken in the far Scottish isles, was perfect.

"If you draw as well as you do this sort of thing, we shall be glad to see the sketches too," cried Nancy.

He beamed, and went to fetch them.

He was evidently a splendid draughtsman, if not particularly good as a colourist, and Ned was impressed.

"Well, Mr. Hench, I have an idea my man will give you an opening if you let me show him a few of these," he said. "I had no idea you were really up to this. I only thought you were a gifted amateur, so to speak."

"It's been the passion of my life," said Hench, slowly. "I am very grateful to you, very. I was beginning to feel that I had wasted my life."

"Well, I'll see what can be done," Ned skated on hastily over this sentimental ice, "Young Rainy would have been another like yourself, if he had lived, Mr. Hench. He was very keen, wasn't he?"

Hench nodded, "According to his uncle he thought of little else."

"Except Miss Rowe," said Nancy quietly.

Hench turned to look at her. "I am beginning to wonder. Inspector Brews has unsettled me. He seems to make it so clear that Mr. Habershon was at the bottom of this tragedy. If he is right, what am I to believe? He even suggested that Mr. Habershon pretended to the young man that I had asked him here that evening. As if I should have gone out when I was expecting guests."

"Of course you wouldn't," said Ned. "It was as well for you in the circumstances, though, that you met Constable Hoggett when you were out."

Hench stared at him in a puzzled way, "I don't quite see that."

Ned shrugged, "We're all under suspicion, even your humble servant has had a temporary shadow. The light in my house that night did it, of course."

"I wish I hadn't mentioned it," said Hench. "I was very restless that evening, and I went out at half past seven for a long walk. But in any case as I said to Brews, if Mr. Habershon had been coming here, why go to the café in Upperton? You might say to wait till I had had my supper. But he knew I have it at eight, and he might in that case have had his own dinner early in town and then come on."

"Of course, he could," agreed Ned. "By the way, he gave you the impression that the young people were mad to get married. Isn't it possible that all he said about them to outsiders was meant only to work up to a suicide fake?"

Hench wrinkled his brows. "If we concede Brews' theory it may have been so. And that letter, or scrap of a letter, found on the girl's dress may have been torn out of some letter she wrote on some other subject. The idea is distressing."

"But not improbable," said Ned. "We form many judgments from what people say. I know a man I once regarded as a bit of a miser, from what acquaintances said about him. When I got to know him I found he was secretly very charitable. Neither young Rainy nor Miss Rowe looked the kind of people to get into a state of hysteria."

Nancy bit her lip. "If it means that, then Habershon simply told a lie about the invitation here to get Rainy to come. You know, Mr. Hench,

Mr. Hope left Fen Court at a quarter to ten that night. He was only a few minutes in the house. But if the time the watches stopped is to be taken as a guide those poor things must have been thrown into the pond a very short time before Mr. Hope arrived."

"The brute may have been hiding in my garden at the moment I went in," said Ned, grimly.

Mr. Hench shook his head sadly. "He couldn't have been hiding, Mr. Hope. He must have been in the pond too."

He began to sort out some of the photographs and sketches as he spoke, determined to plant them on Ned before the latter changed his mind and went back on his offer.

"That's true," said Ned, "it'll come out in time."

Hench nodded. "I have great faith in Inspector Brews. I started with a prejudice against country policemen, but I must say he impresses me as an excellent specimen. Would I be troubling you too much, Mr. Hope if I asked you to take these photographs with you now? Your offer is too good to be lost. Publication will set the seal on my achievement, which you have been kind enough to commend." He hurried to the cupboard for brown paper, millboard and string, and packed up the photographs with frenzied ardour. Ned smiled again at Nancy, and got up.

They got away at last, with a parcel under Ned's arm, and voted for tea at Upperton before they made an attempt to see Brews. On their way to the town ten minutes later, Nancy was very thoughtful. Had little Hench got to the root of the matter? Was it possible that, while Ivor Rainy and his cousin were anxious to marry, the uncle had exaggerated the situation for his own purposes, and proclaimed a state of affairs, and a state of mind in the young people which had never existed? Even the lovelorn may command their impatience with some difficulty but to think of suicide as an alternative to waiting a year or two, when both would come of age, was to exhibit the aberration of a lunatic.

They had tea at the Upperton café, and were almost finished when Nancy started, and drew Ned's attention to a man who had entered the café, and was looking round for a table. It was Inspector Brews, and he spotted them almost immediately, and came over, beaming.

When they had exchanged greetings, Ned asked the detective to sit down at their table, which was in an isolated position. Brews sat down, ordered tea and hot muffins, and said he was glad to see them again. Nancy was privately of the opinion that he had already seen their car outside, and, having an observant eye, had entered with that object.

"We've not been idle, Inspector," she said, mischievously. "In fact, we have something more to swop, if you have."

He grinned and shook his head. "Not yet. But if there's anything you can spare a poor man, he'll be glad of it."

Ned laughed. "We think you're a miser shamming poor," he said, "but before we leave for town, we'll hand you a token of our respect and affection."

The detective nodded, "Good. I knew I wasn't far wrong when I said the fresh eye would do it."

Ned leaned forward. "There were no tracks of a strange tyre near my garden gate, inspector."

"No, sir."

"While Mr. Habershon's car was found near Pudstey, also near the river Lum, which runs past my place."

"That's right, sir."

Ned smiled. "And near the car a punt was moored that night, but it was unmoored by someone who landed on the bank beside my garden. In other words, the bodies were not brought down by car, but by water."

Brews did not jump out of his seat, as they expected. He nodded, genial as ever, and agreed. "I pointed the possibility out to the Superintendent yesterday, sir, when we were looking over the map, he said. "Of course looking for the tracks of the car was routine. Our men do it automatically, so to speak. But I think it was Hoggett who saw the punt downstream, and told the farmer to send word to where it belonged. Well, sir?"

The waitress came up, and Ned received the bill for the tea. He glanced at Nancy, and Nancy at him. Then they both glanced at Brews, who seemed surprised.

"You're not going yet, sir, are you?"

"We are," said Ned. "There's too much routine work up here. We may do better with Scotland Yard!"

Chapter XI

N ED drove the car off in silence, and Nancy sat beside him,
frowning.

"I don't think I like Mr. Brews," she said when they had covered five
miles on the way home. "He's always right."

To her surprise Ned burst into laughter. "Of course, old thing. We
all hate the man who is right. But really I am beginning to have an
affection for Brews."

"An affection!"

"Absolutely. Imagine a young pup from school coming along to tell
me how to write novels, or a student in a hospital showing the star
surgeon the way to use a scalpel! There would be trouble going, and
no free smiles either. Considering what we are, rank amateurs, he takes
us very well. Naturally he's glad to show us that all our inventions and
discoveries aren't as novel as we think them. But Brews is all right. We
mustn't grumble; what we have to do is to get ahead of him."

Nancy agreed, after a moment. "You're right, Ned. And it was
rather a hit between wind and water when he rubbed in the routine
wheeze."

"What next?"

"Some cold thought at home," said Ned. "The blood's got to my head, and stirred up the old brain too freely. Fever isn't conducive to deduction. At any rate Brews was thankful for our coffee tasting."

When they reached a London suburb, an edition of an evening paper was fresh out in the streets. The contents bill hit their eyes at once, and made Ned put the brake on suddenly:

'FEN COURT PONDS SENSATION.

A WILL APPEARS.'

The news boy came running over, handed in a paper, and bolted on. Ned and Nancy put the paper on the wheel, and studied it simultaneously.

"Why, it's only the dead women's wills," said Ned, "Mrs. Rainy and Mrs. Rowe. I suppose they dug them out of a file of newspapers."

"But it brings Mr. Habershon in," said she, eagerly. "You see, I don't suppose either of them thought it remotely likely, but they did make a provision for Habershon surviving the son and daughter."

"That's true. He was to have – or would have through the joint estate – forty thousand pounds; the remainder going to found a home for ancient maiden ladies without means. If he hadn't made a slip between the pond and the fortune—"

"That makes the verdict an easy one. On the evidence they have, the jury will make it murder against Habershon, and accident in his case," she interrupted.

"Not so sure," he replied sagely, as he started the car again. "Juries are notoriously sticky about circumstantial evidence."

He left her at her flat, and went home. He had an idea which he did not care to advance to Nancy at this stage. Hench had taken photographs by flashlight and daylight, and there was just a chance that something helpful might appear on one of the mounted copies.

When he was back in his sitting-room, he laid out those photographs which had been taken near Fen Court – a hawk in a windy sky, a rook diving at a kestrel, a clutch of eggs in a marsh near the hide. But none of them disclosed a clue. He put them away, and lit a pipe.

His thoughts now began to flutter round Mr. Hench. Mr. Hench was the only acquaintance Mr. Habershon had in the neighbourhood. Mrs. Hoing thought it quite possible that Hench had invited Habershon to bring young Rainy down to the cottage. Mr. Hench had apparently been away from his cottage that night, but, apart from one contact with the village policeman, there was no one to prove where he had been, or what he had done.

Further, there was nothing to associate the cottage with the crime. Mr. Habershon's car had been found near Pudstey. How was one to say that Hench had not been over there, and returned by a roundabout route?

For the terms of the will disclosed in the newspaper that day had suggested a point to Ned. If Mr. Habershon contemplated murder, and a plot to stage two suicides, why make circumstances suspicious by converting the investments in house property into negotiable securities, the Bearer Bonds? Had he murdered the nephew and niece, and survived, he would have had to give an account of the estate; even if it was only to the probate officials. His safest procedure would have been to leave the investments untouched, and simply collar the fortune – smaller but still comfortable – which would come to him under the terms of his sisters' wills.

But even this alternative theory was not waterproof. The fact was that he had exchanged house property for Bearer Bonds to the value of sixty thousand pounds, and he was no longer alive to explain the reason for that proceeding.

Then there was another snag. Hench was a small man, and did not look very strong. The punt would give him no trouble under its grisly burden, but could the little man manage the porterage to the punt, and from the punt to the ponds? It seemed unlikely.

Still the bonds were gone, and unless old Habershon had hidden them somewhere, it was possible that a crook was now in possession of them. A love of birds, and expertise in photography, did not rule out Hench. Gilbert knew that the burglar when taking a rest from burgling may have his innocent hobbies. A criminal is not a robot after all.

There was the alibi, of course, and, on the face of it, a very satisfying one. But that might be got round. Probably Hench knew the local policeman's round, and arranged to make his own journeying intersect the beat.

If Hench was in this, then Hench was a clever fellow, and a long-sighted one. He would be quite capable of deciding that you can have no better witness to your whereabouts on any night at any time than a harmless policeman.

The thing would be to see Hoggett and question him. There was always the unpleasant chance that that had also been a bit of Brews' routine, and that the inspector was keeping an amused eye on Hench. But that would have to be risked.

He would go down next day to see Hoggett. That was the best move. If the policeman had instructions not to talk, he would have to try Brews about it. Ned was becoming interested in the study of the alert inspector.

Whether Nancy imagined he was going to steal a march on her, or not, she telephoned him when he was at breakfast next morning, and asked him his plans for the day.

"Same as before, if you are willing," he replied. "We are now on the eve of a new inquiry, and our first witness is Constable Hoggett. Are you on?"

She was so much 'on' that she was waiting on the doorstep for him when he drove up.

"I shall soon be able to find my way to Fen Court blindfold," he told her as they went along. "Last night I had a filthy job trying to write my bit for Bell, while keeping out all the clues. Luckily, as his readers like maundering rather than detection, I filled it up with quotations from a dozen and one scientists."

During the rest of the run Nancy was busy trying to pump him about his new theory, but he refused to divulge it prematurely.

"Probably it's a dud," he said. "If not, you may gather some inferences from my coming pow-wow with Hoggett. We'll try his cottage first."

Hoggett, as it happened, was in, and off duty. He was inclined to lumbago, and night duty among the steamy marshes had not helped him. But he was ready enough to see the visitors, and received them in his little parlour, where he sat before a blazing fire, smoking his pipe. He excused himself from rising, with one hand at his back, like the persecuted figure in a well-known advertisement.

"Getting too much for me, this lumbago is, sir," he told Ned, when he had asked them to sit down. "The wife says it's my job does it, and I shouldn't wonder. Open air's good for them with chestses, but plaguy bad for us with sore bones."

"It must be," said Nancy, sympathetically. "I wonder you don't retire and try for an indoor job."

"Mebbe I will, Miss," he nodded. "My wife she's always going on to me about it." Having allowed him to canvass his woes, Ned decided that he could now venture on a little mild examination.

"If you think of it, I might recommend you to a friend of mine for a job," he said. "In any case, I am sorry to worry you when you are under the weather, but I should like to ask you a few questions."

"Ask and welcome, sir," said the constable, genially, his eyes alert, as he saw Ned shift a ten-shilling note from his pocket-case. "It was hard on you getting that new house – an old house, too, of course – and then this happening."

"I agree that it was a rotten deal," remarked Ned. "I am trying to retrieve a bit by working this case up for a London newspaper. Now, can you tell me exactly where you met Mr. Hench on the night of the suicides?"

"Just by Pulley's farm, sir."

"Good. I brought in a map. Have a look at it, and show me the spot." He unfolded the map on the table, and Hoggett bent over to look at it, rapping out a "damn" as he did so, and then looking apologetically at Nancy.

"Beg your pardon, Miss. I got such a twinge bending."

"Sit back, and let me hold the map," said Nancy.

With her aid, Hoggett was able to get into a comfortable position for studying the map. He looked at it long and earnestly, then put his finger on one spot.

"'Twas here as near as ninepence, sir. I had my bicycle, and got off to light a pipe. I saw a cigarette end glowing along the road, and then heard someone walking softly but quickly. I'm not really supposed to smoke on duty, Sir, so I put out my pipe, and thought I would have a look – see. If 'twas my superior, it would seem right to show I had my eyes open, and if not, well, you do like to see a bit of company on these roads at night."

Nancy thought the constable showed a very human weakness. She smiled at Ned, who grinned back.

"I don't blame you, constable," he said. "But what next?"

"Well, sir, when I put on my lantern I sees it's Mr. Hench, and I pass the time of day. He says he's been over to Hitherland, and is going right along home. I'd have wheeled my bike along of him, only it wasn't my way, so I just said it was amazing mild for the time of year, and after a few words I went on."

"Apart from accident, constable, would Mr. Hench know what your usual route was – the beat you followed?"

"No, sir, he couldn't, as I change it regular, and he wasn't standing waiting. He was coming along from Hitherland, and I was a bit later than usual reaching Pulley's farm."

"Did he look normal?" asked Nancy hastily.

"Normal, miss?"

"His usual self," said Ned. "Would you have said he was worried, or looked as if he had been exerting himself, or was put out in any way?"

Hoggett shook his head. "No, sir, he didn't."

Ned tried again. "If you had been asked to describe how he looked what would you have said?"

"Well, sir, I should say he looked more perky and cheerful than he does generally. He was very affable, sir, and seemed pleased to see someone at that time of night."

"That was about a quarter to ten?"

"Round about, sir."

"And did you see the light in Fen Court, too?"

"Yes, sir, I had a glimpse of a light your way when I left him. But I took no particular notice of it, not knowing what had happened."

"But you knew the house was empty?"

"I did, sir, though I did hear as you had taken it. But there was nothing in it to steal, I knew, so I let it go by."

"Did Hench look as if he had walked fast or far?"

"No, sir, he wasn't puffed, if that's what you mean; and he didn't look hot or bothered; just as if he had done what he said he did, had a bit of a walk and was going home."

Ned nodded. "Good. Did he appear startled when you threw the light from your lantern on him?"

"Not a bit, sir. Some people is when you flash it on sudden, but Mr. Hench just blinked, as you or I would, sir."

Nancy was smiling faintly to herself. She knew now that Ned was on the track of the little ornithologist, and she was amused. The idea of the little man carrying Habershon and two other bodies was rather a joke.

Apparently Ned had much the same impression, for he slid the note across to Hoggett, got up, and expressed the conviction that they ought to be getting on. Nancy added further sympathy for the afflicted one, and they got away and back to the car in record time.

"My dear Sherlock," said Nancy, when she was seated, "this comes of your not confiding in your faithful Watson. How I should like to see Doyle starting a new series on those lines, with Watson giving Sherlock beans, and querying all his clues!"

Ned laughed. "Wait, my Watsoness! That little man is a dark horse. His anxiety to talk about his photographs rather than the crime is distinctly odd. Fervour I can understand, but even ornithologists must be impressed by three in a pond. His anxiety to push his bally photographs off on me before the corpses are cold, is either callous, or significant."

"Have it your own tin-pot way," replied Nancy. "Apart from the physical impossibility, you can't get away from the evidence of Mr. Hoggett. If times mean anything, Hench must have rushed away from the scene of the crime at a tremendous pace, that is, if it was possible in the time to reach the crossroads where the constable saw him. Then he wasn't puffed, or put out, and he was perky and cheerful. Callousness I can understand—" here she smiled provocatively at Ned, " – but if you think a man who has doped two people, and drowned three, would be perky and cheerful, and full of good, easy, deep-breathing soon after the business, I must put in a – what is it?"

"Caveat, perhaps."

"That sounds as if it might be what I meant. Now, having cleared your mind of a futile theory, where do we go?"

"I think we attack Brews again," he observed. "I have more than two ideas to clash together, sweetheart. Now we get on the great watch trail."

"Watch chain?"

"Trail," he said, quickening the car's pace a little. "Here we have two watches. One is a wristwatch, the other, presumably, a gold lever of a respectable kind. The hands of one—"

"Oh, do dry up!" said Nancy. "I know what you are going to say. In fact I thought of it long ago."

"Good. And you thought—?"

"That you can stop watches without water. Pull out the little lever at the top, for instance."

Ned glanced at her sternly. "To examine the insides of the watches is mere routine. My men do that sort of thing on their heads, so to speak. But you have broken my train of thought, and are wrong in addition. Now I shan't tell you my idea."

Nancy folded her hands, "Do, please!"

He shook his head. "No. You have been rude. You ought to be made like your passive predecessor, who ate humble pie with avidity. But if you listen carefully to what I say to Brews, you may get an inkling of the facts."

"Just as I did from your revealing conversation with Hoggett," said Nancy. "Righto."

They drove on in silence, till they were on the outskirts of Upperton. Here they sighted the massive form of Superintendent Langley.

Ned stopped the car, "I'll ask him if Brews is at home."

Superintendent Langley obviously knew that Ned was investigating. He smiled faintly when the latter drew up the car, and asked him if Inspector Brews was at the station.

"Not at present, sir," said Langley, amiably. "But perhaps I could tell you what you want to know."

"That's just the question," Ned replied, grinning. "I thought I might have a look at the two watches found on the bodies."

Langley shook his head. "I am sorry, sir. If you had come to us before your connection with the press, it might have been possible. Anything else, sir?"

Ned shrugged. "You have had no further news, I suppose?"

Nancy gave Langley her best smile, and he visibly warmed under it.

"Let me see, sir. I suppose you heard about the passport. But that would be old news."

Ned started. "If you go on like this, I am getting a friend of mine in the House to move that Upperton police take charge of the Yard, and the C.I.D. come down here! Old news! Why the papers haven't got it."

"No, sir; if I may say so, we do get a little advance news. A newspaper sensation may be three days' old at our stations."

"*Touché!*" murmured Nancy.

"That's what I am beginning to think," said Ned. "But what is it?"

Langley smiled. "Being a part of our—"

"Don't say routine work. Spare me!" Ned interrupted.

"Part of our work," said Langley. "I had almost forgotten it. As a matter of fact, we found a passport in a pocket of the car when our men searched it."

"Habershon's?" cried Nancy, excitedly.

"Mr. Habershon's, Miss. I release that for publication to you, Mr. Hope, so you will be a bit ahead of your friends."

With a little glint in his eye, he saluted Ned, raised his felt hat to Nancy, and walked away majestically.

"We're now going back to town," said Ned. "All the brains of the country have gravitated to Essex, and I feel out of my class. But Bell will devour this about the passport."

Nancy nodded. "While we have to eat our theory about—"

Ned was starting the car when Langley came back, and smiled, "Oh, by the way, sir, though it is not officially that I am giving you the tip, we have evidence that Mr. Habershon posted a very heavy registered packet to Buenos Aires a month ago."

Chapter XII

N ED drove fast, and said little as they went back to town. On
the way through the city he called at Fleet Street, and spent five
minutes at the newspaper office. When he came out again, he looked
and felt better.

"They're beginning to love me," he said, "Langley has his points,
though I am not sure what they are."

"Will you work the passport into your next article?" she asked.
"That and the packet – the Bearer Bonds, I suppose – more or less
prove that Habershon did it. If he hadn't slipped in, he would have
followed the packet, don't you think?"

Ned drove on. "Since I became a journalist I have studied the ways
of the cleverest fellows on the press; the various Captains, Majors, and
other folk who serve out the racing tips. After giving the claims of ten
horses to win a race, they generally hedge all round the shop, and give
so many alternatives that the average man ends with a pin and a list of
the horses."

"I thought you didn't bet," said Nancy.

"I don't," said Ned. "But I know the method. What I mean is
this. As an expert I mustn't come down strong on one side. I have a
reputation. For a man with a reputation a fence is the natural seat. I
shall indicate that the ordinary man – of whom one hears so much –

will be inclined to think that the identity of the murderer is obvious. The expert may have other views. But, as always, the man in the street may be right. If I'm wrong, then I have exhibited humility and flattered the ordinary man; if I'm right, three cheers for the expert!"

"Bravo!" said Nancy, ironically. "What a nasty double-faced fellow you are!"

"Have to be," said Ned. "Now is it home or Mrs. Hoing?"

"Why Mrs. Hoing?"

"To get news about that packet, of course. I shouldn't be surprised if that is where the police got the tip. They are sure to have questioned her. In fact, since she was Habershon's right-hand woman, he may have sent her out with the precious bonds."

"Right. Then we'll go there."

When they reached Gale Street they were admitted by a parlour-maid. The other servants, with the exception of the cook, had been paid off. Mrs. Hoing was at home, and they were shown into a morning-room on the ground floor. The servant lit a gas fire, and left them.

"This house cost money," said Ned, as he looked round.

"Whose?"

"Ah, that's the whole thing," said Ned, and fell to thinking.

Mrs. Hoing came down within a minute, and greeted Nancy warmly. She was introduced to Ned, and extended a firm hand.

"Pleased to meet you too, sir," she said.

"Miss Johnson told me so much about you that I felt I had to come along," said Ned, thinking he might adopt that air of free and easy fellowship, and naïvete, which had proved so successful when exhibited by Brews. "I may tell you that I am trying to investigate the crime for the press, Mrs. Hoing. I hope you don't mind that."

"Mind it, sir; why, I've been reading all the pieces you wrote so far, and clever they were."

"I am tremendously gratified," he returned. "Do you know, I'm a great believer in the common sense of the man in the street. The police have special training, but their training makes them suspicious of simple explanations. People like you and me don't worry about tying knots in our brains. We go straight to the point. I can see that you have formed a pretty sound conclusion about the case already."

Mrs. Hoing beamed, "Perhaps I have, sir, but it isn't one I like."

Ned nodded. "The sentiment does you great credit. Loyalty is a much needed quality nowadays. It isn't taught as it ought to be."

"Go on, Inspector Brews!" Nancy murmured, just above her breath.

"Quite," said Ned, hastily. "Miss Johnson agrees with me. Here you have been for years with Mr. Habershon. He was a kind and considerate employer, and as far as you knew, a good man."

"He was, sir."

Ned warmed to his theme. "And now, quite against your will, and owing merely to circumstances over which you have no control, you have to wonder if you must consider Mr. Habershon in another light."

"You put it beautiful, sir, if I may say so."

"I know how you feel," Ned went on. "This passport first begins to shatter your very natural illusions."

She stared at him. "What passport, sir?"

"You never knew Mr. Habershon had a passport?"

"Of course, sir. He used to travel sometimes, and the young people with him. But what about that, Sir?"

"It was found in the car, Mrs. Hoing," said Nancy.

The housekeeper threw up her hands. "Well, I never! But not all of them surely?"

"You mean those belonging to Mr. Rainy and Miss Rowe? No. I don't think they were found."

"Which suggests that Mr. Habershon later on meant to take a journey alone," suggested Nancy.

Mrs. Hoing looked horror-stricken. Ned went on hastily.

"Then there is another question. The police may have put it to you already. May I ask if you knew about the registered parcel Mr. Habershon sent to South America?"

Mrs. Hoing nodded vigorously. "Of course I do. I took it. Mr. Habershon said it was important, and he wouldn't give it to one of the maids. I was going shopping, so I took it."

"Did Mr. Habershon ask you to fill up a form declaring the contents?"

"No, sir, he said printed papers, but not at printed paper rates. I filled up the form that way. If you'll wait, sir, I'll bring down my diary. I put it down, the hour and the date."

"Oh, that isn't necessary, thank you," said Ned. "I'll take your word for it."

"Was it very bulky?" asked Nancy.

"Very, Miss. Pounds."

"Did you notice the address?"

"Oh, yes, sir. It was Señor something or other – I don't remember that – 8 Calle Perino, Buenos Aires."

Ned noted that down. "Thanks. Rather odd sending off Bearer Bonds like that," he added to Nancy.

Mrs. Hoing stared. "Bonds, sir? It was printed papers he said to me."

"Very likely, Mrs. Hoing. Well, we are much obliged to you for your help."

"What now – dinner?" asked Nancy, when they were once more in the street.

"With me, if you'll come," said he. "Fact is, I intend to go back to Fen Court late, and stay the night. If we can find a decent little café we could have a spot of dinner, and then I could tootle you home before I go on."

She raised her eyebrows. "I say, what for?"

Ned replied at once. "I am wondering again why this nasty business was staged in my garden. Was it because the amenities not only included a garden and four ponds, but also an empty house? In other words, old thing, I am going to search the premises.

Nancy digested that for a few moments as they drove westwards, then: "What weird ideas you have. Are you likely to find anything hidden in Fen Court?"

He shrugged. "Haven't a ghostly. But what I mean is this: If the police deduce anything from the conversion of those investments into Bearer Bonds, it is that old Habershon contemplated a bolt abroad, and wanted stuff with him that he could negotiate without trouble – and without a transfer to be registered, and that sort of thing."

"I see. Obviously they do suspect that he was on the eve of a bolt, and that is why he had a passport with him."

Ned nodded. "Well, I don't say old Habershon did not register a heavy parcel to a fellow in Buenos Aires, but I do say that only an utter ass would send sixty thousand pounds worth of securities in advance to a dago living about four thousand miles away. Why, the gentle South-American had only to take 'em round to a bank, get the dollars, and vamoose.

"You think it was a blind?"

"I do. Habershon isn't proved a rogue yet, but he is not, or was not a fool either. I bet the police will cable Buenos Aires. Do you think old Habershon would give Mrs. Hoing the name of the man to whom he was sending that fortune? Why, he would have known that she would be questioned the moment he bolted."

Nancy agreed now. "Why, I never thought of that. Yes, of course. And your idea is that old Habershon may have hesitated to leave them, I mean the bonds, in the car, but took them along to your house, and hid them temporarily?"

"It's a possibility. He would mean to go back and collect, but slipped up and couldn't. Another thing, I don't quite trust Hench. I can't work out any theory about that night drive by Habershon and Company, unless it was that Ivor Rainy was going down to Pear Cottage. Outside the wonderful photographs of birds, in which Rainy was really interested, what attraction is there in a swampy part of Essex after dark?"

He drew up the car in a square, and manœuvred it into a parking space. When they had parked, they went back to the main street, entered a comfortable little restaurant, and ordered dinner. As the waiter retired with the order, Nancy took up the conversation at the point at which it had been dropped.

"You think little Hench invited them down."

"If he didn't, who did?" asked Ned, frowning. "That's all."

"Then he must have known about the bonds, and the fact that Mr. Habershon was carrying them?"

"Hench's business with Habershon is wrapt in mystery, Nance. We know nothing about their relations except what he chooses to tell us. The whole ornithology business may be a blind. At any rate, it can do me no harm to have a look round generally."

"If you don't mind being in that spooky house, it can't," she agreed, as the waiter approached with the soup.

"The only spooks in this world are the ones you bring with you," observed Ned.

"I don't carry spirits."

They dined rather hastily, and then he drove Nancy home, and started for Fen Court for the second time that day. His equipment for night research consisted of an electric torch, a case full of cigarettes, and a box of matches. There was also a chisel or screwdriver from his tool kit that he meant to use, if he saw any signs that the cupboard or old panelling of the empty house hid unexpected treasure.

The whole trouble about Hench, as he told himself on the way down, was the little man's physical inefficiency. But was Hench necessarily alone that night? What about Habershon?

There might be something in that. It was only necessary to give Hench credit for a little patient cunning to explain what had happened.

"Let me see," Ned mused, "it could be worked out this way. Hench and Habershon are friends. Habershon has converted part of the young things' property into easily negotiable security. Not being sure that he can manage the job himself, he confides in Hench. Hench, who is a fine photographer, and knows a bit about birds, chooses Fen Court for the *mise en scène*. Here there is an empty house, with four ponds in the garden, within reach of a cottage where he lives. It is arranged that uncle shall privately let Hench take photographs of Rainy's collection of eggs. Habershon is to give out that he is financing the publication of a volume by Hench, in which Rainy's collection shall figure. That will flatter the youth no end. But he knows nothing about this. Habershon is keeping it as a surprise for him. One day, when the stage is set, Hench will invite the uncle to bring Rainy down by night to see the photographs."

At this point in his musing Ned had to swerve violently to avoid two blinding searchlights bearing down on him from a corner on the wrong side of the road. When he had scraped the hedge, and straight-ened the car and his temper once more, he went on speculating.

"Habershon and Rainy and the inseparable Miss Rowe go down to the cottage – I can let the punt theory slide for the moment – Haber-shon has put a big dose of mordinal in the thermos, and Rainy and the girl are doped. From some point or other, Habershon and Hench get the bodies to the water, tie their wrists with a handkerchief, and chuck them in, after pinning a scrap of paper to the girl's dress. Then, when they are shivering on the brink, Hench decides that Habershon is supererogatory. He gives *him* a push, and there you are."

Having satisfactorily summarised his latest theory, Ned turned his attention to details. That scrap of paper, for instance. What was it? So far everyone who had seen it considered that it looked like a fragment torn from a letter.

"By George!" cried Ned, suddenly, and accelerated in his excite-ment. "What a dud I am. If it came from a letter, and was in her handwriting, then it was directed to someone else. If it was directed to someone else, how did it come to be in her possession? That's a nasty one! The only question was if it was a bit of a letter. It certainly looked as if it came out of the middle of a sheet. Habershon made a bloomer there. He must have had a letter from her, torn a bit out of it, and fastened it to her dress. But why the dickens should she write to him, when they were living in the same house?"

"Whatever it was, it wasn't suicide," he declared, "Ices and suicide are incompatible, and they had coffee in the car. An appetite and a thirst, kept up to the last moment? No, it doesn't go. If Rainy or the girl had been bright young people, with the incipient lunacy of their kind, they would probably have danced an expressionist fandango on the edge of the pond, and been horribly symbolical about it. But no symbolist or expressionist would go in for anything so objective as ices.

I'll put that in my next article! There's no being clever without weird words nowadays."

When he came at last to the short lane leading to Fen Court, he found the scene enchanting. The moon was high and near full, the river, the water plashes, the ponds, shone like molten silver. The only sad notes in that etherialised landscape were the old house, black against the grey and silver, and the melancholy hoot of an owl.

As he drew up his car at the gate, the owl stopped hooting.

"Please go on," Ned apostrophised it. "I like your round note, though I have no affection for the screamer of your tribe."

He stopped the engine, and walked into the garden. As he turned the angle of the house, he had a slight shock. A man was standing on the near bank of the pond to the right, looking his way. He could see the figure clearly silhouetted against the pale pond.

"That you, Hench?" he called ironically.

"No, it's me, Brews," said a well-remembered voice.

"It would be," said Ned, rather bitterly, then he laughed, and called to the Inspector to come up.

Chapter XIII

"I T was awfully good of you to send me that message by Langley," Ned said, ironically, when Brews had joined him on the terrace.

"Oh, not at all, sir," replied the inspector, his beam visible in the moonlight. "I thought it might help you. You see, it's all proof."

"You mean the passport?" said Ned, offering a cigarette.

"And the registered parcel," replied Brews, taking the cigarette, and lighting up. "Proofs that settle things a bit."

Ned started. "Now, let us suppose that the registered parcel did not contain Bearer Bonds—"

"Do you think it did, sir?" interrupted Brews, suavely.

"I think it was meant to suggest that Bearer Bonds were in it."

The inspector laughed. "Now that was a good shot. As a matter of rout – I mean a matter of fact, we cabled Buenos Aires police at once. That parcel was opened at the post office, they had an idea it might be something smuggled in, you know."

"And what did they find?"

"A great many copies of a pamphlet denouncing the White Slave traffic, sir."

"Whew!" Ned whistled. "Was Mr. Habershon—"

"No, sir, he was not. He was against it, and the man at the other side was the agent of a Vigilance Society."

Ned changed the subject. "I say, Inspector, how do you people regard coroners?"

Brews looked at him for a moment thoughtfully. "More or less like earwigs, sir. They can do some damage in your garden unless you put up empty flower pots on sticks. They crawl into them, and are out of the way. Though, mind you, sir, there are some good coroners, who don't get in our way."

"Are you going to worry about the verdict that will be brought in at the inquest?" Ned asked.

Brews smiled. "No, sir. We never do. We can take our own action. But, may I ask, sir, what brings you down here tonight?"

"I came to look in my house for Bearer Bonds," said Ned.

"That's an idea," agreed the other. "Parcel sent off as a blind one way, bonds pushed off elsewhere to be picked up later, eh?"

"It's a theory that occurred to me."

"And to me, sir."

Ned started. "Two minds with but a single thought, eh?"

"Or but a single start, sir, only my hare seems to be ringing more than yours."

"Do tell me about the beast!" said Ned, eagerly.

Brews grinned. "Now I came here to see the place at night. You can't discover the snags in a night affair by day. Talking about the inquest, what do you think will be the verdict?"

"Murder against old Habershon in the first case, and accident in the avoidance of his avuncular duty in the second," said Ned.

Brews looked doubtful. "Juries are rather like foxes, they'll go for a safe earth generally rather than take a daring line."

"You're full of hunting similes tonight," Ned returned. "But I suppose you mean that they will not like to fix it on Habershon?"

"Quite, sir. An open verdict of murder, and one of accident will fill the bill. It's very hard for people to believe that an old gentleman with a white beard can commit a crime."

"Beards for benevolence?" suggested Ned. "You may be right."

The inspector threw his cigarette butt away. "If the bonds were here, to your thinking, who put them here – Habershon? And why put them here at all?"

"You are overlooking the possibility of an accomplice."

"He's not strong enough," replied Brews.

"But between them they might have done it."

Brews meditated. "Did anything strike you as odd about that passport being where it was?"

"No, did you see anything significant in it?"

Brews looked disappointed. Whether it was because he had expected better from his companion, or because he wanted confirmation of his own views, and had failed to get it, Ned could not say.

"It was proof, sir, real proof. If I get many more pointers like that I shall begin to feel happier."

Ned fished tentatively. "Yes, of course, or proof of a ticket having been taken in advance, Brews."

Brews looked more disappointed than ever. "And I thought you were going to be such a help, sir," he murmured.

Ned laughed. "It's cold out here, and your chill disapproval gets into my bones. Come in, and treasure hunt!"

There was not the slightest doubt that the optimistic inspector was pulling his leg, thought Ned, as he took out his key, and went to the front door. Well, they would see who pulled the last leg.

"If you will work the torch, I'll tap the panels and search the cupboards, Inspector," he told his companion. "By the way, I wanted to ask you about those watches."

Brews took out his own torch, and flicked it on. "Yes?"

"How they stopped," Ned remarked. "Langley was very official. But I recognise you as a kind soul, and communicative on occasion. I rather suspect that you make the occasions, and are not strictly truthful in your communications, but we'll let that pass."

"How can we be truthful, with you gentlemen of the press about, sir? But what was it you wanted to know about the watches?"

"Did the wristwatch stop, or was it stopped?"

"It stopped, sir?"

"By water, or in the effusion of time?"

"Simpler than that, sir. Because the owner forgot to wind it. It was run down."

"Bless your simple kindness, Brews! Now what about the good gold watch worn by Mr. Habershon?"

The inspector pointed his torch at a piece of broken panelling in the hall. "Here's a bit you might look at, sir."

"Becoming official?" Ned asked, genially.

"I like to be truthful when I can, sir."

"Coward!" cried Ned. "Well, I'll find out somehow. But if you want to be an oyster, do! I shan't love you as much, but you can bear that."

They began their search in earnest, and Brews helped Ned conscientiously until he had gone through the house and found nothing.

"He didn't hide anything here, inspector," Ned remarked, half an hour later.

"No, sir. I never saw how anyone could have done. You see, as a matter of – I mean to say, we had a look at the doors and windows here. None of them had been broken or entered, and you had the only key."

"Is there anything your people didn't do, Brews, as a matter of, shall we say, routine?"

Brews laughed. "Several still to do," he observed. "Now, sir, I am quite interested in your theory about Hench."

"Did I say I had one?"

"No, but I say you have. It wasn't the kestrel did it, was it?"

Ned did stare sincerely now, "The what?"

"The kestrel that Mr. Hench was watching," replied the surprising Brews.

Ned shook his head. "If you mean the hen harrier that took wings, and flew away in disgust, I can assure you that it did not give me any hints."

"The hen harrier is rare, but the kestrel is common," said Brews. "Still, if you got nothing out of that, it may interest you to look it up."

"I'd sooner have the number in the index," said Ned. "Be a sport!"

Brews tacitly refused to respond to this appeal. "What use have you for the punt, if you bring in Hench?" he asked.

"Ah, that would be too complicated for you to understand, my dear fellow. Subtlety with us takes the place of routine with you. But, honestly, what is there against the theory that Hench helped old Habershon to do in the two young people, then thought two into one didn't go, and made a simple unit by pushing off Habershon?"

"It's possible, sir. I won't say it isn't. Of course we have Mr. Hench under observation all the time."

"And possibly myself, since I was here that night?"

Brews grinned. "Well, it isn't necessary now. You keep coming up for us to have a look at you."

"So I do. I forgot that. Now I have done what I came out to do, and I shall be getting back. But, before I go, one word. Does it occur to you that a letter written to the wicked uncle would not appear in part pinned on to Mr. Habershon's niece's clothing when she was recovered from the pond?"

Brews was standing beside Ned. He reflected for a few moments, then took his hand out of his pocket, and looked grim.

"Do you mind if I search your inner pocket on the left-hand side, sir?" he demanded.

"Love it!" said Ned. "But why?"

Brews dived a hand in there, and brought it up clutching two crumpled pieces of paper. He straightened them out, flashed the light of his torch on one, and showed it to Ned.

"How did you come to have these on you, sir?"

Ned glared, "I didn't!"

Brews' face relaxed, and he smiled once more. "You're right, sir. I had them. It's a common idea among old lags that we plant evidence on them. Those two papers are bits of a letter, written by Miss Rowe to her uncle. The scrap found on her clothing was the missing bit in the middle."

"Good Heavens!" cried Ned. "Where did you find them?"

"Where they drifted," said the other, putting them back in his pocket. "Well, I must be off. But when you're driving home, you can have something to think over."

"Bless you again!"

"And that," said Brews, as he turned to the door, "is the question of Mr. Habershon's luggage."

"Come back, you ruffian, and be matey!" cried Ned after him, as he strode away. "Don't leave me in the air."

"Goodnight, sir, and a safe journey home," said the voice of that irritating detective. Then the door banged.

Chapter XIV

NED went to the park next day, taking Nancy with him. The weather was still extraordinarily fine, the sky pale blue, flecked with drifting white clouds; the grass was so green, the black traceries of branches so beautiful, that Nancy involuntarily cried that it was a lovely day to be alive.

"That's what the fat fellow just over there is saying," Ned agreed, pointing to one of the incorrigibly impudent and monstrously fat old wood pigeons pecking among the grasses. "He's as confiding as Inspector Brews."

"And why is Inspector Brews so confiding?" asked Nancy.

He lit a cigarette and shrugged. "That is the question that has been worrying me since I first saw his beaming smile."

"Do you think police work makes people callous?" she asked.

"No more than war made men brutal," he said. "The brutes went out brutes, and the others went out, and came back, as they were. The only monument to the soldier that these decadent war novelists want is to look about them. Where are the beasts and savages they tell us about? Have you met them? Have I? Not on your life! And it's the same with the police – decentest lot of chaps you can meet."

"I quite agree, but you haven't answered my question, old thing. Why is Brews so confiding. Why does he tell you all the latest news? It isn't usually done."

Ned nodded. "I can only come to one conclusion, and that is that it has something to do with the Judges' Rules."

"Have they any?"

"Several. The first is not to know what everyone else knows, and there are several others about the taking of evidence by the police. I am not very sure of the terms, but I think generally there is some prohibition about a policeman asking certain questions if he believes the man to be guilty. He must warn him before he goes on in that case."

"I see."

"Now, Brews and I are exchanging information, and he knows that I am investigating in my amateur way. I can ask any questions I like, you see. I may get information from a man he has his eye on, without being hampered as he is. There is no rule binding him not to take notice of something somebody else has said to me."

"In other words, he is making use of you?"

"Absolutely. I never believed that he loved me for myself alone. But don't let that worry you. I hope to be able to make a personal score before I end. By the way, he seems a jolly smart chap. He told me last night to keep kestrels in my mind. You're more of a country mouse than I am, Nance. What exactly is a kestrel?"

"What a juggins you are, Ned! A kestrel is the chap that gets after the country mouse and the bucolic beetle. It's a kind of hawk that never does much work, but hangs in the sky, fluttering its wings, till it sees some wretched little thing below."

Ned grinned. "Why, you're a blinking Buffon, if that was the fellow's name. Is the bird large?"

"It looks large, though it hasn't any pluck."

"Good again. Now what is a harrier?"

Nancy reflected. "A kind of hound. But they couldn't call a hound a hen. A hen harrier is what I am after."

She nodded. "Let's move on. It's too cold to sit. A hen harrier? Why that was the hawk Hench was watching."

He started. "So it was. 'Kestrels are common, harriers rare.'" He added: "A cryptic but poetic line of Brews'."

He had a portfolio under his arm. It contained Hench's photographs, which he intended to take later to his publishers. He now drew Nancy back to her seat, and opened the portfolio.

"None of these illustrations has a legend on the back or front," he told her. "But one is certainly taken near the back of Fen Court. You can't escape the fact."

"Why should I? What do you mean."

Ned now glanced rapidly through the photographs, and selected one. "Here we have a lazy bird hanging in the sky. Give it a name."

"Common or garden kestrel," said she.

Ned raised his eyebrows. "Well, if Hench was taking photographs of that, under the impression that it was some kind of harrier, he's a cheap kind of ornithologist. I wonder if that is what Brews meant."

"That Hench was making it an excuse to hang about there?"

"It seems like it," said Ned, as he wrapped up the portfolios again. "He may have meant too that harriers were so rare that we should not be likely to find one so close to clvilisation."

"A hint to investigate Hench further," she murmured.

He nodded. "Come along. We'll go down Piccadilly and show these nice pictures to the big man in the stuffing line. We may hear his views."

"It isn't long now till the inquest," said Nancy, as they set out across the park towards Hyde Park Corner.

"No, very soon. We'd better go down again for it. They may want us. In any case, I should like to hear the police evidence before I go on. If they have anything up their sleeves, it may give us a pointer. Brews thinks the jury will hedge."

"Will the verdict affect him?"

"He thinks not. I am not very sure if the police can ignore the verdict of a coroner's court in certain cases. You see, the inquest is not directed to punishing a man, but finding the cause of death. You can't try a man twice on the same charge, if he has been acquitted the first time, but I don't see that you can call the inquest a trial."

"Why wouldn't Brews tell you about the gold watch?" she asked, as they approached the gates of the park. "That was funny, especially as he told you the wristwatch had run down."

Ned helped her across the mouth of Park Lane before he replied. "It can only mean one thing – that old Habershon's watch was tampered with, to give the impression that he slipped in accidentally soon after the two committed suicide. But can anyone believe that Habershon, in pursuit of the frenzied young things – and they must have been in a frenzy if they rushed off to commit suicide – reached the pond and fell in just four minutes after they did? Couldn't be done. The car was left ever so far off."

"But if Brews is as smart as you think, can't he see that?"

"He seems to have seen all I have, and about twenty things I haven't glimpsed yet. That's what makes him so irritating. But we must remember that the coroner wants to complete his job, while the police want to make an arrest. I have a feeling that they work an inquest sometimes, so that all their cards aren't laid on the table."

"To prevent the criminal taking the alarm?"

"That's my idea. They may feel that half a dozen adjournments would be necessary before they could get enough evidence to arrest.

The coroner would jib at that, so they give him a flower pot to crawl into, as Brews hinted, and then get on with the business of stalking their man. I may be wrong, but that is how I see it."

Nancy was more or less convinced by his reasoning. "Still," she put a last objection, "he told you plainly that he considered the passport and the registered parcel clear proofs."

Ned patted her on the arm. "Good girl! You have the nicest way of bringing up doubtful points so that I can clarify them in my own mind. Proofs? By Jove, now, what are proofs? Double-sided like records; like criticism, what? Think of criticism. The word has grown to mean censure. But it really may mean praise as well. A proof can be positive or negative. Am I right, sir?"

"As the pudding," Nancy agreed.

He went on more eagerly. "Don't remind me of my pudding head. I see that. I was a dud not to think of it before. Nancy, you make me think! Left to myself I only maunder and burble."

"Well, what are you thinking of?"

"These proofs. They may prove that old Habershon faked a suicide, and intended to bolt with the boodle. But they may prove that old Habershon was innocent of both."

"Prove that proof," said Nancy, severely.

"Easy. Dead easy. And where was old Habershon's luggage, and why did he take a passport with him. And why pinch the money when the fake suicides would have left him heir to a good deal of the gold? Nancy, we may have to start again from the beginning."

She shrugged. "I wish you would clear up what you've said before you start again."

Ned shook his head. "I'm sorry, but I must think it over first. Now we are nearing the taxidermists. We cross here."

For the moment Nancy could get no more out of him. They crossed the road, went on two hundred yards, and entered a shop where stuffed animals and birds filled an attractive window.

They emerged fifteen minutes later with assorted information. The photographs were very finely taken, the sketches were splendid. But the hawk was a kestrel, and the expert gave it as his opinion that the hen harrier was not at all likely to nest near Fen Court, and, if it had been seen so near town, a dozen correspondents would have written to the papers about it.

"But the photographer insists that there was a harrier," Ned had replied.

The expert admitted that it might be so. At the same time he assured them that many expert photographers, even those who might be fond of birds, did not necessarily know much about ornithology.

"Either Hench is a liar, or there was a harrier, or Hench does not know one bird from another," Ned said as they found themselves in the street.

"If he doesn't know the difference, and told us he was writing a book on the nidification of British birds, he's a liar anyway, old thing."

"Finally," said Ned, "if these photos are so fine, why the difficulty in getting them published? Really well done bird books sell like hot cakes."

Nancy reflected. "There may just be one reason. If Hench is not really an expert ornithologist, the letterpress may be the snag. That sort of book must be accurate, mustn't it?"

"I think you may have hit it," said he. "At any rate, I'll put off showing these to my publisher until I can get a squint at the book of words. Meantime I'll shadow Hench. There's something odd about him. It looks, as we thought before, as if he got in the policeman's way to prove an alibi."

"Are you going down again today?" she asked.

"Not till I take you to the next gloomy function at Upperton," he told her. "But I should much like to know when Hench went to Pear Cottage, and where he came from before that."

"Would he tell you?"

"Not very likely. I'll ring up Brews now, and ask him. He always knows what I want to discover, drat him!"

He went to the first telephone office, and rang up Upperton. In ten minutes he had got through, and called Brews away from an important conference with Superintendent Langley and the Chief Constable of the County.

"Well, Mr. Hope, what is it?" asked Brews, good-humoured as ever.

"I want to know how long Hench has lived at Pear Cottage, and where he came from last," said Ned.

"Four months, and was formerly living with his brother at No. 19 Heath Buildings, North Finchley," replied Brews, like an informative automatic machine. "That all?"

"For the present," said Ned, and rang off.

"We'll have an early lunch, and then barge out to North Finchley," he told Nancy when he rejoined her. "But what a memory!"

Chapter XV

A S there was no need for haste, they reached North Finchley by
tube and bus, and set out in search of Heath Buildings. They
expected to find a block of flats; they found instead an agglomeration
of semi-detached houses, one of which, No. 19, boasted a glass struc-
ture running back into the narrow garden.

"Photography," said Ned.

"Genius!" said Nancy. "It was too obvious for me."

He smiled indulgently. "We'll be relatives, neither newspaper nor
police. Cornelius is my second cousin – Got that?"

"Registered and held," said Nancy, as he opened the gate.

The door of No. 19 was opened presently by a middle-aged woman
who, on hearing their errand, bade them come in. They went into an
Edwardian parlour. Mrs. Bray, the owner, followed them, and shut
the door. She was one of those not infrequent people who turn away
no opportunity for fresh conversation, and take on themselves with
avidity the business of local guides.

Having established contact with this amiable woman, Ned success-
fully launched his inquiries.

"Ah, Mr. Hench did live here," Mrs. Bray informed him. "He and
his elder brother. I lived round the corner then. 'Twas them who built
the studio in the garden, for their photography."

"I knew my – my cousin Cornelius was a photographer," said Ned. "But I never heard his brother was."

"Well, indeed, it was he started it, and they did very well for a time; being cheap and good, till they neglected it, and people weren't going to wait months for their photos. At least that was Mr. James. Mr. Cornelius was here, but he couldn't do it all himself."

"Then James went away often?" said Nancy.

"The way of it was this," said Mrs. Bray, licking her lips as if to lubricate them for a long talk. "Mr. James, they say, was mad about birds. He knew all about them, and more than half his time he would be off to Scotland or Ireland or somewhere – they say he had a bit of money that Mr. Cornelius hadn't – to take photos of them."

"Really?" said Ned, glancing for a moment at Nancy.

"True as I sit here. He was always busy over the birds, and some said – anyway the last curate who caught him at it once – that he was writing a book on them."

"How very interesting," said Nancy.

Mrs. Bray drew in her lips. "It may have been to him, but it would have been more sense, I say, if he'd helped his brother more."

"But I thought Cornelius was keen on birds too," said Ned.

"I never heard it, sir, though it may be so. What I heard was just what people were saying. Anyway, when Mr. James died, it came out that he'd had about five thousand pounds in money, and spent most of it gallivanting about the country after birds."

Ned nodded.

"But surely the book which had cost so much trouble would have some value?" he asked.

"Well, I don't know, sir. But the curate I think was asked to have a look at it. Mr. Cornelius asked him, by all accounts. Being a curate, he knew nothing about birds, but he did his best, and took it to show a friend, who was a taxi' expert, they say."

"A taxidermist?"

"Yes, that's it. Anyway the curate was very sorry about it, for the gentleman you mention who does these things said it wasn't worth anything. Spite and jealousy I expect it was, for Mr. James was a good photographer, and cheap too when he stuck to it."

Ned repressed a start. "James was a clever man in his way," he agreed, "but we haven't all got the gift of writing."

"No, indeed. But that's the way it was. Mr. Cornelius came into whatever his brother left by will, and he sold this house (which was all there was), not to mention the photos of birds, and the book, and little things like that that he kept. Meantime the business had gone down, and not enough to keep him, as my husband says, and there was just enough money from this house to bring in a hundred a year invested, instead of what would have been if Mr. James hadn't wasted his money on birds."

Having achieved this long speech, Mrs. Bray licked her lips again, and looked amiably at Nancy, who smiled back.

"Were the brothers much attached to one another?" Ned asked.

"I don't know. I suppose so. Every one liked Mr. Cornelius better, but that may have been because he did his best to get their photos for them, while Mr. James would forget them being busy over his book, that turned out no good, or the birds he was so fond of. Why, he was that absent-minded he sent old Miss Paverton a photo of a hawk, with a letter saying he considered it a good likeness. Never meant any harm, of course, but she is a bit beaky and the upshot of it was she didn't go back any more, things like that being upsetting to trade as you will understand."

Nancy laughed merrily, and was joined by Mrs. Bray. Ned smiled, and rose. "Well, you have been very kind, Mrs. Bray, but we mustn't keep you any longer. Do you know my cousin's present address?"

"I am sorry, I don't. He told no one," said Mrs. Bray.

"Well, do you think she has been interviewed by the police already, for I don't," said Ned, as they walked back to the bus. "If she had been, we should have heard all about it."

Nancy agreed. "No, I think they have left her alone. She's a cheery soul, if a bit gossipy, but she's overturned all our theories."

Ned frowned. "I said from the first that people in my job are too apt to make the circumstance fit the crime. It's true this evidence does not implicate Hench, but it does explain a little how he came to make that mistake about the hawk."

"That's what I thought, old thing."

"As I see it," Ned went on, "James took marvellous photographs of birds, but he hadn't the training or the expert knowledge to write a book about them. A watercolour artist, or a fellow who paints river scenes, may be a poor filter expert. When he dies, Cornelius gets this expert opinion. Probably he, too, puts it down to spite. He thinks his brother, who has spent most of his life and his money chasing birds, must know all about them. Either because he wants to bring out the book as a monument to his brother, or because he has been cheated of his expectations, and hopes to get money by it, he starts to photograph birds himself. For corroboration about the letterpress of the book being unfinished, we have the fact that he doesn't hand it to me to try with a publisher, but just gives me the photographs, which even an idiot can see are top-hole."

"Here's our bus," said Nancy.

They climbed into the half-empty bus, and secured a seat in the corner. Ned resumed.

"The book must be unfinished, or he wouldn't be taking more photographs for it. Probably he has been trying to read up some books on birds, with a view to finishing the manuscript himself."

"But he could get correct information from books."

"And I can get accurate information on relativity from Einstein's works, only I don't understand them, old thing! Research in any subject is not an easy job. No. Cornelius takes a hawk for a heronshaw, or a harrier. Brews is not as clever as he thinks. His hint about the kestrel has fallen down sadly."

"Unless," said Nancy, "he thought you could do the inquiry at this end for him. Also he may be trying to put you on the wrong track. It would be quite like him."

"Absolutely. But this is a side issue. The nonsense about watching a hen harrier may be nonsense without being wilfully untrue. We have proved that Hench may not have lied in this matter, but we haven't proved that Hench had nothing to do with the murders – if murders they were."

"But do you think he could have had something to do with it?"

"He could, of course. You know what a deserted countryside it is down there, and he was the only person old Habershon knew."

"By the way, Ned, someone said Habershon didn't care about birds much. But he was a F.Z.S., wasn't he?"

"Yes, but what of it? Lots of Fellows of the Zoological Society aren't experts. They pay, and they gets tickets for Sundays. By the way, he may have been financing the book to try to get credit for efforts in ornithology. But that doesn't worry me about old Habershon. The point about his affairs that makes me a guesser is that matter of the Bearer Bonds, Nance."

"That he sold out to get them?"

"No, that, having the power apparently to sell the whole caboodle – a hundred thousand pounds worth of property – he didn't sell all."

"His sisters were fools to leave him unlimited power. They ought to have made a—"

"Trust? Of course. But they didn't. What I mean is this. Habershon had the power of life and death over a hundred thousand of the best. He only sold out sixty thou., and invested that in bonds. Was he surprised at his own moderation, like Warren Hastings, or why was that? If he intended to bolt, why not scoop the lot?"

Nancy considered. "On the face of it," she said, slowly, "I should say that he didn't want to leave his nephew and niece quite penniless."

Ned raised his eyebrows.

"Now that is exactly what I want to get at. If he could get clear away, then he was safe to take the lot. If he couldn't, he would be given as hot a sentence for the sixty as he would be for the hundred thousand. Our justice is not measured out in hundreds of thousands. That being so, Portia, you're a Daniel come to judgment! The wish not to be too hard on his young relatives is the only valid reason for his self-denying ordinance."

"I think so."

"Good! Now that brings us, old girl, to the paradox of the strange Mr. Habershon. As things stand, we are confronted with the miraculous spectacle of the man who does not wish to leave his relatives in want, but is quite ready to dope them, fire them into a pond, and stage a monstrous fake. Is he a Jekyll and Hyde, or what?"

"Not quite. That split personality was benevolent on one side, Ned, but Habershon, if we are right, was only a big rogue one way, and a slightly smaller rogue another."

"Good. I agree. Still there is the paradox, and I'm hanged if it doesn't flummox me. Bell and his editor are asses! They really think my work helps me in this. All the time I have been manufacturing a Mr. Habershon who will fit my theories. But Mr. Habershon, with whom we are dealing, is not a fictional figure but a concrete fact. He was created before I was, and what I have to try to get at now is not the Habershon who suits my book, but the man who was alive until a few days ago."

"But Brews is also manufacturing a Mr. Habershon."

"We have no proof of that. He has given me a little mascot of Mr. Habershon to play with, but whether he thinks it's at all like the late Mr. H. I do not know."

"Ask?"

Ned did not reply to that. He frowned severely.

"He may have seen from the first that I was going to hang about, and develop my experiences of criminology. He may have put it to the massive Langley that I would be sure to get in the way anyway, and, if they could provide me with some innocuous occupation, so much the better. Brews is as deep as a draw-well, but he's good-natured. He's more likely to say, 'Go along and play, little man,' than to tell me to go where the coals are hotter."

"Don't give up!" she adjured him.

"Give up? The last thing I thought of. The first thing is to start again from the beginning," said Ned.

Chapter XVI

T HERE was a quickening of local interest once more when the adjourned inquests were proceeded with. The court was very full, the streets hummed, the police and the pressmen conducted their usual activities both inside and outside the official building.

Ned and Nancy watched the coroner with interest. They did not look very much at the jury. The coroner appeared quietly competent. Either he did not know that detectives classed him with the earwig tribe, or he was one of those who earn an exemption by fitting in tactfully with the officers' plans.

As the first inquiry was further unrolled, Ned saw that the police had a hope of getting an open verdict. They failed to stress, or to produce, details that might have firmed up a wavering jury. Their witnesses spoke so impartially that the jurymen looked at one another, and showed perplexed brows, as if they had looked for light and leading and got none. Their inexperienced eyes detected murder, but no murderer.

Even the fact that Mr. Habershon had ordered mordinal, and traces of mordinal had been found in the flask did not topple them from the razor-edge of their fence. Mr. Habershon had had a white beard and now he was dead, so that no one could be quite sure what had happened to him. The evidence was too circumstantial, and there was too much theory about it. Not that individual jurymen objected to theory in itself, only there were eleven of them, and theories are like statistics, each likes to handle them in a different way.

In fact, as the inquiry went on, it became plain that the jury had made up their minds, and wanted to be done. And no one tried to upset this frame of mind by being convincing on one side or the other. Presently Superintendent Langley had a short whispered colloquy with the coroner, and, from his faint smile, Ned took it that the coroner was definitely not in the earwig class. He had been primed with police wisdom, and knew where to check exuberance of theory.

He summed up for an open verdict, and the jury as a matter of form went out to consider it. Most of them thought that the passport looked very bad, and one (who was a small money-lender, and therefore strong on finance), shook his head over the Bearer Bonds. But even he saw that the will which left forty thousand pounds to Mr. Habershon minimised the evidential value of the bond business.

"And then he had no luggage with him," said one.

Their foreman nodded. "It doesn't look too good about Mr. Habershon, but if he didn't do it we don't want to put a slur on his memory, gentlemen. Then there is another thing. No more justice can be done than has been done. If we brought in a verdict of murder against the man, it couldn't be carried into effect. I plump for a fair and truthful verdict, and that is 'Murder against some person or persons unknown.' Mr. Habershon may be the person, but we can't be sure."

A faint look of triumph came to Superintendent Langley's face as he saw the jurymen file back. He knew that look – "Five shillings each way" he used to call it. He was quite satisfied when the record flaunted this open verdict, and the second inquest was resumed.

The inquiry into the death of Mr. Habershon brought out more strongly the possibility of accident. To bring this in as anything but accident would be impossible; to impeach the soundness of Mr. Habershon's mind or morals at the time of his death, indecent. If there was any safe, impartial, and happy verdict to bring in, other than that finally brought in by the jury, the police did not know of it. And yet the jury managed to give it a little twist which saved them from being regarded as a set of complete mugwumps. They found that Mr. Habershon met his death by drowning, but how definitely he came to fall into the pond they were unable to say.

But not one pressed for a more definite finding. The coroner put it in proper form, and the affair came to an end so far as he was concerned.

"What did you think of it?" asked Ned, when he and Nancy were driving back to town. "Not bad?"

Nancy nodded. "I should think it was as far as they could get. And it leaves everything open for Brews."

The atmosphere of an inquest is a complete depressant. After it, for part of that day at least, Ned and Nancy had no more taste for sleuth work. Ned left her at home, promising to come in to see her that evening. The afternoon was partly taken up with an interview with his publisher, who was anxious to capitalise on the publicity Ned had obtained at the inquest. Then Ned went through two rounds of the billiard handicap at his club, dined on the premises and reached the Hampstead flats where Nancy lived at a quarter past eight.

He had hoped to put all memories of the grisly Fen Court business out of his mind that day. But Nancy had a visitor who revived them. Inspector Brews, in a smart blue serge suit, was sitting in the flat, smoking and talking to Nancy, when Ned arrived. He jumped up at once, beamed more broadly than ever, and announced that he had better be going.

"What, before I've had time to look at you?" said Ned, ironically. "Sit down, Inspector, please, and let me know who you're chasing now."

"I'm off duty till tomorrow, sir," said Brews, willingly resuming his seat. "I hoped Miss Johnson wouldn't mind my coming round. You see, after this unsatisfactory verdict, I'm all unsettled again. You and the lady gave me a bit of help before."

Ned grinned. "You call it an unsatisfactory verdict – which one do you refer to, Brews?"

The inspector shrugged. "Just my joke, sir. I call it a model jury. I wish we could always have 'em so easy to satisfy."

"Do you know, Inspector," said Nancy, "that Mr. Hope here thinks he must begin at the beginning once more?"

Brews smiled. "That's right. Now we have that business over, I don't mind telling you that the evidence against Mr. Habershon wouldn't hang a goat. It was very nice to look at from a point of view of orderliness. We had Mr. Habershon getting the Bearer Bonds, getting the passport for South America. We had Mr. Habershon getting mordinal, and mordinal found in those poor young things, and some in the thermos flask. Then we had cousins wishing to marry, and the wicked uncle wanting to stop them, and finally we had the bit of paper pinned on the young lady's dress to show their state of mind. Why, bless me, sir, it's just the kind of plot you would make up for your detective stories, isn't it?"

"Quite," agreed Ned.

"I read one lately and very good it was," went on the detective. "One thing followed another, and you made your detectives more or less like people; not like mugs, or not like wizards either. But the thing that struck me was the nice way everything fitted in."

"Absolutely," said Ned. "I told you. Make the circumstance fit the crime."

"But, now that I'm free to look into the cases sir, and I can't frighten any of the birds away, I may tell you that the sequence of events, while true in each fact, is as tangled and contradictory as it well could be."

"I won't mention what you say outside this room, inspector," Ned promised.

"I knew you wouldn't, sir."

"Then tell us where the sequence goes wrong," said Nancy, smiling. "We have quite an inkling ourselves."

She provided him with a fresh cigarette, and he began: "We'll go back to the Bearer Bonds, since that starts the case. Had you any views about those Bearer Bonds, sir?"

Ned told him what he had told Nancy on their return from North Finchley. Brews nodded approvingly.

"That's one up to you and the lady, sir. I admit I hadn't time to go into that, and it might not have struck me either. But the point I was going to make is this: Bearer Bonds have no particular value as investments, and, unless you keep them in the safe of your bank, or in a safe deposit, they may be stolen without giving you much hope of recovery. In the case of Mr. Habershon, who was dealing with money that did not belong to him, I can see no reason for his action except a rather unpleasant one."

Nancy started. "You don't mean that he committed the murders after all?"

"No, I don't think so. But I can't get away from the idea that he converted the investments in part into bonds which could be nego-tiated easily and safely abroad. Our man, who went into his financial affairs, discovered that, just before this odd conversion, Mr. Habershon had struck a snag. He'd been betting heavily and about half of his original capital had gone west."

"By Jove!" cried Ned.

Brews nodded. "Now that was my idea, and this rather smart deduction of yours about the amount of the money converted into Bearer Bonds saves me a good deal of thought and investigation. I admit that freely. It's my private idea – and unofficial, of course – that Mr. Habershon did consider a bolt; that he took a lot of money, or intended to take it, but did not wish to loot the lot. That is to say, he had some scruples, though not many."

"My idea too," murmured Nancy.

Brews waved his cigarette to and fro. "It wouldn't even have paid him to murder his nephew and niece, in the way they were murdered. That way would leave him alive, if his plans went right, and faced with the probate people, to whom he would have had to show the bonds, when he was accounting for the estate. When that was cleared up, he would have come into forty thousand pounds, less death duties. To put it more plainly, he stood to get less than forty thousand by their deaths, but sixty thousand if he bolted with the Bearer Bonds."

"I can't make out, in either case, why he opposed the marriage of his wards," said Ned, thoughtfully.

"You could, sir, if you had read the full terms of the wills of Habershon's widow sisters. He was to come into the money on the death of both, failing issue. If they had got married, and had children, as most likely they would, he wouldn't even have inherited the smaller sum. Not that I think that matters. He was obviously anxious to get off with the bonds, but not sufficiently determined as a criminal to do it. It's three months since he bought those bonds, but the bolt had not come off."

"Well, we are agreed that he was not likely to commit the murders," said Ned. "What next?"

"The next incongruity, sir, is the use of the car – the particular use he made of it that night. I am not saying that he might not have heard from Mr. Hench of the proximity of your house (which he might think untenanted), or of the convenient ponds. I am thinking of the route he took, which brought him to a café. There half a dozen people, if not more, were able to see the party, discover that the young people were having ices, and note that none of the three was at all hysterical, or worried, or upset. To make things real for a fake suicide, if he had visited the café at all with his wards, he would have created some sort of a scene coming down. He could have made the young man angry, anyway, and perhaps had the young woman looking red-eyed and tearful. Instead of that they all turn up serene and quiet, and linger a bit over some refreshments."

Chapter XVII

O NCE more, as the inspector paused, Ned asked himself why they had been so bountifully blessed with the detective's confidences. The "Judges' Rules" might have something to do with it, but there was another possibility. Did he think Ned knew something, and was keeping it to himself? Confidences breed confidences. Was that his hope?

"You hit it, Brews," he murmured.

Brews nodded, absently. "That is the first time that car takes the wrong turning, from the point of view of the old theory. What is the second? Well, next the car gets to Pudstey—"

"Or is left at Pudstey crossroads."

"Taken there, first or last, sir. It is not on the right road anywhere. You can go on back to Upperton, or swing round, and cross the river. But why was Mr. Habershon out, if not to visit Pear Cottage? However, we'll let that drop and go back to the routine that failed—" here he grinned at Ned, who shook a finger at him, and added "– failed to show what it ought to have shown."

Nancy smiled. "We felt quite disappointed, inspector, because you never even mentioned fingerprints. A detective without fingerprints is no detective at all!"

"Quite right," he agreed. "You'll catch a few out with them now and again, as long as the human mind isn't made to remember everything. Naturally we had a go at that; just as we put on our clothes every morning without thinking of it. But there were no fingerprints."

"No fingerprints – on what?"

"The car, Mr. Hope."

Ned smiled. "We wear driving gloves in March, Brews."

"So we do, sir, and thick ones, too. But the difficulty of thick gloves is handling things. You can't do everything in a car with thick gloves on, lighting cigarettes, drinking out of the cups attached to thermos flasks, for instance. I never saw a car so free from anyone's fingerprints. Mr. Habershon, though he had no need to do it, being the owner of the car, seems to have carefully wiped everything in sight, even the handles of the doors, the wheel, and the spokes of the wheel – I mean the driving wheel. I never saw such a careful man!"

"Gosh!" cried Nancy, excitedly. "Negative evidence."

"That's right. Supposing people had a dinner party and all the glasses on the table after were found to be polished clean? What would you say? Either that the party were brought up as kitchen maids, or dotty, or not anxious to leave their marks where they might be seen. In a way, absence of fingerprints isn't even negative evidence, it's positive."

"Good point," cried Ned. "Someone had evidently handled the car, or the flask, or both, and could not be sure where his fingerprints were. So he wiped out the lot. Does Hench drive?"

"Didn't you get that at North Finchley, sir?" asked Brews.

"No, and you haven't interviewed Mrs. Bray, have you?"

"No. I simply asked Hench, and he admitted that he used sometimes to drive his brother out into the country."

Ned nodded. "That's good. Now let's hear what else is wrong?"

"Well, the most salient thing is the scrap of paper – or scraps, for they were better than the one we found first. Even the man Hench said he thought the first scrap looked like a bit torn out of a letter. From the nature of the wording, it was a complaint or a reproach. To whom was Miss Rowe likely to direct a reproach?"

"To her uncle, since he was against her engagement to Ivor Rainy, and, if Mr. Huston is telling the truth, rather encouraged another suitor," Nancy replied.

"Exactly, miss. Not that we can be sure of it, but that seems the likeliest recipient. But she and her cousin lived in Habershon's house. Why write a letter to him? Naturally I didn't go any further until I had squared that up. My man who went to town asked Mrs. Hoing, the housekeeper, if the young people had been out of town lately. She told him that they had. The two had been asked to a house in Scotland. Mr. Rainy didn't shoot, but he went to look at birds. Both of them only returned three days before the tragedy. More than that. I got a trunk call to their late host, and he said they had both determined to leave a week before the time first fixed."

"They were worried about something?" said Ned.

"I asked that. The answer was that both seemed a bit upset, and were not as good company as usual. Their host said frankly that he did not press them to stay when they told him of the change of plan, first because he could see they were anxious to get home, and next because they were rather wet-blanketing the rest of the house party."

"You got on the right line, Brews."

"Well, it certainly seemed a pointer, so I asked the host if he would mind asking about letters sent off by the pair with him, and let me know. He wrote this morning, saying Miss Rowe had despatched a letter to her uncle, four days before they left Scotland."

"That will be the letter," cried Nancy.

138

"I think so, Miss. Now, taking that as a hypothesis, we get back to Mr. Habershon. He's an educated man, and, if guilty of these murders, a cunning one. What, on the old theory, does he do? He tears a bit out of the letter addressed to him by his niece. He tears out a bit from the middle, he selects a bit that would show even a mutton-headed constable that it was a part of some other writing, having neither a real beginning nor end to it. Then he pins it on her frock."

"Bad staff-work."

"No work at all, sir. If Mr. Habershon was fool enough to do that, he must have had cottonwool instead of brains. The next thing about it is this. A man of sense would know that paper dissolves in water. How long would that scrap last in the pond to explain the suicide?"

"Wait a moment," Ned interrupted. "You made a bloomer there! On the old theory, Mr. Habershon was to rush off for help; say the two had jumped into the pond, and have them got out. Then the paper would be fresh enough."

Brews smiled. "That's a valid objection; only for one thing. How did Mr. Habershon expect to explain how he had seen them go into your pond on a dark night? He could only have seen it if he had been actually in the garden, and pretty near the pond. And how could he have run almost as fast from where the car was to your garden as the young people did?"

"I am not so sure of that," Ned said, obstinately. "I don't mean the running. I mean your particular point about the paper and its dissolving. That reminds me – did they find out what kind of coffee was in the thermos?"

"Brazilian," said Brews. "Mrs. Hoing was right. Though it does not follow that the coffee found in the flask was part of that originally put there. Or why was the flask wiped clean of fingerprints?"

Nancy smiled. "Every day you grow better and better, inspector! If you go on like this, you'll soon catch up on Mr. Hope and myself."

She passed the cigarettes, and Brews took one.

"That's what I want to do," he said. "We country fellows need a bit of smartening up. However, working with the poor brains given to me, I have come to the conclusion that Mr. Habershon was only half a rogue."

"And half a fool," put in Ned. "Or why did he leave those bits of Miss Rowe's letter – where you found them? And why did he leave the passport in the pocket of the car, when he had no luggage for a journey. Wherever you put passports, unless you are actually touring abroad, I am sure it is not there."

"I want to know about the Bearer Bonds," said Nancy. "Are they *spurlos versenkt* – gone altogether, you know?"

"If not lost, they have at least gone before," said Brews, with his head on one side.

"Perhaps he bunged those into the pocket of the car, too, with the passport," said Ned.

The inspector looked pained. "They're a complication in the case. You see, Mr. Habershon may have sent off a bundle of papers as a red herring, and posted the bonds to himself somewhere, for a later flight. On the other hand, he may not. Their disappearance may lead us to believe that they were the object of the crime, while it may be that they were not."

This was rather over Nancy's head, and she said so, frankly. "Go easy, Monsieur Dupin! How could the theft of the bonds have any connection with the crime?"

"To lead us to believe that Mr. Habershon killed his nephew and niece, but got drowned doing it. To let us think that he staged a fake suicide which, from its very nature (that silly scrap of paper and so on), we would *see* to be a fake, Miss. You can do a clumsy crime because you are clumsy, or because you are subtle enough to make it so. If we can be got to believe that the suicides were faked, then we must conclude that it was the wicked uncle who faked them, and was the man who intended to pinch the bonds. If we believe that, then we find him dead, and label him the murderer. If he is the murderer, then that's an end to it. We can't hang his corpse."

"You reason like a book," said Ned. "Really I think you are a dangerous man, Brews. You'll make something next of my having gone down to Fen Court to recover my cigarette case."

"It's just because I can't make anything of it that I am growing so fond of you, sir," Brews replied, amiably. "Your doings there, small as they were, have given me a lot of thinking."

"I call your work low cunning," Ned protested. "Especially your foul tactics at the inquest. I saw your hand in the background, doling out evidence to the coroner, holding back what suited you, spoon-feeding your model jury, and at last getting a right verdict. Where do you learn these things in the country, Brews?"

"From the folk who live there," said the inspector, laughing. "You try to do a yokel down in a deal, sir, and you'll be surprised. Monkeys aren't in it – not wagon-loads of 'em! But to get back to our business, I'd give something to know what you did exactly when you got to Fen Court that night."

"You must warn me, first, inspector!"

"No, sir, I'll appeal to your better nature, as they say, and look to Miss Johnson to back me. Nancy stared at Ned. "Have you been keeping anything back from me? If you have, I call it a dirty trick! Cheating inspectors, who know too much already, is one thing, but—"

"Wait," said Ned. "I apologise to you for that, and to Brews for underrating his eyes. For I suppose he does – or has, come to look at the gas fittings."

"I did look at them, sir, and at the meter," replied the inspector. "In other words, I had a squint at the lamps. But there wasn't one filled, and not a drop of paraffin in the house."

Ned looked thoughtful. "I meant to try an experiment and forgot. We'll try it together tomorrow night, inspector."

"That's right. Keep on being mean!" Nancy reproached him.

"The time has come for complete candour," Ned replied. "The facts are these. There are no gas or electric mains connected up with Fen Court, Nancy. It depends for its illumination on oil lamps. But I did not take any oil with me when I went. I only happened to have brought my little electric torch in the car. I often do, since I can have a glance at any part that goes wrong. When I got into the house, I went to the front room first, and switched the torch on. Within a very short time I found my cigarette case, switched off, and came away."

"Oh; and Mr. Hench saw your light," said Nancy, beginning to understand. "But so did the constable, later."

"They said they saw a light in Fen Court," Ned observed.

"When they might merely have seen a light in Pear Cottage," said Brews. "They're near enough to be confused, looking from a distance, after dark."

"Or again," Ned took up the tale, "Mr. Hench may have had visitors, and left the light burning."

Nancy saw that. "What is your experiment, Ned? Well, I vote we all go over tomorrow night, and enter Fen Court – at least you and I will, while Brews hoofs it over to the crossroads so intimately connected with Hench's alibi. From there he will try to discover if he can detect me flashing a torch in the front room."

"It's worthwhile, sir," agreed Brews. "If you only flashed it on and off, and that just a little, the constable couldn't see it after he had left Hench. You weren't looking long enough for that. So it is pretty clear that he, at any rate, mistook for yours a light showing in Pear Cottage."

"We'll see that tomorrow night, Brews. It's possible."

The inspector looked well satisfied. "I was sure you would respond to kind treatment, sir! That was why I was nursing you gently along. I had an idea there was something dickey about that light business, but couldn't be sure what it was, or why you were concealing it."

"There was just a chance, you see, Ned, that you were the criminal," said Nancy lightly.

Brews agreed. "You're quite right. If the police were to take it on themselves to make exceptions, a lot of crooks would get away. I had to look at everyone."

Ned grinned, but said nothing. Nancy went on. "It seems to me that you have to look for someone who knew the country well, and knew Mr. Habershon well. That ought to narrow the field."

"It does, Miss Johnson, decidedly."

"And you have to remember that, though the river Lum does not come nearer Pear Cottage than two hundred yards, there is a drain, six feet wide, and about four feet deep, that does pass one side of the orchard, and debouch into the river," added Ned.

"Quite navigable for a punt," murmured the inspector. "I saw that at first. But I am not sure yet how I can fit it in."

Ned shrugged. "Since murder is about as beastly a game as there is – almost worse than writing dirty novels – I don't like to throw suspicion on a man who may be innocent. But I can say that there is one man down in Essex who knew Mr. Habershon, who pretends to some knowledge he doesn't possess, who promptly put in an alibi, and lives within reach of a navigable drain. He is also the only man we can think of who might have invited Ivor Rainy and his uncle down at night with some hope of success."

Brews looked thoughtful. "I've given that full weight, and will look into it further. At the same time, what you and Miss Johnson discovered at North Finchley mustn't be forgotten. The little man may merely be trying to complete his brother's book, to work it off as his own."

"Since your men are practically robots at routine, Brews, I need hardly ask if they traced all the tramps."

"You needn't, sir. There is no road there between two workhouses, and in addition the part round Fen Court is the hungriest spot in the county. Tramps don't walk for their health, but to pick up a living. Lonely fen-farmers don't encourage tramps. They keep savage dogs. There was only one stranger out that night in that direction, apart from a few cars, and he was a carpenter going to a job at Upperton. Besides tramps wouldn't know about Mr. Habershon's private business."

"That's why I asked," said Ned, as Brews rose to go. "The circle of suspects is going to be jolly narrow."

Brews nodded, made an appointment for the following night at nine, thanked Nancy for her hospitality, and went out.

Chapter XVIII

"YOU don't know much about boxing, Nance," said Ned, as they drove down to Upperton after an early dinner, next day, "but I expect you know that a man may appear to advertise his intentions by feinting with his left, while the right is the fellow he means business with. But if he made a feint at his second, the second would know that he was not to be the receiver of a blow. Therefore he would not put up his hands to defend himself."

"Muddled, but still not too cryptic," replied Nancy, judicially. "What's this all about?"

He laughed. "I was just thinking that Brews was not only exceedingly confiding, but he took pains at first to explain to me, and to Hench, what might be the ideas and theories on which he would base his plan of campaign. Did he expect the guilty one to consider what the police hypothesis was, and then take steps to counter it? Did he expect this counter, or camouflage, to give him a clue to the guilty man?"

"If you would give your innocent Watsoness a clearer clue to what you mean, it would be one good deed," murmured Nancy.

He nodded. "If you will be dense, then here you are! Suppose, in Brews's outline, the guilty man saw that he had left a weak spot. His first step would be to repair that breach in his defences. Brews might watch the repair, and so light on the man he wanted. If you were a murderer, and the police told you that the guilty man could *not* have worn a black beard—"

"I couldn't wear one in any case."

"I'm speaking impersonally, you juggins! If they did that, and you were the murderer, you would try at once to show that you had been wearing a false black beard that night, and all that night. In other words, the police would have led you to try to prove something that would let you out, while, all the time, you were letting yourself in. The question is: Did Hench do anything significant after he had been given Brews's theories?"

Nancy shrugged. "I see what you mean, but I haven't an idea what Hench did, or Brews thinks. What I should like to know is this – does Hench also use Brazilian coffee?"

"We'll have a look at Hench tonight, and ask him," said Ned. "Our first job is to settle the question of the lights. Can a torch flash be seen from the crossroads near Pullen's farm, and can the lamp in Pear Cottage be seen from there too. Hench has a hanging oil lamp, as you may have noticed."

Nancy reflected for a few moments. "I am trying to remember the map we looked at," she said, presently. "Unless I am much mistaken, a man looking towards Fen Court from the crossroads would find Pear Cottage very little to the side of it – behind, of course, but visible from that angle. They would seem pretty near together."

Brews was waiting for them at Upperton, and wasted no time getting into the dickey. He was the passenger to be dropped at the crossroads near Pullen's Farm, and then Ned and his companion were to drive back to Fen Court to work their end of the experiment.

As they drove past the empty house, Brews leaned forward and whispered, "Hench is at home. I can see his light anyway."

"We'll pay him a call later, if you're game," Ned returned. "I want to know what kind of coffee he drinks."

At the crossroads Brews was put down, lighted a pipe, and settled to wait for the flashes from Fen Court.

Ned drove back fast, turned the car into the lane, and helped Nancy down. They entered the house a few moments later, and the girl shivered.

"Cheer up, old thing! There aren't really any spooks," he said, noticing her shudder.

"I was thinking it was a beastly cold time of year to be in empty houses," she retorted.

"Well, you would come, you know. Stamp your feet, and swing your arms! My next car shall be a saloon. I can promise you that. But now to repeat my innocuous actions on the night of that beastly business."

Nancy watched him as he reconstructed with every regard for accuracy the scene on the night of the murders. He flashed on his light near the door, then jetted the beam into various corners, finally projecting it on the spot where he had found his cigarette case. Then he shut off the torch, and the séance was over.

"Now to pick up our friend," he said, as he led the way out of the house and locked the door behind him. "If Brews did not see that when he was watching for it, it's unlikely that Hench did by chance.

Brews was waiting for them when they drove up. "I thought I saw what looked like a quick spark now and then," he told them, "but I should not have called it a light – that is in Fen Court."

Ned wrinkled his brows. "But what about Pear Cottage?"

"Oh, I saw that all right, Mr. Hope. If I hadn't known there was a cottage near, I might have said it was yours. But it was a steady light, not a flash, so it must have been Mr. Hench's lamp that we saw burning as we passed."

Ned felt satisfied. "Then Hoggett must have seen the Pear Cottage light. What actually happened I take to be this: When it came out that I had been at Fen Court that night, Hoggett, who had really believed it to be Hench's lamp, accidentally left on, concluded that he had been wrong. So he admits that he saw a light in Fen Court."

"Which explains why he did not go to see," agreed Brews. "If he had suspected that there was some unauthorised person in Fen Court, he would certainly have gone there to see what was up. He's a careful officer, but, like so many men, he is anxious to see what he thinks his superiors wish him to see.

"In other words, he is a human being," said Nancy. "Now, Ned, don't stop here all night. Let's get on to Mr. Hench's. He may offer us coffee, and so save me from dying of cold, while helping the inspector here to another clue."

"The Brazilian coffee? I am not sure I can tell it from the other kind, Miss."

"I can!" said Nancy.

"I suppose you haven't any good news for me about that publisher," said Mr. Hench, eagerly.

These were almost the first words he did say, after he had welcomed the party to Pear Cottage, and provided them with seats round his welcome fire.

Nancy looked down. Brews lit a cigarette, and appeared quite at home. Ned shook his head.

"Well, no," he said. "The fact is, Mr. Hench, that my publisher says he isn't in the habit of publishing books with illustrations only. He thinks well of your photographs and sketches. In fact, he agrees that they are extremely good. But he must see the manuscript of the work before he can go any further."

Nancy looked up now. It struck her that Ned was a good liar; at any rate in a good cause. Then she turned her eyes on Hench, who looked a trifle uncomfortable, and from him to Brews, who was beaming in his most fatuous fashion.

"The letterpress – yes, of course," said Mr. Hench, stroking his chin. "Some of it's done, of course, but not quite half. He might see that. By the way," he added, "are there no publishers who will get out the book as an illustrated book, without letterpress?"

"There may be, no doubt there are, but I don't know them, so would have no influence," said Ned.

He had got all he wanted, so Nancy took a hand. "How perfectly ripping your fire is, Mr. Hench!" she cried. "We were almost frozen in the car. What asses we were not to bring some hot drinks with us."

Mr. Hench smiled at her, no longer uncomfortable. "How remiss of me not to think of it. But here the kettle is nearly boiling. I was thinking of making a cup of coffee when you came in. May I offer you some?"

Nancy thanked him warmly, as did Ned and the inspector.

"Is it Brazilian?" asked Nancy, as the little man began to make his preparations. "I love Brazilian."

"I don't know what it is, but Mr. Habershon gave me a pound of it to try, Miss Johnson, the last time I visited his house. It seems to me very good, but then I am not an expert, I'll put the milk on to boil, if you will wait a minute."

The three exchanged glances while he went for the milk, and put it over the fire in a little saucepan, where Nancy promised to watch it. Then he went to his cupboard, and produced four cups and saucers and an ancient coffee-pot.

"We were all wondering about that light you thought you saw in Fen Court some nights ago," said Brews, when Hench sat down again. "Could you tell me anything more about it? Was it, for example, a strong or bright light; a steady light or a flickering one."

Hench stared at his questioner. "To tell you the truth, Inspector, I have been thinking of that light, too, since. I remember wondering what kind of light it was. It went in and out, and it wasn't very strong. It struck me that there would hardly be lights in working order in a house that had been empty so long."

"That is easily explained," said Brews, slowly. "We know now that Mr. Hope here simply used his flash – an electric torch. Did it look like that?"

"Now that you mention it, it did," said the other.

"I was wondering," said Brews, frankly.

Presently the milk was boiling, and Nancy volunteered to make the coffee; for which the little man thanked her, explaining that he could do for himself pretty well, but did not claim to be a cook.

"Jolly good this coffee," said Ned, when they were all supplied, "I must try Brazilian myself – it's a greener bean, isn't it?"

Hench got up and fetched the tin in which he kept it. He handed it over to Ned, who examined it and then passed it on to the inspector.

Brews managed to palm a few beans before he passed the tin back. "Mr. Habershon was rather proud of his taste in coffee, Mr. Hope tells me," he murmured, sipping at his cup.

Hench shook his head. "I don't know. It was very good of him to think of me, but I'm sure I don't know – or didn't 'til you told me."

Brews nodded, and turned the conversation. Half an hour later, they took leave of Mr. Hench, and went back to the car, Ned carrying a parcel of typewritten MS. Which represented half the book on the nidification of birds. He asked Mr. Hench, before he went, to write his name and address on the parcel.

When they were hurrying to Upperton, to drop Brews before going back to town, Ned looked over his shoulder.

"I say, Inspector, what do you think of our point about the coffee?"

Brews replied at once. "I thought it odd that Hench didn't know Mr. Habershon's tastes. If a man is very particular about his coffee, or his wine, or his tobacco, and offers you some which he gets from a particular source, he generally tells you all about it. I should have expected to hear from Hench that Habershon had told him about his friend in Brazil, who sent him that particular coffee."

"But what do you make of it?" Nancy asked.

"I should be inclined to think that Hench bought the coffee. Mr. Habershon is not alive to tell us otherwise. But then I can't be sure. It's a point I'll have to consider."

"He admitted that the light he saw might have been the flash from a torch," said Ned.

Brews agreed. "Well, he's either innocent, or very cunning. I'll have an eye kept on him. But the next job I have in hand is to search Habershon's house from top to bottom. There's just a chance that the bonds are still hidden there somewhere."

Chapter XIX

"MY dear editor is very pleased with my last article," said Ned, as he and Nancy walked down Bond Street next day. "He says half his highbrow readers have been congratulating him. And all because I reinforced my stuff with slabs from Professor Madle's *Influence of Psychopathic Neuroses on The Criminal Instinct*, in the original German."

"But I didn't know you knew German, old thing?" said Nancy.

"I don't. Surely, though, you know that the public loves a foreign language? Why, a man can pig it abroad in an *estaminet or albergo*. If he was in the same place at home, he would call it a 'dirty pub.' A rose with a foreign name smells twice as sweet."

"I wish we could get on with the case, though," Nancy said.

"It's all because of the mathematicians, and their beastly habit of sticking X in equations," he returned. "X is the chap who is holding us up here. Just consider how few suspects we have. Myself for one; Hench, two; Mrs. Hoing, three, and loathly X, four."

"I suppose Mrs. Hoing must come in?" said Nancy. "She was in touch with Mr. Habershon."

He nodded. "Of course. I have been considering Brews's point about the coffee, and I think it is good commonsense observation. There is no doubt that people who make a hobby of something do tell you about it. The man who smokes a weird tobacco and asks you to try some always tells you how he discovered it. Mr. Habershon must have talked about his Brazilian friend so much that the housekeeper knew all about it. There was no need for her to tell you how particular he was about it, or where he got it."

"I rather thought that at the time, old thing, but I couldn't see any relevance in it."

"No, I expect not, at that stage. But this is how I have been arguing. According to Mrs. Hoing's tale, Habershon must have said something like this to her: 'You know, Mrs. Hoing, I am very particular about my coffee. I like Brazilian best, but not the ordinary Brazilian. The stuff they sell you is as like it as "Russian Blend" cigarettes are to Russian. Please make my coffee carefully. It's expensive stuff that a friend sends me direct from Brazil.'"

"Or words to that effect," said Nancy, laughing, as they turned into Piccadilly.

"Absolutely. Then he sees Hench, and offers the little man a pound. If he acts like any other human being with a similar hobby, he won't say: 'Here's a pound of coffee, old chap!' He will say: 'You must try some of my coffee. I am very particular about it, and get it sent to me, etc.' What do you think?"

She reflected, then nodded. "People do go on like that. But what does it mean here?"

"Well, little Hench thinks it may be Brazilian coffee, but he is not impressed, and he doesn't know where Habershon got it from, or that Habershon is accustomed to making a song about it. That suggests two alternatives to me. Either Habershon did not make a song about it, or get it from a friend in Brazil, or Hench bought the coffee himself. If he bought it himself, we may suspect that he doctored some coffee that night, put it in an identical flask – I mean the same size and shape as that carried by Habershon – and doped Rainy and Miss Rowe. If it was actually sent from Habershon's, while at the same time no attempt was made to prove to him that this was Heaven's own nectar, sent by a pal of H's from Brazil, then we may suspect that the coffee was sent not by Habershon, but by Mrs. Hoing."

Nancy stared. "Much thinking has made thee mad, Ned!"

He smiled. "The people at the back of those murders are cunning as they make 'em. It was a fake suicide, but I imagine them long-headed enough to erect a second line of defence in case the first failed. If mention of the use in the Habershon household of Brazilian coffee did not lead the police to believe that old Habershon doctored the thermos and destroyed his wards, the fact that Hench used the same coffee might enable them to stick the crime on Hench – the only local who knew Habershon, and was in touch with him. It's only a theory so far, but I vote we go into the business of investigating it now. So we'll turn about and take a bus to Bloomsbury."

"And what then?" asked Nancy, somewhat impressed.

"Well, I suspect the friend in Brazil may be a figment of Mrs. Hoing's imagination. If she wanted to impress the Brazilian origin of the coffee on your mind, she might have got up that story. If she is at the back of the plot, Mr. Habershon and his doctored coffee is the strong point to push."

"But why suspect her at all?" Nancy asked, as they got into a bus.

"Because there are several fishy things in her evidence, as I see it. On investigation the fishiness may disappear, but we must make sure one way or the other. In the first place, beyond a vague remark made by the weed Jimmy Huston, Mrs. Hoing is the only one who really furnishes evidence that there was serious trouble between Habershon and his wards. Secondly, she stresses the point we have been discussing; the coffee. Next, as I heard from you, she took the theory of dope having been used as if it was quite likely—"

"But Brews's colleague had evidently gone into the question of the mordinal," said Nancy. "He may have asked her about it. In fact he would have done, as she was the chief person in the house."

Ned looked doubtful. "I am sure Brews's man did ask her, but I am inclined to think that his inquiries were made *after* you had seen Mrs. Hoing. I can check that easily. Meantime, we must follow common practice. Leave out the picture of Mrs. Hoing guilty, and think of her as Mrs. Hoing innocent – the respectable, decent housekeeper and trusted family servant, with nothing to hide. You come along and ask her about possible dope, say mordinal. The normal woman with no axe to grind would, I think, reply that it was funny you had mentioned it, since that was what the policeman had been questioning her about. Do you agree?"

Nancy nodded vigorously. "I think you are right."

"I think so too. I am taking it that she, in her anxiety to show that Mr. Habershon had staged two suicides, which were really murders, assented readily to your suggestions and told you that Mr. Habershon had had mordinal."

"But she may have been in it with Habershon?" said Nancy.

"Or Hench, or X," he agreed. "All I say is that Mrs. Hoing must be watched. In her evidence at the inquest she says that Mr. Habershon went for a drive with his wards. When you interview her, it turns out that Mr. Habershon did not leave the house in the car, but walked to the garage—"

"But she told me to inquire at the garage."

"Quite. And at the garage you got corroborative evidence that Mr. Habershon was carrying the thermos flask which, on our theory, was presumed to be doped. But the fact is that Mrs. Hoing gave the court the impression that Habershon had started from home in the car with his wards. Actually she tells you later that he left afoot, that he must have gone to the garage for his car, and that she deduced the joint drive, and the presence of the nephew and niece, from the fact that she had been asked to put coffee for three in the flask. She's more of a swell at deduction than most housekeepers of my acquaintance."

"It does look rather thin," Nancy admitted.

"Very much so. But don't take it that I feel sure she was in the game. The coffee, if we can get on the track of it, may be a help. I wonder where she shops?"

"She went round to Oxford Street the morning I called," said Nancy.

"We'll have a glance at Gale Street first," said he. "We get off here."

They had walked halfway up Gale Street, and were within fifty yards of the crossing, when a tall man in a blue suit emerged from Mr. Habershon's house, and came towards them. Ned pulled Nancy up. He was pretty sure that the man was one of Brews's emissaries, from his style and bearing.

"I'm going to have a word with this chap, Nance," he whispered, and waited till the man came up.

"Well, sir?" said he of the blue suit, as Ned approached and stopped him. "What can I do for you?"

"Nothing, thank you, old chap," said Ned, promptly. "But I think you can put in a job of work for Inspector Brews, if you are not too busy. Saw you at the Upperton inquest, didn't I?"

The detective bit his lip. "May I ask your name, sir?"

"Edward Hope. Brews and I are great friends, my dear fellow. Ask him if we aren't."

The detective looked thoughtful. "Well, sir, what is it?"

Ned smiled. "Ask at the post office, which sends parcels round to Gale Street if they have ever delivered parcels from Brazil to the late Mr. Habershon's house. Tell Brews what they say, and ask him if he will be kind enough to let me know."

The detective had seen Ned at the inquest. He nodded. "Very well, sir. Is that all?"

"Telephone Brews first, if you like, for his permission. That's all. I am much obliged to you."

"Not at all, sir," said the detective, saluted, and moved away.

"Parcels of coffee?" inquired Nancy, a moment later.

"Certainly not nuts," replied Ned. "Now back to Oxford Street and district. We are going to ask if we can get any of the splendid Brazilian coffee Mr. Habershon liked so much. If I do one shop, and you another, we may come on it before teatime."

"There aren't many grocers in Oxford Street," said Nancy.

"The fewer to see then, my dear. We shall also telephone the five great stores, asking if they supplied Habershon with groceries. If we draw blank there in the main, we'll try the side streets. London is a wonderful place for delicacies in dingy alleys."

They divided when they reached Oxford Street, and spent the next hour in an unsuccessful quest for Habershon's coffee merchant. When they met again, Ned decided to telephone the various stores. Ten minutes later, having drawn a blank at all of them, he took Nancy to tea.

After tea, they set out again to explore the many side streets, and cross streets within half a mile of Gale Street, Bloomsbury.

They were to meet again at six at Oxford Circus.

"A hopeless dawn, old thing!" said Ned, when Nancy joined him opposite Peter Robinson's at five past six.

"Eureka, to you, sir!" replied Nancy, who was all eagerness now. "You're a pretty good guesser, Ned."

"We call it deduction," he informed her. "But don't tell me you've struck oil?"

"I've discovered coffee anyway," she retorted, "in a little street behind the Museum. They specialise in tea and coffee, and supplied Mr. Habershon—"

"With coffee?"

"Brazilian coffee. But he said it was for the servants. It seems that it's cheaper than the other coffees."

Ned shrugged. "That's a snag, but we'll know better when we hear from Brews about the parcels from abroad. Mrs. Hoing no doubt bought the coffee at this place, and she could say what she liked. I am still sure she only invented the planter story to impress the coffee on your mind. She knew the information would go to me, and that I was temporarily connected with the press."

"But then she might have expected these importers to come forward and say they had not supplied Habershon's coffee, but some Brazilian friend."

"They did not come forward, my dear, but if they had she was still sufficiently safeguarded. She said the coffee was for the servants. Why tell the man that? Shops don't care who drinks the stuff so long as they can sell it."

Nancy agreed now. "But that suggests a long premeditated plan, doesn't it?"

"It does. If Mrs. Hoing was in this, she must have been doing a certain amount of spying and prying for some time. She must have had an idea that Habershon was losing heavily on the races. She must have had an idea that he was tinkering with his wards' money."

"But how could she know that?"

Ned pondered. "That's where we shall need expert opinion. If Habershon brought those bonds to his house, and put them in his safe, we want to know what kind of safe it was. Lots of people keep valuables that a crook could get at with the aid of a stout hairpin. I've seen one or two Silly safes myself."

"You think that she would have dared to tamper with his safe?"

He raised his eyebrows. "My dear girl, if she was in this, she is a perfect terror and would stop at nothing. She's a trusted servant, and was with him for years. She had the run of the house, and might even have had a chance to get a squeeze of his safe key. There's nothing in that. Brews will tell us what he thinks of her chances."

"But she would require an accomplice?"

"Of course. But the business of getting the bodies down to the bank alongside my garden would be comparatively easy, granting the use of the punt in that drain leading to the river."

Nancy nodded. "I see. But if Mr. Hench made an alibi, by meeting the policeman at a quarter to ten, then – the murders must have taken place much earlier."

"Between eight and nine, in that case," said Ned.

Chapter XX

"I 'VE had two nice little letters this morning, Nancy," said Ned, when he called for her next day. "One from a film company offering to buy my house, to stage a crime play there—"

"But are you?" Nancy began.

"No, I'm not. I think it's a rotten idea. T'other letter was a note from Brews. He's rather bucked about our idea, and says he can assure me that no parcels from Brazil were delivered to Mr. Habershon's house in the last year, at least by the post. He is circularising the express and parcel companies now, and will let me know."

"I believe we're on the right line," she said, eagerly.

"Hope so," he said, and called her attention to the parcel under his arm. "Here we have part of the great work on the nidification of British birds, the letterpress. I read some of it last night, and was delighted to find that old Hench had packed a bit of his own in by accident. He was in a hurry to let me have it. There are eight pages on a different style altogether."

"What does that mean?"

"I don't quite know yet. But, having my little suspicions, I went carefully over the photographs again. Hench was watching a nesting hen harrier from a hide, wasn't he?"

"So he said. He told us the people coming had frightened her away."

"Well, if he made a 'hide' to watch a bird on its nest, the 'hide' must have been made within sight of it. How is it that there are no photographs of a hawk on a nest in a marsh? There's only the silly kestrel showing, and that is on the wing. The fact is that there was no hen harrier, and no nest! Either Hench was telling the tale to explain why he was hanging about there, or else he mistook the kestrel for a harrier, and thought when it stooped down on some prey in the marsh that it was dropping on to its nest. He's a bad man, or a bad ornithologist, as we said before. But why bring in a hen harrier at all?"

Nancy reflected. "Perhaps because it is known to nest in marshes, while other hawks don't."

"Well, I am going to waste a fee on that expert taxidermist we saw the other day," he replied. "Come along, and we'll get into town and pay him a visit. I am going to ask him to read the last typewritten chapter (which I think was written by Hench's brother), and then the loose sheets which are Hench's own contribution."

Half an hour later found them in the shop in Piccadilly. Ned explained what he wanted done, and said he would call back in an hour for an opinion. He was willing to pay an adequate fee if the matter was attended to at once.

Then he and Nancy went the round of the shops, took a turn in the Green Park, and returning to Piccadilly, were soon in consultation with the taxidermist in his office at the back of the shop.

"What do you think of it?" Ned asked, as the expert thoughtfully turned over the leaves of the manuscript on his desk.

"I should be inclined to say, sir, that the original writer had been taken ill, and handed his work over to some inexperienced collaborator," was the reply. "I read the last chapter. It was rather original, but quite sound, so I dipped in here and there further back. I should say the author was not a trained man, but had a natural love for the work, and keen observation."

"You mean the original man, not the one who began the extension?"

"So there was another hand, as I thought?" the expert murmured. "Of course, it's palpable. The loose pages are nonsense, where they are not copied verbatim from books on the subject. But I had better not say more, in case you had a hand in it, sir," he added, with a smile.

Ned laughed. "My withers are unwrung. You confirm the impression I formed. I suppose the book would have no chance if finished by the latter hand?"

"No, sir, it would be laughable. It would be as funny, to a man who knew the subject, as a grouse stuffed and fitted with the head and neck of a snipe. But I can assure you that the first part, with the excellent photographs you showed me the other day, would sell. Our firm here would be quite willing to publish it. Of course the original writer would have to finish it himself."

Ned took out his note-case. "He's dead, poor chap," he said. "That, however, is all I want to know. What's the damage, may I ask?"

He paid the fee; the parcel was handed to him again, and he and Nancy walked out into Piccadilly.

"Looks as if we should have to acquit Hench after all," said Nancy. "He's simply a muddler, not a murderer."

Ned looked rather disappointed. "It certainly looks as if Hench was merely down there trying to finish his brother's manuscript, and not quite knowing how, but we can't let him out yet. He may have stuck in those loose leaves to give that impression; not because he was in a hurry last night. The fact is that Hoggett must have seen a light in Pear Cottage; and there's the navigable drain. We must have a look at that before we come to any further decision about the little man."

162

"Brews will be at Gale Street," Nancy said, suddenly.

"So he will. I forgot that," cried Ned, "Well, we'll run over at once and see him. This is our chance to get a tip about old Habershon's safe."

They went by tube to British Museum station, and then hurried to 11 Gale Street. When they rang the door was opened by a plain-clothes man, the one Ned had accosted the previous day. He smiled, and asked their business.

"I want to have a talk with Inspector Brews," Ned told him. I saw him at Upperton the night before last, and this morning I had a letter from him."

He drew the envelope from his pocket. The plainclothes man nodded.

"Come in, please. Mrs. Hoing, the housekeeper, is away for the day, and the inspector has sent the servants out. They're going at the end of the week anyway."

He admitted them, closed the door behind them, and took them upstairs to what had been Mr. Habershon's library. From the footfalls and other noises they heard in the house, they concluded that Brews had a small army of his myrmidons searching the house from cellar to attic.

When they entered the library, Brews was on his knees amid a pile of books and papers. He beamed up at them, and got to his feet.

"As you see, I am pretty busy," he told them. "But I can spare you five minutes. Shut the door, Haselden," he added to the plain-clothes man who had shown them up. "Don't let any pressmen in on any excuse whatever."

When the man had gone, he looked expectant, but waited for Ned to speak.

"I've come about the safe, that's all," Ned told him. "Miss Johnson and I thought we should like a look at it."

"The safe?" Brews stared at him thoughtfully. "Well, that's easily done. It's in the wall over there. You can see the handle."

"But we want to see inside," said Nancy.

"Still easier," said Brews, taking a key from his pocket, and crossing the room. "One turn does it. It's empty, I'm afraid, but perhaps you don't mind that."

"Not a bit. What kind of safe is it, Inspector?"

Brews shook his head. "A very nice, straightforward little bit of metalwork. It will keep papers clean and dry, and proof against the ordinary pilferer. These safes give confidence without protection, and are much liked by burglars!"

"Could be opened by any knowledgeable person, eh?"

"Even by a plumber, sir. But most house safes are like that."

"So you didn't expect to find the bonds there?"

The inspector smiled. "No. I asked Mrs. Hoing if she knew anything about the bonds. The only information she could give me leads me to believe that the bonds were deposited here, for a short time at least, after Mr. Habershon bought them. But she was quite sure he did not take a parcel, other than the thermos, with him on the night of his death."

"I don't suppose he did, or the man at the garage would have mentioned it," Ned remarked. "But how did Mrs. Hoing know the bonds were ever put in the safe?"

"She simply said that Mr. Habershon went to the bank one morning, and came back in a taxi-cab with a large, sealed parcel. That day, as I know, was the day he purchased the Bearer Bonds. The bank did the business for him. Mrs. Hoing says he took the parcel straight up here. She had occasion to go to him half an hour later for orders. He was still in this room, and the parcel was not visible. Naturally enough she assumed that he had put the parcel in the safe."

"Naturally enough," Ned agreed. "Well, Inspector, do you think it would have been possible for Mr. Hench, when he visited Mr. Habershon here, to open that safe, and see what was in it?"

"If he was left alone here for ten minutes, sir, and knew how to manipulate a simple lock, it would be possible, of course. But you mustn't let Mrs. Hoing's slip about the coffee make you suspicious of everyone, Mr. Hope; you really mustn't!"

Nancy started, and Ned stared. "Are you on to that, too?" he cried.

Brews feigned surprise. "You will have your little joke, sir. Why, of course; it stood out plain from the beginning that whoever did the murders knew a lot about Mr. Habershon's private affairs. No use killing three poor things for the mere sake of making an unprofitable sensation, was there? We don't know the extent or intimacy of Mr. Hench's relations with Mr. Habershon. He may have known all about the bonds. So we have to watch him closely. But Mrs. Hoing was in a position to know something, too. Or may have been. That is the wisest way to put it. We have few enough straws to make our bricks with in this case, Mr. Hope; we can't afford to throw away a straw, you can take it from me."

Ned nodded, dejectedly. "Then you think it possible Mrs. Hoing may have had access to the safe?"

"I don't know if she had. But she was in a privileged position here. She had dozens of opportunities to open it, if she had the will, and the means."

Nancy smiled. "Inspector, you don't know how hateful you are! Please complete our destruction by telling us that you know Mrs. Hoing was near Fen Court on the night of the murder."

He laughed. "I know she was here all that evening and night, Miss. She has a cast-iron alibi. I'd go bail on it myself."

"Then who—" began Ned.

Brews interrupted him. "There's your chance, sir. The field's open, and the chances even."

Ned grinned. "All right. Miss Johnson and I are going down this afternoon to see Hench again. What'll you bet we don't get something out of him?"

"I won't bet; but I'll raise my hat to you, if you do," said Brews. "Good luck to you."

"Did you notice that Brews only guaranteed a cast-iron alibi for Mrs. Hoing as far as Fen Court was concerned?" said Ned, as they set off in search of lunch. "The Commander-in-Chief of an army always has an alibi for the trenches. It isn't his business to go there, but he directs operations all the same."

Nancy smiled. "Brews is a beast – but a very agreeable beast. We'll see his hand one day, but not yet."

Two o'clock found them once more on the well-remembered track to Fen Court, and as they drove Ned instructed his companion in the part she had to play.

He reminded her that a man in a corner, like a rat in a corner, is a painful as well as a dangerous sight. If she did not mind, she would get down short of Pear Cottage, cut across the fields to where the broad drain met the river, and beginning there, investigate the bank very carefully.

"That will take you twenty minutes at least," he added. "By that time Hench and I will have come to some sort of understanding."

The programme being agreed to, Nancy was eventually dropped at the point mentioned. Ned drove on, until he was at the entrance to the field intersected by the path to the cottage and orchard.

In theory, he had a very good weapon for a duel with Hench. But as he got down, he felt that really skilful fencing would be necessary to avoid wounding the little man unnecessarily. That is to say, if Hench was innocent of the crime, he must not be allowed to suspect that he was under surveillance.

Mr. Hench was in. He received Ned warmly, and almost at once inquired about his book.

Ned dropped into a chair, lit a cigarette, and rubbed his chin, while he studied Hench's face thoughtfully.

"I came to speak to you about that manuscript," he said slowly. "But did I understand you to say that it was yours?"

Chapter XXI

"WHAT do you mean, Mr. Hope?"

Hench had turned rather white, and there was a sickly smile on his lips. Obviously he was uncomfortable and uneasy. He dropped the cigarette he had lighted, and picked it up again with fumbling fingers. He shifted his feet as he sat back.

Ned did not look severe. He smiled faintly, as if he knew human weaknesses and was prepared to indulge them.

"I was just asking, Mr. Hench. You see I took the trouble to have the manuscript read. Most of it was typed, a few pages—"

"Did I enclose those?" Hench cried with exasperation. "But of course that means nothing, my dear sir. I have no typewriter, you see, and I have not collected enough new material to—"

"Wait a moment," Ned interrupted. "Let me be frank. It wasn't a question of that. It was pointed out by the expert who read the typewritten portion that the work showed keen observation, and an original method, though he did not consider the writer to be a trained ornithologist."

"Perfectly true, Mr. Hope."

"The last few pages, however, he said were laughable," Ned continued, his eyes steadily fixed on the uneasy features of the little man.

"Absurd!" said Hench, and threw his cigarette angrily into the fire.

"My trouble is this," went on Ned, comfortably and easily. "You asked me to do something which is the business of an agent – to try to market the manuscript for you. I was quite willing. I think those photographs and sketches are too good to be lost. But the publisher's allegation is a serious one. He practically tells me that the person who wrote the final eight pages that I showed him must be trying to pass off someone else's book as his own. Now if he had accepted it, and that was the case, I might have been included in any action taken for infringement of copyright."

Hench bit his lip. "How can he prove that? Why, it's libellous!"

"It may be. I am not an expert on ornithology. But the man who is an expert says that the eight pages, where they are not copied verbatim from standard works, show that the writer does not know his subject."

Hench lit a fresh cigarette, and puffed smoke gustily. "One can quote to a certain extent, Mr. Hope. I intended to give the sources in footnotes."

Ned shook his head. "I am afraid you are not meeting my point. If the first part of the manuscript passes with the expert as accurate, and more or less valuable, we may take it that the writer knew what he was talking about. If he did, why descend into inaccurate nonsense at the end?"

Hench scowled. "I know what I am talking about."

"I don't think you know what you were writing about then," said Ned, irritated by the little man's obstinacy. "Why all this mystery about it? I am speaking to you in confidence, and you may do the same with me. But you put me in an awkward position with the publisher, and I insist on having an explanation."

Hench got up. He took a turn up and down the room. He looked more dejected and troubled now than angry.

"I don't see what more I can say to you."

Ned shrugged. "Now, Mr. Hench, it won't do! I am not the only person who saw that you were not a trained ornithologist – not even an average amateur at the game. You told me, and the inspector too, I think, that you were watching a hen harrier. Now what you were looking at was a kestrel. There are no hen harriers here."

"You never saw the bird, Mr. Hope."

"No, but if you can tell me which of your photographs represents a hen harrier, on the nest or off, I'll apologise to you."

Hench sat down. "I don't deny it. I was unable to get photos of the hen harrier."

"Because we frightened her away, eh? But, surely, since you were watching her nest, you have a picture of the nest."

"Go to the devil!" Mr. Hench retorted with extraordinary ferocity.

Ned laughed. "Perhaps then you will draw me a hen harrier? I suppose those sketches were really yours?"

Somehow, looking at Hench's sullen eyes, he felt that they were not. The little man drew in his lips.

"You're impertinent."

"I am actually trying to be helpful," murmured Ned. "But, if you take that line, perhaps I had better leave you to the tender mercies of Inspector Brews."

The phrase acted like a bomb. Hench sprang to his feet, frightened and anxious.

"What has he to do with it?"

"Nothing so far, but I'll tell you what it may come to. Brews is investigating the murders, and you are the only man living here who had relations with the late Mr. Habershon."

Hench's face showed relief. "Does he think I killed him – the man I was depending on for money to get my book published?"

"That is just the point. So far Hench hasn't roped you in, because you are supposed to be living in this seclusion to study birds, and that common interest explained your connection with the dead man. But if Brews discovers that you are a fraud as an ornithologist, he'll put you through it. How would you like to be confronted with an expert, who would examine you in ornithology? He wouldn't handle you as tentatively as I have done."

Hench winced. "Whatever my reason for living down here, it does not connect me with the murders. How could it?"

"You will have to ask Brews that. Possibly he might say that you were living here as one of the agents in a plot. This flapdoodle about bird-watching in itself proves that you are not – shall I say, strictly veracious."

That shot went home. Hench did not fire up this time. He resumed his seat, and sat crumpled in it, looking from the fire to Ned, and from Ned back to the fire.

"On the other hand," said Ned, looking away from him, and speaking very slowly and distinctly, "there may be an explanation of your bluff. If you think fit to let me know the truth, I am quite ready to take it into account. But I resent the idea of being the agent for the sale of a book you are passing off as your own."

"Inspector Brews must know that I have an alibi – if I needed one." The words came desperately from the little man hunched up in the chair.

Ned nodded. "For a certain hour. You went to Hitherland, you say you saw a light about here at a quarter to ten. But how do you know that the murders took place at a quarter to ten, or before that hour?"

Hench looked alarmed. "The watches. I understood—"

"The watches were tampered with – one at least was. No, Hench; the inspector will want to know how you could say you had an alibi, if you don't know when the murders took place. An alibi covers time as well as place, you know."

Hench drew a long, deep breath. He sat for quite five minutes, staring into the fire, his face a kaleidoscope of chaotic and ever-changing emotions. Then he looked at Ned, bit his lip and surrendered at discretion.

"You're right, Mr. Hope. I am sorry I deceived you. I did not know that my deception might involve you in trouble. I never thought of that."

Ned smiled faintly. "Good. Now we are getting at it. I won't prompt you, or hint at my theories. Just carry on with your explanation, if you don't mind."

Hench sighed, then he began to speak rapidly, his face flushed now, and his eyes ashamed. He explained with a sort of melancholy pride that his elder brother had taken most of the photographs, and had done the sketches. He himself, while quite as expert a photographer, had no knowledge of birds, and no interest in ornithology until James's death. James had had a certain amount of capital, and Hench admitted that he had been disappointed and upset when the valuation for probate of his brother's estate disclosed the fact that most of the capital had been spent. His brother had, he said, not pulled his weight in the business they had set up together. He had let it down, and when he died, it was hardly worth carrying on.

"But he left you what property he had, including the book?" said Ned, when Hench had got so far.

"Yes, he did. I was very proud of James, though he did let me down," Hench replied. "I couldn't help seeing that the photographs were magnificent, almost unique; but, of course, the written part stumped me. My first idea was to get it published in James's name. But the people I submitted it to said it had no value unless it was finished. Well,

I thought and thought. I knew what I could do. I felt sure I could photograph birds as well as James, and it seemed to me I could get information from books to complete the letterpress. I didn't realise that it would be such a job."

Ned reflected. "But why try to pass it off as your own work?"

Hench looked abashed. "I don't know. I did a lot of photos myself, and you couldn't tell them from James's. Somehow, I began to wonder if I couldn't make a name for myself. Conceit, I suppose, if it comes to that."

He broke off and resumed again in a curious tone. "I suppose it never occurred to you, Mr. Hope, that little people want to be big ones? People don't think of that! They never seem to imagine that butchers, and bakers, and candlestick-makers, yes, and suburban photographers, want to be anything else. But they do often enough. I did! When I looked at those photographs, I asked myself why shouldn't I be famous? James started knowing no more than I about birds. He taught himself. Why shouldn't I study birds, and bring out a big book in my name on them? It couldn't hurt poor James, who was dead."

"No," said Ned, looking at him in some surprise, finding indeed a puzzled, half-sympathetic interest in the dreams of this little would-be climber.

Hench went on quickly. "Yes, I thought what people would say. When I went back to North Finchley where I came from, they would think differently about me. It would not be the man who used to take their photos for thirty shillings a dozen, but 'Mr. Hench, who is so famous with that book of his.' And it would have been half mine!" he added.

Ned lit a fresh cigarette. "So you didn't know the difference between a kestrel and a hen harrier?"

"No, I didn't."

"Neither do I," said Ned, smiling. "And, of course, your brother had not started to do the hawks and falcons for his book."

"No. That's it! If he had, I could have had a better notion. But I saw it once said that hen harriers were hawks that nested in marshes, and when I came down here I saw a hawk drop down in the marsh. I thought, as it was nesting-time, it was dropping down on its nest."

"So you waited for days under the impression that the bird was sitting? Why didn't you look for the nest?"

"I was afraid to disturb the bird. I took some photographs of the place with a telephoto lens, hoping inspection of the finished pictures would show me the nest."

Ned stared. "Were those sketches not yours either?"

Hench shook his head ruefully. "No. I can't draw. My brother was naturally gifted that way."

"I see," said Ned, doubtfully. "If we can square this out, I may be able to place the illustrations and sketches for you, but not the letterpress. Let me see now. You went to Hitherland that night about seven. You did not take supper at your usual time."

Hench shook his head. "No. The fact is, Mr. Hope, I made the acquaintance of a man there a fortnight ago. He had been a professional wildfowler, but is now retired. He lives in a cottage near the shore. I hoped to get some information about the habits of birds from him. I had promised to look him up one evening, so I had supper early, and went over."

"You are sure you sent no invitation to Mr. Habershon or his nephew?"

"Of course not. I went to see Daly."

"And you left his cottage about nine, eh?"

"Yes, about nine. I walked home then."

Ned pondered. So far, Hench's explanation held water. But was it all true? Had the tragedy taken place after ten o'clock that night, and not before?

"You did not think that there might be a light in your cottage which you mistook for one in mine?" he asked.

Hench shrugged. "No, of course not."

"I suppose you lock up your cottage when you leave it?"

The little man began to show signs of restiveness. He felt that Ned was usurping the functions of the police, and resented it.

"Need you ask all these questions?"

Ned quite understood, but endeavoured to explain. "If you think it over, Mr. Hench, you will see that if we can eliminate you from the case, all the better for you. The sooner Brews lets you out, the sooner you will be free to carry on without being worried about the affair."

Hench made an impatient gesture. "Well, I never lock up. I have no valuable possessions, and few come this way."

Ned got up. "Well, I won't bother you any more. But just one thing before I go: Did you see anything in this cottage that worried you when you came home?"

Hench stared. He hesitated for a moment before replying. Then he shook his head vigorously. "No, Nothing! Of course not."

When Ned left him, and went off to look for Nancy, he was not so sure of Hench's innocence as he had been ten minutes before. It seemed to him that his last question had frightened Hench a little, or worried him. He had hesitated for a moment before replying, and then spoken with vehemence.

Nancy had examined the banks of the drain most carefully, then she went back to the car. She felt that she did not want to meet Hench just then.

Ned joined her after a little. "I say," he said, as they got into their seats, "I am beginning to wonder if the murders took place before ten, or if Habershon's watch was set back to help out the alibi. Hench seems straight enough, and his story tallies with our conclusions about the bird book, but I don't quite like to drop him yet. What did you find – anything?"

Nancy nodded. "If one dare judge by the torn water weeds, and that sort of thing, it seems pretty certain that some kind of boat or punt came up the drain. Where it joins the main stream, there is a bed of floating weeds, and that is not growing smooth as it would be in ordinary circumstances."

Chapter XXII

WHEN they reached Nancy's flat again, the porter said that a gentleman called Brews had called to see her. He had promised to call back about six.

"Stay and see him," Nancy said to Ned, as they went up, "I'll make tea now. He may have some clue to the thing."

"Or simply want to pump me about Hench," Ned suggested. "The beggar seems to know all my movements.

He sat down to smoke, while Nancy made tea, and after tea they talked over the Hench interview until both felt that there was no more to be said about it. But Brews thought otherwise, when he came in at six, and was accommodated with a chair and a cigarette.

"You're not one to let the grass grow under your feet, Mr. Hope," he began, beaming at Ned. "Make anything of Mr. Hench?"

"I'll tell you, if you promise to let me know the result of your work at the house today," Ned replied.

The inspector nodded. "That's a bargain! Carry on, sir, if you please."

Ned told him briefly all that he had learned from the owner of Pear Cottage, and added that Hench's explanation squared with his own and Miss Johnson's theories. "But perhaps not with yours?" he added.

"Oh, I don't know that, sir. A great deal of it must be the truth. The only question is, how much fiction, if any, has been added. I know he did visit Daly, and stayed 'til nine or so. But, as you say, the watch may have been set to show the deaths took place before ten, whereas they may have taken place later. Hench would be back after ten. As for what Miss Johnson here says about the drain, it looks to me as if the punt had been used there. Did you ask Hench if he said he would go that particular night to visit Daly – I mean make the arrangement in advance?

"No, I didn't ask him that."

Brews smiled. "Well, I know he did! He told Daly he would go to see him that night. He fixed it up some days before his visit."

Ned shrugged. "Trying to strengthen an alibi, eh? That looks odd. But now you have my news. What's yours?"

The inspector stared into the fire. "Well, sir, to take first things first, I know none of the parcel companies delivered packages from Brazil to the house in Gale Street, and we know that the Post Office didn't either."

"That nails Mrs. Hoing down in a lie, I think."

"It seems to. Next, sir, I may tell you that I found no sign of those Bearer Bonds in the house. They're gone right enough, and I am pretty sure Mr. Habershon did not take them with him in the car. If he took a passport, ready to do a bunk when the murders were done, you would think he would have the boodle with him, too. But I don't think he had. Then our inquiries at the banks and safe-deposits have drawn blanks. He had no deposit anywhere."

Nancy stared. "Then you think the bonds have been stolen?"

"Of course. But now I am going to tell you something bearing on the negative evidence as we called it. As you know, there weren't any fingerprints on the car, so I've been reversing the usual routine and looking everywhere for the absence of fingerprints."

"And you found the absence?" Nancy asked and smiled.

"I found lots of absences," said Brews, with a grin. "Lots of little fingerprints seem to have been playing truant; on the handle of the safe, for instance, and on the phial where the mordinal was kept!"

"By Jove!" cried Ned. "Bottles are fine for impressions generally."

"Splendid, sir. But the phial was as clean as a whistle. I was told the housemaid polished the handle of the safe regular, and naturally I couldn't object to that. But I didn't ask Mrs. Hoing if the housemaid was instructed to polish up the medicine bottles! That seemed to me to be a bit too thorough."

"It looks black for Mrs. Hoing."

"It looks thoroughly nasty for her. You see, so much turns on her evidence about Habershon and his relations with his wards, and what he did, and where he went. Take the case of Habershon's drive that evening. The two young people are going to tea at their friend's. Mr. Habershon, before his dinner, goes for his car, calls for the two, and rushes them off to the country. Now why does he do that? Has he had a telephone message from Hench? No! The telephone people say he was not called up that afternoon, and Mrs. Hoing says he wasn't."

"We can't take her word for it, but the exchange ought to know."

Brews nodded. "They do know. On the other hand, as we are investigating the possible complicity of Mrs. Hoing, we can ask ourselves what happened – not merely what she said happened."

"A sound idea, but what exactly do we ask ourselves?" ventured Nancy.

"If Mrs. Hoing told Habershon there had been a telephone call for him! There is just a chance that she went to him—"

"The telephone is in the hall, isn't it?"

"Yes, and he may have been in his library. Or he may have come in from somewhere. What was there to prevent her from telling him that Hench had rung up, and was very anxious for him to bring young Rainy over to see the photographs of his collection of eggs? He might say, or be made to say, that he was taking the lot to a publisher next day. Isn't that possible?"

"Quite. Indeed it seems probable, Brews. Mr. Habershon wouldn't go there at night on chance. This is how it seems to me to work out. Mrs. Hoing got to know that Habershon was gambling, and in need of money. She had a false key to his safe, and made herself familiar with his financial affairs. She knew he had invested some of his wards' money in negotiable securities, and suspected that he had an idea of bolting. She had an accomplice, and between them they worked it out to get Habershon and the two wards down to Pear Cottage that night. There Habershon was knocked on the head, and the two young people, being doped with mordinal in their coffee, were drowned. The whole affair was staged to make it appear that there was a suicide, and an accident, or that Habershon had committed murder, faked the appearance of a suicide, then spoiled his own plans by tumbling into the pond."

"But how were they carried to the pond? Do you mean by water?" asked Nancy.

Brews intervened. "If we adopt the theory that a visit was paid to Pear Cottage, we can rule out the ponds as the scene of the drowning. It is more likely that the drowning took place in the six-foot drain. The punt was very wet when we examined it. Some of the water had dried up, but there was too much for an ordinary trip in a calm river. I am going to assume that the drowning took place in the drain, that the bodies were then shifted into the punt, the punt poled down to the river, and finally taken to that spot on the bank opposite your garden at Fen Court, sir."

"But why put them in my ponds?"

"Because, otherwise, questions would be asked about Pear Cottage and its occupants on that night. Also, because, while Mr. Habershon could not get out of a deep pond, with a slimy edge, he might have saved himself from a mere drain."

"But the blow on the back of the neck might have stunned him," said Nancy.

"It would. But he could not get a blow on the back of the neck by falling into a drain from the clay bank. It was supposed by us at first to have been caused by the back of his neck striking the stone, as he slipped and went in."

"That was the work of the accomplice then," observed Ned. "Mrs. Hoing, as you admit, was at home, and has an alibi. Do you think the bonds were stolen – if they were stolen – before or after Mr. Habershon left his house?"

The inspector pursed his lips. "After, I am inclined to think. Mrs. Hoing dared not remove the bonds from the safe until she was sure that he would not come back to the house."

"That he would never come back to the house, you mean?"

"Yes, that is what I do mean. The bodies were not discovered till the following day. Mrs, Hoing went out early, with a closed basket, nominally to shop, on the morning you found Habershon floating. We have not yet been able to trace where she went."

"By Jove!" cried Ned. "She may have had the bonds with her then?"

"Quite possible. Though she did not post them. But we have one find, that may be a clue. An elderly woman deposited a parcel in the cloakroom at Liverpool Street Station that morning. She called for it on the day of the inquest."

"Nerve!" Nancy murmured.

"If it was Mrs. Hoing, yes. But I met her on the platform at our end, and she had no parcel then."

"Could she have disposed of it *en route*?"

"That's the point, sir. She may have done; but how, or when, we cannot say yet." Ned started. "Hench was not at the inquest. Could he have waited somewhere by the side of the line, to pick up a parcel dropped from the train?"

Brews jumped. "You may have hit on it, sir! We'll go into that. There are several places where a man might clamber on to the line, and pick something up. Mrs. Hoing was alone in a third-class carriage when the train came in."

"One up to you, Ned!" said Nancy. "Pear Cottage ought to be searched from top to bottom."

Brews shook his head. "I hardly think he would be fool enough to leave the bonds there."

Nancy had been thinking of another phase of the case, one on which Brews had never satisfied their curiosity. She wondered if he would tell them now, when he seemed in such an expansive mood.

"How did you come by those scraps of the letter, Inspector?" she asked suddenly, smiling at him appealingly."

"They came by post, Miss Johnson," he said, readily. "I know you both have an idea that I make use of you without giving anything away. People get the idea that we are so anxious to make a personal hit that we either suppress ideas from outside, or make them our own. It's a mistake! If I get help from you, and pull off the case, I get credit for it anyway. My superiors would take the view that it was smart of me to rope you in. I admit you have been a help, and I shall say so in court if I unravel this business. But one or two things I have had to keep to myself for a certain time. I can tell you now that the remains of that letter were sent to me in an envelope, by post, with the address in capitals."

He pulled two envelopes from his pocket as he spoke and handed one to Nancy. It was addressed to Brews, and was a cheap, whitey-brown envelope.

"This other envelope," he went on, holding it up, "contained a reply to a note I sent Mr. Hench. Apparently he hadn't the sense to see that the two were the same."

Ned smiled. "Perhaps not. What impression did the letter give you when you pieced it together?"

Brews shrugged. "A pettish sort of letter, and rather exaggerated in its terms. She and Rainy wanted to get married at once, and she thought the uncle was wilfully standing in their way. They had 'almost given up hope, and there must be an end to it soon.' If Habershon would not consent, they might take matters into their own hands."

"Why should Hench send that to you?"

"Well, sir, it showed that the scrap of paper pinned on the poor thing's dress was not a genuine message from someone about to commit suicide, and, since Habershon had received the letter, it would hint that he had torn a bit from it, and pinned it on. In other words, it would confirm the theory that Habershon made away with the two."

"Have you finished your job in town, Brews?" Ned asked, nodding assent to the last proposition.

"As far as I can see, I have, sir. Tomorrow morning, first thing, I shall put men on to search the railway line, both sides, to see if there are any traces of a package having been thrown from the train Mrs. Hoing went by, or a man having clambered over to pick it up. I expect it will be too late, but I can't afford to neglect it. Then I must see if I can trace any of the passengers who travelled by that train, and ask them if they saw a parcel thrown out."

"And the guard, driver, and stoker, of course," said Ned.

"Of course. That will be an easier job. The railway people will know who were on duty on the train. The passengers may be more difficult to find."

Chapter XXIII

"THERE is one thing that still puzzles me about the case," said Ned, next morning, when he and Nancy were again on the road to Fen Court.

"I'm more modest – there are a dozen things that puzzle me, old thing," she replied, thoughtfully.

"I'm crushed," he said. "I meant that one thing hasn't really engaged my attention enough. That is the car, and the position it occupied when it was found. As we know, it was in that little field bay near Pudstey crossroads. I suppose it was a pretty good car, if it belonged to Habershon, and was usually chauffeur driven. It must have had decent lights. Were they on, or off, when the car was found?"

"Can't we ask Brews?" she suggested.

"He'll be busy. Wait a moment! I believe the car was taken to that big garage at Upperton after the police had examined it. I think we'll go round by Upperton, and make sure."

"Do you think it will help, Ned?"

He frowned. "It may. After that, I have a good mind to stay at Fen Court for a few nights. I meant to before, but found Brews there, and changed my mind. I would go down quietly after dark, take a camp-bed, and spend the time nosing round the district. I really think those bonds have left town, and are hidden somewhere not a hundred miles from my house."

"Any more offers for your house, by the way?" she asked.

"No. But my publishers say there is a new demand for my books! They are getting out cheap editions of the old ones. That's on account of this newspaper work. But I'm hanged if I know how I am going to write many more articles, unless I can say something definite. So far they've gone down like milk, but I was really commissioned to unravel the murder tangle, not to generalise."

When they reached the big garage at Upperton, they got down, and had an interview with the manager. He readily admitted that Mr. Habershon's car had been left with him. He had since had instructions from the executors of the dead man to offer it for sale.

"May we see it?" Ned asked.

"Certainly, sir. It's a twenty-horse 'Bellum' saloon. Come this way."

They went into the garage, and inspected the comfortable five-seater in which the tragic three had taken their last drive. Ned walked round to the front, and inspected the lighting-set. There were two big headlights, and the ordinary sidelights.

"Were any of the lights on when the car was found?" he asked.

The manager considered. "Not when it was found, sir, but they were on. Naturally, if the old gentleman ran after his nephew and niece, he would be in too much of a hurry to turn them off."

"*Did* he run after his nephew and niece?" asked Nancy.

"That's what we think here, madam. All that complicated business about murder, and so on, may do all right for the police. *I* think they committed suicide, and the old gentleman tried to stop them."

"You mean that the lights were turned on, but had gone out?" asked Ned, who had not been listening to the manager's views about the cause of death.

"That is what I mean, sir. I should say from what I saw that the lights were turned on, and left on, after the car had stopped. But the engine wasn't running, and the supply of juice gave out. In fact, I know it did, from my examination."

"Thank you," said Ned. "That is exactly what I wanted to know. But, since it was being driven up to the time it reached the crossroads, may we assume that the lights were on at that time, and would be alight for some considerable time after that?"

"I don't deny it, sir," replied the other. "If they gave light enough to drive by, we can say that they would be alight for hours after the car was abandoned. But the car was there all night on that very lonely road, and part of next day, before it was found."

Ned thanked the manager, and left the garage with Nancy. She looked amusedly at her companion as they got once more into the car.

"What about it, Dupin?" she asked.

"Pudstey crossroads and the farmer who owned the punt," said Ned. "Possess your soul in patience a little longer, darling, and you can then help me dissect the new evidence."

"If Hench drove the car there, after murdering them, why would he leave on the lights?" asked Nancy. "You see, even women have gleams of intelligence."

"Whole searchlights, not mere gleams, I admit!" He rallied her. "But that remark of yours isn't one of them. If Hench committed the crimes and meant to throw the onus on old Habershon, he could argue, as well as you and I, that a man pursuing two people hastening away to drown themselves would not wait to cut off the lights on the car! Did you observe the set of the headlamps?"

"No. What about them?"

"They were set pretty high. We may also take it that they were on. An experienced driver in these narrow roads at night would have them on."

When they reached the farmhouse, they interviewed the farmer's wife for the second time. Her husband was in Upperton.

"There is a question coming up about the car that was found at the crossroads," said Ned. "People are beginning to wonder why it was not seen before."

"After dark, sir?" she questioned.

"Why not? The lights had been left on."

"Mortal few folk come this way, sir."

"Evidently, but I wondered if you or your husband had not seen it," he replied. "I mean the beam from the headlights."

The farmer's wife shook her head. "We're early to bed here, and I don't know that we could see it anyway; not from here."

She led her visitors outside, and pointed to the gable of the house facing to the crossroads. It was a blank wall, with a cowshed against it to the height of the first storey.

"If the lights were on, and someone had been sleeping here, they might have seen it, only there's no window," she told them. "I don't know if they would have bothered though. Cars aren't the strange sight they used to be," she paused, then added, "Aren't you the gentleman who came the other day about our punt?"

Ned nodded, "Yes, how much do you want for it?"

"I told my husband after you had gone, and he said you could have it for two pounds, sir." Ned hesitated for a moment, then pulled out two notes. "Very well. I'll buy it, if your husband will have it sent down, and moored opposite Fen Court," he agreed.

When she had made out a receipt, they thanked her and left.

"I'd like to examine the thing," Ned explained, as they drove on. "I can sell it easily enough."

"But aren't you going to Fen Court now?" asked Nancy, as he turned the car presently down a side road that led south once more.

"Not today – I've changed my mind," he said. "I am going home. Can I drop you anywhere, or are you doing anything today?"

"Leave me at home," she said. "I must really put in a call or two this afternoon. Bob Jameson has sent me an S.O.S. He's fallen in love again, and he doesn't know if Ferda will release him! Then Mrs. Gay has asked me to a tea-fight. I haven't been near her for ages."

"Good enough," said Ned. "I have lots to do myself, old thing. Tomorrow, at the hour of ten, I'll call for you, and we'll get on the trail once more."

"Watchman, what of the light?" asked Nancy.

"Still foggy," said Ned. "From where the car was left, the headlights ought to have been beaconing over the hedge, and visible as a ray from the crossroads where Hench sets his alibi. He did not mention seeing a light there, did he?"

"I did not hear him mention it, but, if he was asked about a light at Fen Court, he would naturally not worry about the beam of a car away to the west."

"That's true," said Ned, and suddenly announced his intention of going about once more to call on Hench. "Even the worms are allowed to turn," he added.

"But then they don't boast of their intelligence," she retorted.

"No; they're like sententious people; they make silence serve for wisdom," he said. "Pax, my dear! We won't fight till we have settled this business one way or the other."

189

Mr Hench was walking in the neglected orchard when they arrived. Though, apparently, he hoped Ned would help him to market the photographs, he was not so pleased to see him as on earlier occasions.

"I am afraid you think me an awful bore," Ned apologised. "But I am doing my best for you, and once I can convince Brews that you are about the most harmless man in this district, I shall be able to go ahead with those photographs of yours."

"I am sure Inspector Brews has never worried me," said Hench, rather sulkily, "I don't feel at all anxious about him."

Ned pursed his lips. "Ah, Brews is on a new line. It appears someone sent him two scraps of a letter addressed to Mr. Habershon, in a whitish-brown envelope. He's going carefully into that. But what I want to know is something you can answer cheerfully."

Hench looked immediately perturbed and anxious. "What is it?"

"When you were at the crossroads that night, where you met the constable, did you see the lights of a car?"

The relief that showed on Hench's face was unmistakable. "Only one car passed me that night."

"I don't mean passing you, or on that road at all. I mean did you see what looked like a steady, fixed beam from the headlights of a car near Pudstey crossroads; in short, the lights of Mr. Habershon's car?"

Hench was not put out. "Now I come to think of it, I did. After I had spoken to the constable, I was looking about me, and I saw a sort of ray in the distance. It's so flat here you can see a headlight for miles. But I thought it might come from the car owned by the farmer up there. In any case, I did not pay much attention to it."

Ned thanked him. "That's all I wanted to know, and I think you will find it helps our case. Well, see you again sometime, Mr. Hench. Miss Johnson and I have to scoot back to town now."

Chapter XXIV

"I'M making a night of it, Nancy, so I go home to bed in an hour," Ned told the girl next day, when he called for her. "By the way, I had old Brews on the telephone this morning, and told him what we had done yesterday about the car inquiry. He seemed grateful, though I have a notion that he had an inkling already."

"About the lights," said Nancy, as they walked down the hill, "and the farmer's wife."

"Yes, and our talk with Hench. Hench, of course, is a puzzle. Sometimes I think he has cleared himself completely, and at other times I can't see that the job could have been worked without him. It was such a brutal and beastly business anyway that the man who gets hanged for it won't get a scrap of my sympathy. If it's Hench, he's an oily hypocrite as well."

"I wish we could decide one way or the other," Nancy murmured.

"I am going to have a shot at that tonight," Ned told her. "I look at it this way: if we can get at the whereabouts of the stolen bonds, we shall discover at least one of the brutes. I have an idea that my guess about the parcel being thrown from the train is the right one, and I believe Brews thinks so, too."

"A needle in a haystack," Nancy said, doubtfully.

He agreed, but added: "If I only take one man at a time, I shall narrow it down. I am going to see if I can make up my mind about Hench, Now there can only be two theories about what he was doing down there. One is that he was trying to get material to finish his brother's book, and blunderingly made a 'hide' in the marsh to watch what he thought was a hen harrier. If that was all, then he is clear."

"But the proof, Ned, how are you going to get that?"

"By investigating the other alternative, that he went down there as accomplice in a conspiracy of a criminal kind. Which ever way it works out, one thing is certain, and concrete, and that is the 'hide' itself. I can see, by studying two of the photographs he took, and comparing marks, the general position of the 'hide' itself."

"But he filled it up when the hawk flew away."

Ned smiled. "I know. If he filled it up, it suggests that the 'hide' was a hole he dug in the ground; camouflaged no doubt with reeds and rushes. If he dug a hole, and stayed in it all day, it was in a comparatively dry part of the marsh—"

Nancy started. "I say, you don't think he hid the Bearer Bonds there, meaning to dig them up again when all was clear, and the excitement had blown over?"

Ned shrugged. "I can't say that I think he did. If I thought so, there would be no question of his complicity in the business. What I do say is that I am going to take a spade with me to Fen Court, and do a little digging tonight after dark."

"But would the bonds not be damaged or destroyed?"

"I don't suppose they were simply buried in a paper parcel. Whoever picked up the bonds must have packed them more strongly before he put them underground."

"*If* he did."

"Well, tonight will show that, one way or the other."

Nancy reflected. "I think it's a bright idea of yours, but will Brews take it for granted that the finding of the bonds there can be linked up with Hench?"

"There will be the presumption that he did it; especially as we are sure Hench sent those scraps of the letter anonymously to Brews. But that's the inspector's job. I told him what I thought of doing, and he was quite keen on it."

"He won't interfere?"

Ned shook his head. "No. As a matter of fact, he goes this morning down to Hampshire to investigate another bit of the case. He wouldn't tell me what it was."

"I wonder what he can want down there, Ned? He never mentioned Hampshire before, did he?"

Ned shook his head. "No, but he's a weird bird. Look here, Nancy. Do you mind doing a bit of shopping for me, before I go home? I want some stuff that won't need to be cooked. You see, I may be a few days at Fen Court. What do you think I ought to have?"

"I can get you tinned tongue, and things like that," she replied. "You had better get some fresh bread at a village going down. Milk you can get bottled, and it will keep for a couple of days at this time of year. I'll see about the other things for you now."

She went into the first grocer's shop they came to, and came out again in a few minutes with a large parcel.

"That ought to satisfy you, even if the marsh air gives you a whale of an appetite," she told him, as he took the parcel. "What about the camp bed?"

"I won't need it. I found an old sleeping bag I used to have when I was camping. I'm taking that in the car tonight."

He left Nancy ten minutes later at the foot of Heath Street, and went back to his flat. He was rather more excited than usual, though he had not cared to exaggerate the potentialities of his theory to Nancy. He might be mistaken about the hide in the marsh, but it did seem an ideal place in which to conceal the bonds.

Who would be likely to look there for them? So far, not even the astute Brews had suggested it; but he had caught an approving note in the inspector's voice that morning, when he had spoken of his intentions, and Brews had replied that there might be something in it. Brews was a sport. He felt sure that he would not rush in and make the discovery himself.

If the 'hide' drew a blank, Ned intended to spend the next few nights spying on Hench's house, so he turned in ten minutes after he reached the flat, and managed to put in seven hours sleep, before he rose, had a bath, and sat down to a late tea.

He took a thick coat with him, and a pair of woollen gloves, carried his parcel of groceries and the sleeping bag down to the car, and then went back to study the photographs of the marsh in conjunction with a large-scale ordnance map.

"I think I can place it," he mused, as he smoked contentedly, and studied the map lines. "It must have been where this ridge is raised a little above the level of the marsh. That comes just in the line between the windmill past Pudstey and the west side of my garden. Making a cross mark from Poljohn to the – Yes, that's it, as near as may be."

He pencilled a cross on his map, worked out two easily identified lines of approach to the spot marked, and rolled up the map again.

He concluded that, as Hench was a small man, the hide would not be more than four feet deep. Probably he crouched in it, and concealed his head behind a fringe of reeds and rushes stuck round the side of the pit. It ought not to take much more than half an hour to dig down to the bottom of it.

He dined early, and set off in his car at a quarter to eight. At nine, he was within a few miles of Fen Court, and switched off his headlamps; driving slowly and cautiously with side lamps only. He met one car, but passed none when he had come to the marsh country. And, for the last seven miles of his drive, he did not encounter a single traveller on foot.

When he turned his car into the tiny lane leading to the house, he put out the lamps, and went quietly into the grounds, with his sleeping-bag and parcel of groceries. He left these in the silent, gloomy house, suddenly recollected that he had not brought a lamp of any kind, and growled impatiently at his own forgetfulness.

He had also forgotten to get bread or milk. Excitement, and eagerness to get on with this new quest, had driven such material matters out of his mind.

The house struck cold. Even in his thick coat, he shivered as a draught from the open door came in. He shut the door.

Switching on his pocket torch, he went into the sitting room. He was not a nervous man, and far from superstitious, but he told himself that there was something beastly about the house. It smelt musty, it was icy cold. The dark rooms were intimidating. As he moved over to the window, a board creaked, and made him start. The echoes of his footfalls were uncanny.

He repressed an impulse to look over his shoulder, pulled out his cigarette case and lit up. Ugh! What was the use of standing there, looking into the dark garden, where the sinister ponds now lay invisible, and the damp wraith-like mists were creeping and drifting over the neglected paths, and derelict bushes. It would be better to tackle the job of work he had to do. Digging would warm him. If he came upon the bonds, he would go back to town; or rush over to Upperton and sleep the night there.

If he didn't find them, at least the exercise with the spade would have driven out some of the chill engendered by the cold drive and the creepy, empty house.

He threw his cigarette into the rusty grate, and turned back to the hall. The spade was still in the car. He went out for it, and felt sensibly relieved when he shut the door of the house behind him, and heard the last of the faint echoes that the clang had made in the deserted rooms.

Taking the spade from the car, he stood still for a moment or two to get his bearings. Hench's 'hide' had not been far away, some hundreds of yards behind the house.

He climbed through a gap in the low hedge bordering the little lane, and found himself on a bit of marshy ground. It was not very wet, and here and there clumps of stunted gorse and brambles were dotted about.

Though he was not anxious to make himself conspicuous, he had to flash on his torch twice to get the line.

"I can't be very far from it now," he said to himself presently, shifting the spade from one shoulder to another, as he came abreast of some gorse bushes. "I saw these in the photograph. Must be somewhere within twenty yards of this."

Chapter XXV

THERE was a curious singing in Ned's ears. His head was throbbing, and there seemed to be weights on his eyelids. He had the sensation of a man in a dentist's chair, who comes slowly to after gas, and, in a few seconds, that appear like æons, goes through the weighty and depressing business of coming again to life.

Yes, he must be at the dentist's, he decided. He could hear the man's voice speaking as through many folds of cloth. But no rays of light filtered through the tissue of his eyelids. The room must be dark. What the dickens did it mean? Dentists couldn't operate in a dark room. And what was the matter with his body? It was so heavy, laden, and unresponsive.

He felt himself lifted suddenly. He knew he was being lifted almost in an upright position, arms about his thighs, he felt a shoulder in his chest, and then his head drooped down. Were they hanging him? For what? Someone had killed someone. But it was all a mistake. Now he was being joggled along. He opened his eyes for a moment, but saw nothing; it was all dark about him.

What world was he in? The question answered itself absurdly. Within an inch of his nose was something that smelt faintly of cloth, mildly of perspiration; the pressure of the shoulder which was now on his stomach gave his awakening senses the impression that he was being carried slung over someone's shoulder, like a sack. Quite near him there was heavy breathing. He swayed regularly.

With awakening came the ache in his head again, something at the back, and, with that, realisation that somewhere was wrong. He must cry out, give an alarm. He tried several times without success, and then, at the fourth attempt, a curious strangled shrill cry broke from his lips. The jolting ceased. He was put down, his shoulders rested on a hard knee, and a familiar voice spoke.

"It's all right, sir. It's all right."

"Is it *out*?" said Ned, and then began to laugh rather hysterically.

"Out for good," said Brews. "Easy now, sir! I'm here. You're fit to take a drop of brandy now. I thought you had gone west at first."

Ned stared up at the face invisible above him in the dark. He must be in Hampshire. That was where Brews had gone. Somehow, he must have driven down to look for the inspector, and had a crash.

A flask was put to his lips, and a few fiery drops of brandy were doled into his mouth.

"Swallow that," said Brews.

Ned swallowed. A few more drops came, and he swallowed those.

"Where am I?" he asked, weakly.

"On the road," said Brews. "I've sent Hoggett off to scout round. "But don't worry. I'm going to carry you into your house in a minute or two. Just a drop more, and we'll go on."

Ned drank. He realised now that the less he exerted himself the sooner he would be able to move and recover. He knew where he was at last. He had gone down to Fen Court, gone out to look at the hide.

Brews took him up again, and carried him along very carefully down the short lane. Outside the door of Fen Court he felt in Ned's pockets, produced the key, and laid his burden down while he opened the door. Then on again. He heard someone beyond, and a crackling sound. He was taken into a sitting-room, and there was brushwood burning in the wide old grate, and a burly man on his knees by the fire, feeding it.

"Going all right, Sankey?" Brews asked, gently, letting Ned down, so that his back was against the wall.

The burly man got up. "Fine, sir. Is the gentleman all right?"

"Will be," said Brews, cheerily. "Cut out for more wood. Leave your lantern here!"

"Yes, sir," said Sankey, who was evidently a policeman. "Did they get the fellow yet, sir?" "Not yet; but we shall," said Brews.

Sankey went out. Ned had his eyes open now, and was gazing curiously about him. It was a strange scene in which he found himself; the big, bare room, the little lantern throwing a pale and scanty beam on the floor, the flames from the dry brushwood leaping up and throwing dancing shadow on the walls, and, in the half-light, Brews, his face beaming, staring at Ned, and rubbing his hands together.

"Feeling better, sir?" he asked.

Ned felt a different man already. "Rather!" he said. "What happened to me? Can't have been very serious, or I shouldn't have come round so soon?"

Brews nodded. "Good. It wasn't. But an inch further up, and there might have been a different tale to tell."

Ned moved his feet and legs, moved his arms, and was chiefly conscious now of a dull ache just at the nape of his neck.

"Did I crash?"

"You were crashed," said Brews, grimly. "You must have shifted a fraction, or the back of your skull would have been bashed in. But don't worry about that now. As soon as you feel like it, I'll drive you to Upperton in your car. We'll make arrangements for you to spend the rest of the night at the 'Blue Boar.'"

Ned looked puzzled. "What time is it?"

"Round about half-past eleven, sir, not more."

Ned put a hand to the back of his head. He withdrew it, and stared at it. There was a little blood on his fingers, and he bit his lip.

"It's very little; just broke the skin," said Brews, watching him. "We'll fix it up when we get to Upperton."

Ned shrugged.

"I feel heaps better already. I say, put me in the car and let's get off out of this."

"Sure you can manage, sir?"

Ned nodded. "Yes, I think I can."

Brews came over, and helped him up, scientifically supported him, and walked him out. The policeman met them at the door. He dropped the brushwood he was carrying.

"Can I help, sir?"

"Yes, crank up the car, and get her started, see? We shan't need the wood. We're going into Upperton at once."

"Very well, sir. I'll see to it."

"And tell the Superintendent we've gone, if he comes along."

Brews helped Ned into the car, while the constable whirled the crank viciously. The engine was cold, but, within a couple of minutes, the car got into gear and started off, with Brews at the wheel.

Ned felt a bit sick at first, but that wore off, and he congratulated himself on having come off so lightly. He did not attempt to question Brews further about the matter, but worked it out for himself in silence as they drove along.

He remembered now that he had taken a spade, and gone out to look at the hide Hench had made in the marsh. What had happened after that? He puzzled for a few moments, then had it. He had been very near the place for which he was searching, then he had passed a clump of gorse bushes – or had he passed them? No. It was at that point that his senses had left him.

Surely he had not tripped and fallen, and struck the back of his head on the blade of the spade? No; he did not remember falling. Besides, Brews had told him that he had been 'crashed' or 'bashed.' That meant an outsider; someone who had hidden in the gorse clump, and attacked him when he came level with it.

"Hench!" said Ned under his breath. "The little beast has been keeping an eye on the place, and thought I was after the bonds! Got away too! Didn't that constable ask if they had caught him?"

It was very puzzling and worrying, and yet it wasn't. They knew who they were after now, and Hench would not get very far.

"Have you sent someone to dig up the hide?" he asked Brews, suddenly.

Brews turned towards him.

"Hoggett will dig it up, sir; don't worry about that," he said. "If he gets the bonds there, we can make our arrest."

Ned felt happier. Things were moving. He had an extra grudge against the murderer now for giving him this sore head.

"Does anyone know who hit me?" he asked.

Brews grunted. "Hoggett says he saw a man running like a hare; a small man. We'll see."

Ned found that talking and thinking made his head ache more than ever. The shaking of the car was bad enough without that, and he sat back in his corner, closed his eyes, and did not speak again until they had driven into Upperton, and were at the 'Blue Boar.' The little hotel was closed, but Brews soon had the door opened, and the half-dressed proprietor busy brightening up the kitchen fire. Ned was placed before it in an easy chair, and promptly asked for a light. When he had got a cigarette going, Brews announced that he must run round to the police station.

"Sit quiet and rest, Mr. Hope," he said, "I shan't be ten minutes." He was less, by many minutes. When he got to the door of the inn, he heard two men come stumping down the street, stopped and hailed them.

"Constable Hoggett there?"

The footsteps stopped. "Here, sir," said Hoggett's voice.

"Come into the 'Blue Boar,' constable. Bates can get back to the station," said Brews.

Ned was surprised a few moments later, to see Brews step into the kitchen, followed by Hoggett, who was mopping his brow like a man who has had a hard run.

"You didn't catch the little man you saw, Hoggett?" said Brews, sitting down.

Hoggett shook his head, disappointedly. "No, sir, what with my weight and the lumbagy I had recent, I didn't. But he had a start of me. I stopped to see if the gentleman was dead before I give chase."

Ned smiled faintly. "Not quite dead yet, Hoggett," he remarked. "Still it was kind of you to look. I wish you had gone on, though, and arrested the brute."

Brews nodded. "What actually happened, Hoggett?" he asked. "I haven't had time to get your report properly."

Hoggett scratched his head, "Let me see, sir. I was patrolling down the main road near Fen Court when I thought I saw a flash or two in the marsh – the marsh."

"That would be Mr. Hope's torch," assented Brews, "well, you went towards the spot—"

"Not at once, sir. I asks myself what it could be at that time of night, and wondered if it wasn't one of those marsh lights. But it seem more like a torch, and I hide down and keep low."

"In the roadway?"

"Just at first, sir, I did. Then I got in through the hedge, and crept along towards where the light was moving. I was pretty sure then t'was someone with a torch, and it might be the man we wanted, so I thought it would be wisest to fall in some distance behind him, to see where he was going, and what he was up to."

"You didn't suspect that it might be Mr. Hope?"

"No, sir, of course not. Well, I was about fifty yards behind, and going very cautious like, when I saw the gentleman fall. I run up, and as I runs up, a little man jumps out of the gorse, and cuts off. I stopped to see what had become of the man who'd fallen, and there he was, lying on his face, and looked mighty bad. I had just set off to chase the little fellow, when I ran into you and the Superintendent—"

"Wait a moment," Ned interrupted. "Weren't you going down to Hampshire, Brews?"

"I did go," said the inspector. "But I was on a false trail, and came back at once. The superintendent wanted me to have a look round the marsh with him, and we set out. That's where we came on Hoggett."

"Pity you weren't a minute earlier, sir," said the constable.

"We both felt that, but it's too late now to worry over it," Brews replied. "All right, Hoggett. Get back to the station, and give your report to the station sergeant."

"Now, sir," said the inspector, when Hoggett had gone. "You must get to bed, and no bones about it. Tomorrow will be time enough for talk. No doubt you feel better; what with the brandy and the excitement and all, but tomorrow you'll feel the reaction, and worse, if you don't rest now. The landlord's made a bed up for you."

"Bed for me, and me for bed," was the reply. "I feel fuzzy and silly. Perfectly putrid, to be honest! Give me an arm up."

Brews took his arm, helped him out of his chair, out of the kitchen, and up the stairs.

"You've done well, sir," he said, as they entered a bedroom where a fire had been recently lit. "Now I'll help you off with your clothes, if you'll let me."

"You'd make a dashed fine valet, Brews," said Ned, as the inspector gently helped him to get ready for bed. "I'm glad you think I have given you a leg-up in the case."

Brews nodded and smiled. "You have, proper, sir. When you get near a plover's nest, the plover comes out to dash at you. You lit on the nest of eggs tonight, I'll swear! But now I must get on. I'll be round in the morning to see how you are."

Chapter XXVI

F OR some reason which she could not explain, though it was obvious enough, Nancy slept ill that night. She had gone to bed still thinking of the excursion Ned proposed to make after dark, and though, at first, she was pleased with the idea, and thought it an excellent one, doubts had begun to assail her later on.

If Hench had really hidden the bonds in that hole in the marsh, was it not possible that he kept an eye on the place? Suppose he saw Ned making his way there, spied on him as he began to dig? She knew that Ned was capable of taking care of himself in any ordinary scrap, but a man who had callously murdered three people would hardly expose himself to an open attack. More likely he would strike from ambush, and against that kind of thing Ned would have no defence.

It was this thought, subconsciously working while she slept, that gave her a disturbed night, and wakened her early in the morning with an ominous but inexplicable sense that something was wrong. She jumped out of bed at seven, took a hasty bath, then dressed quickly. Of course she must be mistaken. If anything had happened to Ned she would have heard of it. Brews or someone would have notified her.

She kept saying that to herself, as she ate her breakfast, but the consolation became less and less convincing. Ned had gone out by night on the marsh in that lonely place. Brews and his men would have been busy all day; it was unlikely that they would have occupied themselves patrolling the marsh after dark.

It was now just before nine. A man lying out in the open country near Fen Court might remain undiscovered till late in the day, for more than a day perhaps, in that unfrequented spot.

She finished her breakfast and went to the telephone. She found it impossible to wait any longer for news of Ned. In ten minutes she got through to Upperton Station. The station sergeant answered her call.

"I suppose Inspector Brews is still away?" she asked, when she had made herself known.

"No, Miss, he came back yesterday evening," said the sergeant. "But he is over at the 'Blue Boar' at present, talking to Mr. Hope."

Nancy started. "Is Mr. Hope at the inn?"

The sergeant assented. "The gentleman got a knock on the head last night, Miss. Nothing to hurt, but the inspector thought he would be better at the inn."

Nancy turned very pale. "Are you telling me the truth?" she cried, almost shrilly. "You're sure he is not hurt seriously?"

"I am quite sure of it, Miss," was the reply. "Mr. Hope is all right this morning."

"Tell him I am coming down – Miss Johnson is coming down at once," said Nancy, and rang off.

She was very white and a good deal shaken when she ran upstairs to get ready. The sergeant had reassured her somewhat, but there was always the possibility that he had minimised the injury Ned had received.

How right she had been in her fears, she said to herself, as she hurried in a taxi to Liverpool Street Station. Ned had been seen and followed, attacked and hurt. What an ass she had been not to ask the sergeant who had done it, and if they had taken the man.

If Ned was not much hurt then it was obvious that he had put up a fight and not been taken altogether unawares. Of course Hench was a little man. He might be effective from ambush, but he would have no chance with Ned in a rough-and-tumble.

She caught an early train with just a few seconds to spare, and felt better when she was rushing along towards Upperton. Ned was at the 'Blue Boar.' He was not unconscious, if Brews had gone over to talk to him. That was something. And Brews had come back early from Hampshire. Since he had only started yesterday morning, he could not have been there very long.

When the train drew into the station, she poked her head out of the window and looked about eagerly. Then she saw Brews, and beside him Ned, who was waving to her. She drew her head in again, and wiped her eyes. By the time the train had stopped, and Ned was opening the door of her compartment, she was smiling gaily, and showed no traces of the emotion which had threatened to overwhelm her a few moments before.

"Been in the wars, I hear, Ned," she said, as he gripped her hand.

"Not a word!" he cried, grinning. "Here's Brews. He'll tell you that my little private war is to be kept completely dark for the moment. No one, outside the police force, knows that the skirmish took place. But come along. We're going to see Hench now, and the car is outside."

"Why, haven't you arrested Hench yet?" she asked Brews, in a low voice.

Brews smiled. "Not yet, Miss Johnson. Mr. Hope didn't see who hit him. We must go canny and make inquiries before we act."

They hurried out to the station yard together, and Brews bundled into the dickey leaving the driving seat for Ned.

"You are a fraud," cried Nancy, as Ned took the wheel. "I believe you made up the skirmish because you were afraid to sleep in the haunted house."

"Far from it! But I was nearly put to sleep in the haunted marsh," he replied, gaily. "If you take a microscope and examine the back of my head, you will see where the ruffian's club impinged. I'm sorry my cap is over the scar at the moment."

Nancy leaned back to look at Brews. "Is it true, Inspector?"

"Quite. Mr. Hope had a lucky escape. He must have moved his head forward as the blow came, and just took the count, instead of going out unpleasantly. But not a word of that to Hench. We must just see how much he knows."

She turned again to Ned. "But wasn't this near his house?"

"Not so far off," he replied. "But Hench did not show up. Leave him to Brews. We'll soon see what part our little friend had in the show."

Nancy nodded. "Oh, I shan't interfere, if this is an official visitation."

They drove on in silence, and presently they came out into the road that ran near the orchard of Pear Cottage. They stopped the car presently and got down, to enter the field path, the inspector in the lead.

Smoke was rising lazily from the chimney of the cottage, and as they approached Hench opened the front door, and came out, a camera under his arm. He stopped as he saw them, hastily leaned the camera on its tripod against the wall, and stared at them.

"Good morning," Brews greeted the little man, cheerfully.

"Good morning, inspector," said Hench, looking past him at the two serious faces staring into his own. "How d'ye do, Miss Johnson. And Mr. Hope, too. I – will you all come in, and sit down?"

"Thank you," said Brews. "We will."

He led the way into the room, and Ned and Nancy followed gravely. Hench hurried in after them, and began to set out and marshal chairs round the fire with anxious haste.

He himself remained standing, and Brews stretched out his long legs, and looked at him dispassionately.

"Just a few questions, Mr. Hench. Before I ask them I must tell you that the matter is a serious one, and I hope you will take it seriously. If your replies are satisfactory I shan't trouble you again, but I want the truth this time."

Hench looked white. "I have always told you the truth, Inspector."

"Some of it, sir, some of it, but not all! I want it all now. It's a serious matter to give false evidence, but it is quite as serious to suppress evidence; a fact of which you don't seem to be aware."

Hench fired up. "That's not true, and you know it!"

Brews leisurely extracted two envelopes from his pocket. "You posted two letters to me; one properly addressed, the other addressed in capital letters, and anonymous. Is that true?"

Hench shifted and bit his lip.

Brews bluffed. "Do you wish me to produce proof, and convict you of suppressing certain knowledge you had?"

Hench's defences broke down; he cried eagerly, "No. I did send them. I admit it. But it was not suppressing evidence. It was giving you evidence. You can see that for yourself."

Nancy shrugged and glanced at Ned.

Brews pursed his lips. "Proof of what?"

"Proof that the scrap of paper pinned to the girl's clothes came from a letter."

"What of it, sir? We already knew that. The scrap in itself was only of importance in relation to the place, time, and manner, in which the rest of the letter was found. In an investigation of a murder charge every moment counts, and you have held us up for days by this suppression of yours."

"I am sorry," said Hench, biting his lip.

"Well, it's done now, and can't be helped," Brews replied sternly, "but you may repair a little of the damage by telling me frankly what are the facts. Come now! Where did you find those fragments of the letter?"

Hench winced, and blurted it out. "Here. I found them here in the grate."

"But they weren't burned."

"No, they had been rolled into a ball, and thrown at the fire. They hadn't gone in."

Nancy gave a start, then smiled scornfully and sceptically. She could see from Ned's face that he was not so much surprised as excited and expectant. Brews nodded, and asked another question.

"I see. You found the scraps here, but were afraid to say you had found them. Why?"

Hench stammered. "Because that was after I had heard about the tragedy. I was afraid someone would think I had had a hand in it. I was the only one here who knew Habershon."

"Very well. I take that point. But did you notice anything at all out of the way that night when you returned to your cottage after visiting Hitherland?"

Hench nodded. "I did. That was what made me afraid next day when I knew what had happened. I could say I had seen the policeman, but I was not sure that would let me out. They – you might have taken me for an accomplice."

Brews raised his eyebrows. "What did you see?"

"I thought – in fact I was sure that the chairs were not quite as I had left them."

"That all?"

"Yes. Do you know what I thought too?"

"No. What was it, sir?"

"I had seen that light at Fen Court. At first I thought Mr. Hope here had visited his house after dark, and come in here to borrow something, but found me out. I spoke to him next morning in his car, meaning to make myself known as his nearest neighbour, and to ask him if he had called on me the previous evening."

Ned looked puzzled. There might be something in what the little man had said. But Brews went on again.

"I see. Mr. Hope was in a hurry that day, and did not stop to talk. You returned on the night of the crime after ten o'clock, suspected that someone had been in your cottage, and picked up the fragments of a letter which you sent to me later on. Is that right?"

"Quite right, inspector."

"Thank you, sir. Now I will go on to the morning of the inquest; the first inquest held on the bodies. You did not attend that?"

"I was not subpœnaed."

"No; at that time your evidence was not thought essential. I merely want to know what your movements were that morning. You were not, for example, on a road near the railway between Upperton and Tankton?"

"Certainly not; but let me think," said Hench. "I – wait a moment – no; I certainly was not. I went inland that day, quite early, to Mereham. I am sure you can check that. I was in Mereham at ten, and did not leave until three. I got permission from Lord Mereham to take photos of herons in his demesne. The keeper could tell you."

Brews laid a big notebook on the table, and took out his fountain pen.

"Good, sir. I can check that easily. Now we have two witnesses here, and, if you will be good enough to write down all you have told us; in other words, make a statement, and sign it, that will be all for today."

Hench sat down at the table. "Why not?" he said.

Brews bowed. "And you might add a statement as to your movements last night between ten o'clock and one," he said. "Now, then, sir."

As Hench scribbled down his statement, Nancy stared at Ned. To her surprise he did not look surprised or displeased. He appeared to be speculating, and once looked up to bestow a glance of admiration on the grave-faced Brews.

Hench finished, signed, and had his signature witnessed by Nancy and Ned. Then the inspector rose, thanked him, and made a sign to the others that he was ready to go.

Hench stared at them nervously as they got up. "Good morning, Inspector," he said, and then advanced to Ned, and held out his hand, "Goodbye, Mr. Hope."

To Nancy's surprise, Ned shook hands.

"I'm going to hustle on that business for you, Mr. Hench," he said. "But I'll let you have the manuscript back."

Hench began to thank him rather hysterically, when Brews cut in.

"Come along, Mr. Hope. We have another job to do."

Nancy did not take Mr. Hench's hand. It was all right for Ned to be suddenly so cocksure about it, but she was not at all certain that Hench was innocent. She merely bowed stiffly, and went past Brews, who was holding the door open for her.

"Well, you two are easily contented," she said, when they were out of earshot of the cottage. "He didn't give you an atom of proof."

"We'll prove it tonight," said Brews, as they reached the car, and added to Ned. "If I were you, sir, I should leave Upperton for the day.

212

Why not take Miss Johnson for a run into the country, and come back in time for dinner."

"I don't think he is safe to go out alone," said Nancy, smiling. "He might not move his head at the right moment next time."

Brews smiled broadly, "Well, I meant both of you to come back here," he said. "By the way, Mr. Hope, we had a light on the flight of those bonds this morning. The guard of that train says he was looking out of the window of the rear van, and saw a parcel lying on the edge of the six-foot way, about ten yards this side of the Colley railway bridge. Probably it was thrown out just as the train drew in under the arch, and the way of the train carried it on a yard or two."

"Then you were right about Mrs. Hoing!" cried Nancy.

"Looks like it," said Ned.

Chapter XXVII

"DOES Brews really imagine that Hench had nothing to do with it?" Nancy asked, as Ned drove her towards Cambridge.

"He does, and I am inclined to do," said Ned. "The fact is, old thing, that I spent an hour this morning trying to pump Brews, and he was as dry as a draw-well after a drought. All I can get out of him is this: He thinks the fact that I was attacked last night shows that my guess about the bonds was correct. The hider had seen me with the spade and got on my tracks, meaning to put me out before I could find them."

"Well, I think he is right. But surely it is easy to prove, Ned. All they have to do is to dig."

"They are going to. Brews said Hoggett was to dig to the bottom of the hide."

"But how will that show who hid the bonds?"

"Heaven knows, my dear! Perhaps there may be fingerprints on the parcel, or the bonds themselves. I leave that to Brews. I am quite prepared to find that Brews wants us away, to make his dramatic coup, and exhibit it to us on our return."

Nancy nodded. "He's a brainy beast, Ned."

"Absolutely. I underrated him at first, but after this I give him the Palmer without hesitation. He admits we helped, and that's more than

I thought he would do. I gather that my brain wave about the batteries of the car being exhausted is my chief merit. We'll see how that has panned out when we come back."

They drove rapidly down to Cambridge, and had lunch on arrival. Then Ned took Nancy to see the 'Backs,' and afterwards out to Grantchester to revive memories of Rupert Brooke, and have tea.

But, in all their sightseeing, they could not get quite away from the Fen Court mystery. Both of them were determined loyally to observe their compact with Inspector Brews, to return at six and not before, and their growing excitement and anxiety to know what had happened in their absence, made the intervening hours drag.

At a quarter past five they climbed into the car.

"If Brews disappoints me, I'll kill him!" Ned announced.

He drove fast. The sun would soon set. Already the flat country was gilded by the low rays of the sun in the west, and the mists were beginning to creep over the land.

They were silent going back. The end of the case was in sight, and they were at once relieved and regretful. Nancy sat close to Ned. Since last night she had felt more intimately concerned with him than ever before. Her emotion that morning when the train pulled into Upperton Station had been a revelation, too. Short of living with Ned at Fen Court –

There she pulled up in her vagrant romancings. How merciful it was that people couldn't tell one's innermost thoughts. If Ned only knew!

They drove on, Ned's foot now well down on the accelerator.

"Inspector Brews's compliments, sir, and would you and the lady wait in for him here after dinner," said the landlord of the 'Blue Boar,' when Ned and his companion got down from the car, and entered the inn. "He left a note for you too, sir," he added, as Ned nodded assent.

"Thank you. We'll wait," the latter agreed, taking the note. "You might give us dinner at seven. We'll go into the coffee room now."

In the coffee room, which looked cheerful enough with its blazing log fire, Ned sat down to look at the note from the inspector. It was brief but pregnant.

"Don't please go away till I come. It may be later than I expect. But there is quite a chance that I may have some news for you of the greatest importance. If so, you may wish to drive to London at once to give it to your paper. There will be no other journalist in the know."

"Awfully generous of him to hand me a scoop for nothing," said Ned, as he passed the note to Nancy, and lit a cigarette. "Does that mean an arrest, or does it not?"

She looked across at him eagerly. "It does, of course. I don't care about the scoop, but I shall be glad if they can catch that rotten murderer. It doesn't look like you're having a hand in the coup though, Ned."

He shrugged. "Well, I can't help it. The police can do what they like, and I am an outsider after all. I can't butt in unless they are willing."

She shook her head. "Oh, I'm not grumbling. We'll wait, however late it is."

The 'Blue Boar' gave them a better dinner than they had expected – soup, a sole, excellent beef, with Yorkshire pudding, a tart, and Stilton cheese; sound English food decently cooked. After dinner they ordered coffee, and it had just been served to them when another visitor entered.

At the sight of him Nancy gave a little involuntary gasp, and Ned stared. It was Mr. Hench, who looked nervous and ill-at-ease, as he shut the door behind him, and hesitated just inside.

Ned jumped up and rang a bell. "Sit down, Mr. Hench," he said, politely. "We're going to have coffee. Will you have a cup with us?"

216

Nancy bit her lip, but said nothing. Mr. Hench replied gratefully that a cup would be very welcome. It was dreadfully cold outside now.

"I had a visit from the inspector," he added, as he took a seat near Ned. "He suggested that I should come over and spend the evening here with you, I hope I don't intrude?"

Ned suppressed a burning desire to ask what Brews meant by pushing the little man on to them, but he replied calmly enough, "Yes, that's all right. Brews knows his business. Have a gasper?"

Hench accepted a cigarette as the waiter came in.

"Another cup. This gentleman is having coffee with us," said Ned.

"Yes, sir. Immediately, sir."

"I don't really know what the inspector is up to," said Hench to Nancy timidly.

"I am sorry I can't help you there," she replied, rather coldly.

Ned gave her a significant glance. "We'll know in good time," he said. "Did you hear that they were going to dig up the hole you filled up in the marsh, Mr. Hench?" he added.

"What for?" Mr. Hench's face wore a puzzled look. He stretched out his legs towards the fire, and stared thoughtfully at his feet.

But it was obvious that he was neither alarmed nor anxious. The exploration in the abandoned "hide" did not appear to interest him. Mere appearances might have gone for nothing had he been a better actor, but they had already seen that the little man was no expert in hiding his emotions.

"Looking for the stolen Bearer Bonds, I imagine," Ned murmured, as the waiter came in with another cup. "Nancy, will you pour out coffee for Mr. Hench, please."

Nancy's rather stern face relaxed. She was still very much interested in studying Mr. Hench, but much less convinced of his complicity in the murders.

"Sugar?" she said, poising a lump.

"Thank you," replied Hench, and added, as the waiter closed the door. "The Bearer Bonds? But surely no one would put them there?"

Ned shrugged. "That is the theory anyway. At a guess, I should say that is why Brews asked you to come on here. He wants everyone out of the way while he investigates."

Hench stared. "How extraordinary! I thought his request very odd, but imagined from the way he put it that you had suggested—"

"Brews has his own way of doing things," Ned interrupted. "You must know now that he suspected someone had been in your cottage that night while you were over at Hitherland."

"I see that now. But how could they – they know I was out?"

"He, or they, may have watched you go."

Hench nodded. "Of course it may be that. I was rather worried, as you know. I am afraid I was rather less helpful than I might have been on that account."

"I am afraid so," said Nancy. "Surely, Mr. Hench, you might have realised that the mere fact that you knew Mr. Habershon would not involve you in the murders?"

He bit his lip. "I ought to have thought of that. But I was the only one he knew, and the whole thing upset me very much. I am not used to things of that kind. I couldn't even say that I knew someone had been in my cottage. I merely thought so, but I could not prove it. To this day I can't imagine what they wanted there."

"You never thought of the navigable drain that runs from your place to the river?"

Hench started. "Never. Why?"

"Or that a punt might have been brought up there?" Hench turned white. "You don't surely suggest that the crimes were committed in my cottage? Why, they were drowned."

218

"Isn't it possible they were drowned in the drain, and then taken down to the river, and carried in the punt alongside the garden of Fen Court?"

Hench gave a little gasp. "What a foul thing! But – but, Mr. Hope, then it must have taken place while I was away."

"Obviously between half past eight and ten."

Hench sat thinking for a minute or two. There was hardly a doubt that he was staggered by Ned's revelation.

"Then you think that letter must have been taken from Mr. Habershon's pocket while in my cottage?"

Ned assented. "I think there is no other solution."

Hench, who was apparently rather sensitive, had seen Nancy relax a little of her stiffness, and lost some of his own timidity.

"It is a dreadful thought," he mused. "But, even then, it is very hard to imagine what can have happened. Granting a callous ruffian, or ruffians, who had no scruples, Mr. Hope, the mordinal business perplexes me. Surely I heard that the mordinal was found in the thermos flask brought from town by Mr. Habershon."

"There is no doubt that dregs were found containing mordinal," Ned agreed. "I know no more than you about that. I can only suggest an hypothesis as an alternative theory."

Nancy frowned at him. Was he going to give this away to Hench? Ned went on, without looking at her.

"The flask had no trace of fingerprints. They would have been on it when it was found, if someone had not taken the trouble to clean them off. Even if Habershon had doped his young relations, he would have left the prints, since it was his flask and they would naturally be there. What about an outsider, who lured Habershon and his wards into your cottage while you were away, substituted a flask similar to that owned by Mr. Habershon, a flask filled with coffee doped with mordinal—"

"Yes, but how would he know that Habershon had set out with a flask?" Hench objected.

"He knew," said Ned, who did not enlighten him with regard to the suspicion under which Mrs. Hoing lay. "Having substituted the flask, he might have put Rainy and Miss Rowe in the water, knocked old Habershon on the head—"

"But why, if he was already doped?" asked Nancy.

"Aye, that's the question," said the little man. "Miss Johnson has hit it."

Ned shrugged. "I am only stating a theory. I see the snag, but there is one way of getting round it – merely supposititious, as the whole theory must be. If Habershon and the others came into your cottage, it may be assumed that they came to see you—"

Hench protested hotly. "I deny it, Mr. Hope. I never invited them. I must really ask you—"

"Oh, do wait a moment!" Ned cried, impatiently. "I am not suggesting that you did invite them. But someone did, possibly in your name. Why the dickens should they go there otherwise?"

"I am sorry. I see your point. Though it amazes me."

Ned continued. "Very well. Rightly or wrongly, they went to Pear Cottage to see you. You are not in. Obviously the man, or men, who lured them there must have told them you would be in presently. Isn't that possible?"

"It's obvious, if they came there thinking to see me."

"As no doubt they did. But they are asked to wait, and I suppose they preferred to do that, since they had come so far to see you. But we may assume that your fire was low – you had left it to visit Daly for the evening. Isn't it just possible, too, that the murderer heard Habershon refer to the thermos in the car. That would be left on the road outside. Can we swear that he did not offer to go and fetch it, and actually did so?"

"No, that seems possible, Mr. Hope. Do go on."

"He brings the flask, or one which is identical with it, but in which the mordinal has been placed. Now Habershon had had coffee at Upperton, while Ivor Rainy and Miss Rowe had plumped for ices. Either because he did not feel the cold so much while waiting, or wished his niece and nephew to have more, he did not drink as much as they, and, consequently, took less of the dope in solution."

"Seems logical," murmured Hench.

"And likely. But, that being the fact, he may have recovered, or began earlier to recover, from the effects of the dope, and been stunned by a blow from the murderer, who saw his plan in danger."

Hench seemed at once convinced and astounded. Nancy needed no further proof of the soundness of the argument. She knew that Ned himself had been struck on the previous night in much the same spot, a blow aimed at the back of the head just above the neck.

Ned looked at his watch. "I wonder what is keeping Brews?" he said.

Nancy frowned. "It is getting on. Had he anyone, any other detective with him when he called at your cottage, Mr. Hench?"

"No; he was alone, Miss Johnson."

"Probably he had sent Hoggett and the man Sankey to dig up the 'hide'," said Ned. "Anyway it looks as if we must wait here some time. What about a game of dummy whist? Do you play, Hench? I am sure the landlord will have cards."

Mr. Hench did play. The cards were obtained, and they began a game. None of them played very well that night. They had one eye on the fall of the cards, and the other on the door.

Nine came, then ten. They were all growing impatient. Hench thought he must soon be getting home. He had come on a bicycle, but even with that nine miles is nine miles. But Ned felt that Brews meant the little man to stay, and dissuaded him.

"Wait till eleven," he said. "You're helping us to pass the time, and you may hear something interesting too when Brews does arrive. We ourselves are going back to London tonight."

Hench sat down again, and they resumed their interrupted game. At ten minutes to eleven, just as Ned had dealt, they heard the front door open, Ned sprang to his feet, spilling the cards over the table as he bumped against it. Nancy turned excited eyes on the door. Hench sat still, twiddling his fingers restlessly.

"Inspector Brews to see you, sir," said the landlord, opening the coffee room door suddenly.

Chapter XXVIII

WHEN Inspector Brews came into the room, and hurriedly shut the door behind him, Nancy gave a little cry, and even Ned started, and swore.

Brews looked like a man who has been playing half-back on a muddy Rugby field against uncompromising opponents. He was muddy, hot, bruised, and had a handkerchief tied round his forehead. But he smiled a little as he saw the sensation his appearance had created.

"I have only a moment, sir," he said to Ned, his voice rather thick, "I have to get over to the doctor's to have my head bound up—"

Nancy burst out before he could finish. "What is it? Are you badly hurt, Inspector?"

"Missed it, and no more!" said he. "Edge of a spade," and he tapped his bandage. "Here you are, Mr. Hope." He made an almost imperceptible movement of his head towards Hench, as if to warn Ned that the news was not to be communicated, put a leaf of his notebook in Ned's hand, and bolted again before they could stop him.

Hench found his tongue first after Brews's disappearance. "Has he been fighting?"

"With wild beasts at Ephesus," said Ned, glancing at the paper, and then excitedly at Nancy. "We must get to town as quick as we can. Come along."

Hench was quite bewildered now. "But what is it? What has happened?"

"Look in the papers tomorrow," replied Ned. "Nancy, get your coat on! I'll go out and start the car – I'm sorry, Mr. Hench, but we haven't a moment to spare."

Hench remained staring and stupefied for a minute after they had gone. But Ned and Nancy had no further thought to spare for the little man. Already the engine was turning over, and Nancy was restraining her impatience with the greatest difficulty. She wanted to ask what had been written on the leaf from Brews's notebook, but knew that Ned would not satisfy her curiosity until they were on their way to town.

But once clear of Upperton, and she would take no denial. "Who was it, Ned?" she asked urgently. "Don't be a pig!"

Ned told her. "Hoggett! They arrested Mrs. Hoing at six today, and Hoggett not half an hour ago. I know no more than that."

Nancy gasped. "The policeman! But what could he get out of it?"

He was as astonished as she. "There you have me, old thing. All I know is that I must get this to the office as soon as I can. Brews said I would be the only journalist in the know, and I am."

He opened out then, and the car flew. Nancy said very little during the journey to London. Sometimes she thought Brews must be mistaken, and sometimes that a man of his experience would not risk an arrest of that kind on flimsy evidence. Hoggett, of all people! Then it must have been Hoggett who had struck Ned from behind on the previous night.

She could not doubt that the constable had been admirably situated for a job of the kind. The marsh was on his beat, and on many nights he might be the only person walking the roads after dark in that region. It was the lack of apparent motive that puzzled her.

Otherwise, if the motive was granted, there was evidence that pointed to Hoggett. It was the constable who had found, as he said, Ned lying by the gorse bushes. He had spoken of a little man who had burst from the shelter of the gorse and fled on his approach. But no one else had seen the flying man.

Their first stop was in Fleet Street, at the newspaper offices. Ned made Nancy come in, and sit by the fire in a waiting room, while he saw the news editor, and handed in his report. He came back in ten minutes, glowing and satisfied, and took her back to the car.

"You're going straight home to bed, and then I'll go home, and do a bit of the same," he said, as he started the car once more. "I expect you are dead to the world. I know I am!"

"What did they say to you," Nancy asked, as they rushed off towards Hampstead.

"I had difficulty in preventing them from embracing me," Ned replied. "And I have an order for a serial at my own figure. I didn't make a bad deal, buying Fen Court, after all. Sooner have those poor devils alive than all the deal, though," he added.

"Are you going down to Upperton again tomorrow?" she asked.

"I am never going down to Upperton again if I can help it," he returned. "My recollections of the place are too ghastly. Tomorrow I take a real holiday, and so do you. We're going to the Chilterns. I'm going to look for a house there, which doesn't require heroes to live in it. I say, Nancy, are you game?"

She smiled at him. "No; I'm dead, and half asleep. I can't take it in yet. But tomorrow I'll go with you, and tell you if I like the house. I can't say more, can I?"

"You can, tomorrow," whispered Ned. "If you can make up your mind, it may help me to make up my own."

"So you aren't sure yet?" she rallied him.

"Not about the exact house, but perfectly sure about everything else," he retorted.

"Does one go with the house?"

"I can't tell you till we see it," he said. "But be ready at ten tomorrow morning when I call."

Nancy was ready at ten next day. By that time she knew more of the mysterious arrest of the previous night than either of them had been able to gather from Brews's exiguous scrap of paper.

The *Record* had made a scoop with Ned's news, and the other details two pressmen had been able to gather, after rushing down to Upperton in a high-power car.

From the account in the newspaper Nancy knew that Superintendent Langley had arrested Mrs. Hoing at the house in Gale Street about six on the previous evening. She had refused to say anything at first, but, it was reported, had made a statement when she was told later on of the arrest of Police-constable Hoggett near Fen Court.

The scanty details about the actual arrest of her male accomplice explained very little, but it was clear that the Upperton detective force, headed by Brews, had come upon him after dark, digging up the 'hide' once used by Hench. He had resisted arrest, and almost felled the inspector with a spade in the course of the struggle. But he had been finally mastered, and taken to Upperton.

Excavations in the hole, made after his departure, revealed the Bearer Bonds which had played such an important part in the Fen Court mystery. They were wrapped in a small waterproof sheet, and apparently undamaged.

"I have no more idea of the connection between Mrs. Hoing and the constable than you have," said Ned, later on, when they were driving towards High Wycombe. "And I don't intend to spoil a perfectly good day by inquiring. The weather report says that rain is coming tonight. This is to be a picnic, with 'all the world well lost for – '"

"For a house!" said Nancy, with a demure smile, "All right. I expect we'll hear soon enough."

"I dropped a note to Brews, asking him to come and see us when he has time. He'll come. Then we shall know what Americans call the inside dope. Meanwhile; what sort of a house do you favour?"

They spent the rest of that day very pleasantly indeed, and at precisely half an hour to tea time, when Nancy stood in a hilly lane, looking at a charming half-timbered cottage, in a sunny garden, and announced that, if she wanted a house to live in, this was the exact and predestined house.

Ned looked at her earnestly. "Do you want a house to live in, Nance darling? If you do, then it's yours."

"Without encumbrances?" she asked, half-mockingly, half-tenderly.

"With me," said Ned. "Oh, my dear, you don't know how I love you, and want you."

Nancy dropped her guard at once. "I think I do, dear," she said. "Yes, I know; because I want you, too, and I – I think this is my house."

"Have another cup of nectar?" Ned asked, half an hour later, as they sat at tea in a cottage at Perlingham. "I'll be hanged if it tastes like tea!"

Chapter XXIX

I NSPECTOR BREWS came to town on the day following their house-hunting tour in the Chilterns. He had business at Gale Street, and was there until six in the evening, in consultation with Langley, and a representative of Scotland Yard.

At seven he dined with his Scotland Yard confrère, and at a quarter to eight he announced his intention of going to West End Lane.

"That where these amateurs of yours live?" asked the C.I.D. man.

"One of them," said Brews. "I promised to let them know what happened. I owe it to them. They're the first civilians who ever gave me a tip you could put your necktie on, let alone your shirt!"

"Unusual," the other admitted. "I saw the fellow's pieces in the paper, but there was so much blather about psychology, and that kind of tripe, that I thought he was one of the usual criminologist duds. Well, you seemed to have pulled off quite a strip this time. Our people got a shock when they heard of the arrest. I don't mind admitting that we thought that little bird blighter did the dirty work."

"So did I at first," replied Brews, as he rose. "But my sideline expert got on to the lighting failure, and put me right."

"Have a coffee before you go," said the other, smiling.

"I'm invited to coffee at Mr. Hope's flat," said Brews. "I said I would be round after eight, and I don't want to disappoint them. Many thanks for the grub. Come down and see me any time at Upperton, and we'll see what the 'Blue Boar' can do for us."

When Brews presented himself at Ned's flat, and was sitting with a cup of coffee before him in the cosy sitting room, he relaxed into a smile.

"Got a neater bandage on tonight, Mr. Hope," he said, as he foraged in the box of cigarettes handed to him. "You must have thought I had been acting for the movies last time you saw me."

"You certainly gave us a shock," Nancy told him. "I congratulate you on your escape, Inspector. There are nicer weapons than a spade!"

He nodded as he lighted up. "Much! But it wasn't Hoggett's spade that brought Mr. Hope down, or Habershon either. That was his baton."

"Don't tell us in scraps; let us hear all about it," Nancy protested. "How did you come to arrest Hoggett?"

Brews leaned back in his chair. "Let me see. You knew as well as I did that Mrs. Hoing was probably at the back of the plan."

"Yes. Did she make the promised statement?" Ned inquired.

"She turns King's Evidence, though I don't see that it will do her much good," Brews replied. "But she was our starting point. At the same time her alibi was incontrovertible. There was no chance of proving that she was out of London, or in Essex, on the night of the murders."

"That meant an accomplice."

"Obviously. An accomplice who knew Habershon and knew the country. Hench filled the bill better than anyone else. He knew Habershon, and he had told lies – though not with any evil purpose – and got himself suspected on that account. But then there was the fact that he was visiting Daly that night. We assumed that he spoke to the constable to fake an alibi, but we did not realise that it was an alibi for Hoggett too! How could we? There was nothing earlier in the case to connect him with the murders."

"We want to know how you did that."

"I didn't directly. Mr. Hope put me on the track with his inquiries about Habershon's car, and the fact that the batteries had run down. As we agreed, a criminal cunning enough to do the thing, would argue that a man running off to prevent a suicide would not wait to turn off the lights of the car from which he jumped. So he left them on. Mr. Hench, as we hear later, saw the beam of the headlights, but paid no particular attention to it; first because he thought it came from the Pudstey farmer's car, and next because it was so far to the west of the scene of the crime discovered next day."

Nancy looked interested. "That is true. But how did the batteries show you what had actually happened?"

"Well, Hoggett left the lights of the car on to make it seem natural. Mr. Rainy's wristwatch had stopped at twenty past nine, so he stopped Mr. Habershon's watch at four minutes past that; to suggest that the old man had been drowned soon after his nephew and niece. But that fixed the hour of the drowning at some time after nine, and Hench saw the headlight of the car nearer ten."

"Still, I don't see," protested Nancy.

"I do," said Ned.

Brews smiled faintly, and went on. "You couldn't know as we did, Miss. Hoggett perhaps expected that the lights would go out before next day, but he forgot that that road was part of his beat. He says he rode down on his bicycle, and did not see the car, because it was in the dark bay behind the projecting hedge. But if the light was beaming across the road he must have seen it. When Mr. Hope mentioned the batteries, I saw the flaw, and began to wonder what Hoggett had been up to.

"But it would be a waste of time to investigate Hoggett's affairs unless I could prove that he had some direct or indirect connection with Mrs. Hoing. I did not go to Hampshire, I went to the office where were kept the regimental records of the regiment Hoggett served in during the war. He only joined the police in 1922."

"What did you find?" asked Ned.

"I found that the records tallied with the police records at Upperton. Hoggett was apparently his right name. I was doubtful if he had joined under his own name when I came to suspect him. But I also found that he came from a village in Surrey, and I went there, and got a little further light on the subject. Hoggett was the illegitimate son of a Miss Panger; at least born out of wedlock. He was given a proper name when his mother married the village carpenter, and went with him to live up in Westmorland. Miss Panger, now Mrs. Hoggett, had a sister. This sister went out to service, and was promoted later to be housekeeper to a family in Warwick. There she married the butler, who died in the last year of the war. Hoing was his name. Mrs. Hoing ended up, as we know, as Habershon's housekeeper, and Hoggett was her nephew."

"By Jove!" cried Ned. "That does give one a line, doesn't it?"

Brews nodded. "Now that alone could be taken as evidence, I mean his relationship to Mrs. Hoing. In court – at the inquest – he showed no signs of recognising her. It might be that he had not seen her for years, but surely her name, which is not a common one, ought to have produced some impression on him. However, it was not good enough for proof, though it was sufficiently illuminating to make me follow up the matter with more eagerness.

"Hench, of course, stood in my way, until you had given me a theory to account for his movements, and I had it confirmed by the man himself. Outsiders rarely consider how helpful it is to us to eliminate suspects. But we think a great deal of it, and that is why I am particularly grateful to you, Mr. Hope. Once I could clear Hench, I felt that half the job was done. The next thing was to see if Hoggett could be induced to make a false move. If he was innocent whatever he did would not hurt him; but, if he was Mrs. Hoing's accomplice, then I might scare him into the open."

"You mean over the 'hide'?" asked Ned.

"Exactly. That was a brainwave of yours. He must have noticed that Hench had filled up the hole in the marsh so that the appearance of freshly turned earth would not excite curiosity. I assume that he dug it up again by night, buried the bonds, and intended to leave them there until the affair blew over."

"I wonder if that is why he got lumbago?" asked Ned.

Brews smiled. "I think it was. There was no report of his complaining before, but, just after the murders, he began to talk about it, and actually told Sankey he might have to retire from the force if the trouble got worse. In other words, he was preparing the ground for a quiet and safe retirement with the loot. But to come back to the 'hide' itself. I am afraid I used you as a stalking horse there; though, if my plans had gone well, you wouldn't have come to any harm."

Ned stared, then grinned. "You mean you sent me out to get killed by Hoggett?"

"Well, not quite that, sir. You remember you let me know where you thought the bonds might be hidden, and I agreed that you might have a shot at it. That seemed a fine chance to test Hoggett. I did not say that I thought there was anything in the idea; indeed I rather scouted it; but I did let Hoggett know that you wondered if the bonds were in the hide, and were going to poke about that night."

Nancy started. "What a beastly idea of yours!"

Brews shrugged. "Wait a moment, please. I told the Superintendent, and he and I were to lie out for Hoggett, and prevent any mischief from being done. Sankey, who was not told about Hoggett, was to wait in the road, and rush up if I whistled. The trouble was that, on account of the level ground, we could not keep near enough to Hoggett. We heard him come in off the road, but then he vanished, into that clump of gorse, no doubt. If we tried to follow him up, he might spot us, and the game would be up. So we lay low where we were till you came along with your spade."

Ned raised his eyebrows. "All ready for execution."

"Well, what were we to do, sir? A dozen times I wished I hadn't thought of the scheme, but there was just a chance that Hoggett was not our man, but had just gone into the marsh to investigate something he saw there. At any rate it was too late for us to do anything. A few moments later we heard a thud, and your cry—"

"Did I shout?"

"You gave a proper scream, sir, though you may have forgotten it. The moment we heard that, the Superintendent and I dashed out and ran your way. We hadn't gone ten yards when Hoggett rushed up. He was shouting 'Stop him! Stop him!' and running like blazes. I stopped him instead, and he said there was a dead man lying by the gorse bushes, and he was in chase of the man who did it; a little man who had already bolted. I gave him permission to continue the chase, whistled up Sankey, and sent him to Fen Court to put a fire on. I forgot to give him your key, but I think he got in by pushing up a sash. You know what happened after that."

"Why didn't you arrest Hoggett there and then?" Nancy asked.

"We hadn't any visual evidence that he had struck the blow. It was dark then. And we wanted to link him up with the murders, too. By letting him run off, we made him believe that he was still unsuspected, and that was a useful point. You see, Mr. Hope here had the back of his head cut. That was where his wound differed from that on Mr. Habershon. I had a pretty good idea that there would be a slight stain from it on Hoggett's truncheon. That, of course, he kept usually in its case, and it would not occur to him that he would be asked to show it. He certainly imagined that he had thrown dust in our eyes, and when we had a look at his truncheon later on, we found a slight stain of blood on the thing, and a hair or two sticking to it. He had just stuffed it back into the case, and forgotten about it, when the Superintendent and I breezed in."

"Then you knew it was he who had struck Mr. Hope?" said Nancy.

"I assumed it before, of course, but this was proof, and it led me to stage the final bluff. If Hoggett had attacked and tried to kill Mr. Hope, because Mr. Hope was going to dig up the hide, it was obvious that the bonds were there."

Nancy laughed. "How deceitful you are, Inspector! I remember you told us Hoggett would dig up the bonds."

"But I didn't say officially, Miss Johnson; so you must forgive me," he replied, with a twinkle. "We knew that Hoggett would be uneasy. He could never be quite sure if I would not take it into my head to dig in the marsh, and if he wanted to remove the loot, the sooner the better, and safer. So we laid our dispositions, and had men posted in hiding round that particular bit of marsh after dark. I got Mr. Hench out of the way by telling him you were anxious to see him at the 'Blue Boar' We did not want him hanging about, and giving the show away by accident."

"Rather not!" Ned agreed. "But where did you hide?"

Brews smiled. "I was lying flat for an hour and a half in the rushes within twenty feet of the 'hide,' and a jolly uncomfortable job it was. I was as cold as a motherless iceberg, had a crick in my neck that gave me gippo, and was in deadly fear that Hoggett would come that way, and tread on me, before he got to the 'hide.' But things went well enough after all. We heard him come quietly along through the rushes presently, and he went by within two yards of me, while I pricked my face jamming it into a tuft of rushes."

"Then he got to work with the spade?" cried Nancy, excitedly.

"That's right, Miss. He had a spade with him, and began to dig. I raised my head, gave a flash of my torch, to let the others know I was about to get on the job, and then hopped up, and went for him. If I hadn't rushed him, he might have laid me out. As it was, he seemed as quick as a ferret, and made a jab at me with the edge of the spade. Luckily, as the spade struck me, I kicked out at his knee, and brought him down. The knee is the spot to put a man out of action for a bit. I was nearly blinded for a moment by the blood running into my eyes, but I managed to wipe it away, and jump on him before he could rise. We were at it hard and fast on the ground, when Langley and Sankey came up and pinned him. After that all went according to plan. We took him back to Upperton, I nipped in to tell you that we had got our man, and then over to the doctor to get a few stitches put in my noddle. So that was that!"

Chapter XXX

WHEN Inspector Brews had finished his narration, Nancy offered him a cigarette. "Have a smoke first – before you go on," she said. "You deserve a rest."

"And then I want to know how you think Hoggett worked it," said Ned. "I should like to know how far your ideas square with ours."

Brews lit up, and nodded. "So far, of course, I can only give you what the known facts indicate," he said. "Mrs. Hoing will let out a bit more when she has to make an amplified statement for the Crown Prosecutor, but I do not think that will do more than throw extra light on some small details."

Brews finished half his cigarette and threw the rest into the fire, glancing at his watch as he did so.

"One of the points that troubled you, and me too," he resumed, "was the fact that Pear Cottage seemed to have been the scene of the first act in this crime. Hench had left it to visit the man Daly at Hitherland. How was it possible for Hoggett to know that Hench would be away that night? Obviously the first question was where did Hench go, but the second was, why did he go? He went, he says, to see Daly, who was a professional wildfowler. I decided to see Daly too. The man is a very decent fellow, and agreed that Hench came to him, very anxious to hear his views on the habits of birds. Naturally I asked Daly how he had got to know Mr. Hench, seeing they lived some distance apart. He replied that Hench had asked Constable Hoggett if there was any local who was interested in birds, and Hoggett mentioned him. That was good, but there was better to come. When Hoggett gave that information, and introduced Hench to Daly, he made a later appointment for their meeting. In other words, Hoggett told Hench that Daly would see him on the night of the murder at his cottage in Hitherland."

Ned frowned. "But why didn't Hench say that it was Hoggett who introduced them, and Hoggett who fixed an actual hour and date for the call at Hitherland?"

"Because, sir, Hench had no reason to connect Hoggett with the crime. He could not be expected to understand that his visit to Daly, and the means by which it was brought about, would be of the slightest interest to the police. When you ask a witness questions with regard to a case, he only gives those answers which appear to him to have a bearing on the point at issue. Irrelevant matters only become relevant when you have a fresh set of facts. But when I knew that Hoggett had arranged that Hench should be at Hitherland that night, there was the chance that his motive was to get the cottage free for a certain purpose.

"Hench was the only man there who knew Habershon personally, and might induce him to come down that evening with his nephew and niece. There is no doubt that Mrs. Hoing told Habershon that Hench had rung him up, and asked him to bring his niece and nephew down to Pear Cottage that evening. Though, in her statement, she denies suggesting murder, and pretends that Hoggett must have got the mordinal, we know that he was never in the house, and was certainly not the person who rubbed all the fingerprints off the phial. I assume that she either doped the coffee in the thermos, or sent the mordinal to Hoggett. At any rate, we may take it that Habershon went down by car with Mr. Rainy and Miss Rowe, and we can take it, too, that he must have remembered, when on the way, that Hench did not take supper till eight. As the times show, he drove very fast from London, and obviously via Upperton, not by the lower road. His visit to the café can only be explained by the theory that he arrived there earlier than would be convenient for Hench, and realising the fact, took the two young people into the café for refreshments. They had had a late and heavy tea with a friend, so they plumped for ices. Mr. Habershon had a cup of coffee."

"He meant to waste a little time before going to Pear Cottage?"

"I assume so. At any rate, he left the café, and must have driven to Pear Cottage. You can't drive a car up to the door, as you know, so we can presume that Habershon left his car at the stile that gives access to the field path, and went down that path to the cottage."

"The car being on the high road?"

"Yes, that is it. Now it was at this point that Hoggett had an advantage – that of being a uniformed policeman. The fact made it possible for him to be found anywhere without suspicion. We may take it that, when the car arrived, he had gone into Pear Cottage and was waiting there. Habershon and party, when admitted, would naturally want to know why Hench was not present to receive them. Hoggett explained no doubt that Hench had to go out for something and would be back soon. Perhaps he adds that he had met Hench, whom he knows pretty well, and Hench had asked him to explain, and to request Habershon to stay until he could get back. Coming from a country constable, that would sound reasonable enough. Habershon and his nephew and niece sit down to wait. It's a common human weakness that, if you wait anywhere, with nothing much to do on a cold night, you want to eat or drink. Mr. Habershon may have suggested the thermos of coffee out in the car, or Hoggett may have suggested making them some tea.

I have little doubt myself that he had the mordinal tablets in his pocket at that moment.

"What probably took place was this: they wanted a hot drink, and mentioned the flask, which Hoggett no doubt knew would be in the car. Hoggett, with apparent helpfulness, says he will go and fetch the thermos. He goes, dopes the coffee with the tablets, which he has crushed in advance, for easier solution. The three drink the coffee, and presently it has its effect. It was not necessary for Hoggett to be there all the time to watch them. I have little doubt that he had already secured the punt, taken it down to the junction with the drain, and had it within reach. He returned to the cottage, to find Miss Rowe and her cousin asleep, and Mr. Habershon struggling to awaken. He felled Habershon with a blow on the back of the neck, and then drowned the three in the six-foot channel outside."

"Filthy brute!" said Nancy, shuddering.

"And callous too," said Brews. "But there is no other way out of it. No one who wanted to commit suicide would jump into a shallowish drain, and if he did, a would-be rescuer – the part Habershon was cast for – could rescue them by wading in. So Hoggett chose the ponds, instead. They were deep, the edge was slippery and slimy, and there was a rim of stone flags that would account for the bruise on the back of Habershon's head. The wetness of the punt, when found, in itself told us that some dripping objects had been laid in it.

"Having managed the ghastly business to his satisfaction, we can take it that Hoggett got the punt down to Fen Court, and landed the bodies there, afterwards throwing them into the pond."

"But what about the scrap from off the letter?" Nancy asked.

"Mrs. Hoing asserts that Hoggett must have taken the letter from Mr. Habershon's pocket, but there she lies. There was her finger-print on one of the two scraps found crumpled up in Hench's grate.

It is much more probable that she found the letter in Habershon's wastepaper basket, and sent it on, with a hint for its use. As we know, Hoggett pinned on a fragment which suggested suicide. After that, he had to act quickly. He had let the punt drift away when the last job was done. But Mr. Habershon's car was standing on the road by the stile, and probably his own cycle was hidden behind the hedge at that point. He thought he had met every eventuality by stopping Mr. Habershon's watch at a certain time. At that time, normally, he himself would be on the further side of Pudstey crossroads.

"He went back to the car, got his cycle, and put it in. Then he drove off to Pudstey, and placed the car in that bay. Getting down, he must have mounted his bicycle, and hurried down to the other road. That was the road down which Mr. Hench would return from Hitherland, and Mr. Hench was necessary to his alibi."

"But wouldn't his uniform be soaking?" asked Ned.

"If he had exposed it, yes. But he has a civilian mackintosh at home which comes to his heels. I have no doubt he took that with him, and hid it before he saw Hench, picking it up again on his beat next night. Well, it came off. He was in time to speak to Hench, who could swear that he met the policeman two and a half miles from Fen Court at about a quarter to ten that night. He finished his round, and went home at the usual time. And next day he saw the bodies being brought up without turning a hair."

"I am sorry for his wife," said Nancy, after a long silence had followed Brews's story.

"I'm not!" said Ned. "This will release her from the most savage brute I have ever heard of."

Chapter XXXI

"WHAT about Mrs. Hoing, Brews?" said Ned, lighting a cigarette and passing over the box. "What she hopes to gain by a statement beats me hopelessly."

"She would never have made it, if we hadn't got her rattled," said Brews, looking at his watch again, and buttoning up his jacket. "The Superintendent told her about Hoggett the moment after he had warned her, and she jumped to the conclusion that Hoggett had squealed."

"She would."

"The result is a statement that admits her knowledge of Mr. Habershon's private affairs, and a concerted effort with her nephew to get hold of the Bearer Bonds, but shies at the idea of murder. In her anxiety to clear herself of that, she puts up a tissue of inconsistencies and flawed statements that make her case as bad as an open confession. The truth is that she is one of those people who are for ever prying into other people's business. She used to amuse herself, for instance, prying into her employer's private correspondence, and came to know that he was gambling heavily, and anxious to get money."

"Her first plan of campaign was undoubtedly blackmail, but she was not quite sure how to work it; seeing that he had a more or less free hand with the wards' investments. Then she went a step further, had a false key made for that simple old safe, and found that the old chap had sixty thousand odd in Bearer Bonds locked up there, while he was also inquiring about South America, and acting like a man who contemplates a bolt. With the key to his safe, she came into possession of many facts she could never have learned by ordinary spying. She looked up an encyclopædia about Bearer Bonds, and saw that they were the easiest things to get away with. But Habershon might bolt any day, and that would be the end of her get-rich-quick schemes.

"Then Hench came into the picture. He wrote to Habershon, whose name he had seen as a Fellow of the Zoological Society, asking him if he would publish the book on birds. The book would be dedicated to him, if he agreed to finance it. Habershon was having trouble with his nephew and niece, over the ban on their marriage, at that time. Habershon saw Hench and agreed to advance a hundred towards the publication of the book, if it included photographs of his nephew's egg collections. This was to be kept dark, and only disclosed as a pleasant surprise for the lad when the book came out – at least that was the first idea.

"But Hench was down near Upperton, and Mrs. Hoing's nephew was the officer on the beat near Pear Cottage. She and Hoggett met once or twice in town, and she told him about the bonds, and found that he was as quick as she to see the profit in the affair. But there her statement gets muddled. She tries to prove that she had some idea of drugging them, while she got away with the money – forgetting that there was no need to drug them at all if a few hours' start was all she required. The death of all three was necessary, if the affair was to look natural.

"I think we may take it that she was as deeply in as Hoggett," said Ned, "But did she take those bonds down by train to Upperton?"

"On the day of the inquest, yes. Hoggett attended the inquest, but he was not on duty 'til it began. He left home after breakfast, saying to his wife that he had to fetch a parcel of official documents from somewhere up the line. He returned home just before the inquest, as unconcerned as you please, with a large parcel, which he put in a cupboard. I need hardly tell you that it is not there now! He must have been waiting on the railway bridge this side of Upperton, and seen the parcel of bonds thrown from the train. All he had to do was to see that the coast was clear, then get down the embankment, and recover the parcel. If he was seen with it, that meant nothing. A country policeman carrying a brown paper parcel arouses no comment."

"But what nerve!" cried Nancy.

Brews' lip curled. "Sheer brutal callousness, that's all. But there it is. Mrs. Hoing took the bonds from Habershon's safe, left them next morning in the cloakroom at Liverpool Street station, called for them on the morning of the inquest, and took them in the train to throw to her waiting accomplice."

He rose as he finished speaking, and held out his hand to Nancy, "Well, Miss, that's that. If I had a hat on, I would take it off to you both! I'll do it in words at the trial, you may be bound. It was just the little bit over routine that—"

Ned jumped up. "Brews, if you mention routine again, I'll brain you! Why, you handled the case splendidly."

The modest inspector beamed on them. "Thank you, sir. I did my bit, of course, but you finished it off. Well, I must run, sir, and so I'll say goodnight. But I hope I may see more of you, if you come to live down at Fen Court."

Ned grinned. "Then we may as well say goodbye altogether, Brews," he retorted. "As it happens, I – that is to say we – are going to live in the Chilterns."

"*Where there are no ponds in the garden!*" added Nancy.

THE END

OREON titles in this series:

The Boat Race Murder
by R. E. Swartwout
ISBN 9781915475039

USA   *UK*

Murder at the College
by Victor L. Whitechurch
ISBN 9781999900489

All

Who Killed Alfred Snowe?
by J. S. Fletcher
ISBN 9781915475015

The Yorkshire Moorland Mystery
by J. S. Fletcher
ISBN 9781915475008

Fatality in Fleet Street
by Christopher St John Sprigg
ISBN 9781909349759

The Charing Cross Mystery
by J.S. Fletcher
ISBN 9781909349711

The Doctor of Pimlico
by William Le Queux
ISBN 9781909349735